To the

Stendwick, ___ ____

May 20, 2001

The Bermuda Indenture

Forsan et haec olim meminisse iuvabit.

(Someday this will be but a pleasant memory.)

The Bermuda Indenture

Strudwick Marvin Rogers

COURT STREET PRESS
Montgomery

THE BERMUDIAN PUBLISHING CO., LTD.
Bermuda

Court Street Press
P.O. Box 1588
Montgomery, AL 36102-1588
and
The Bermudian Publishing Co., Ltd.
P.O. Box HM 283
Hamilton HM AX
Bermuda

ISBN 1-58838-011-4

Design by Randall Williams
Printed in the United States of America

To my parents

NAN AND ZACK ROGERS

who taught me to take an interest in everything

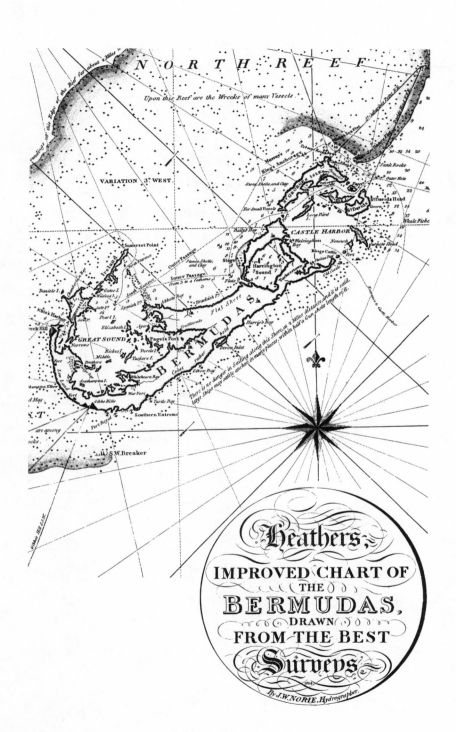

N O R T H   R E E F

Upon this Reef are the Wrecks of many Vessels

VARIATION 3° WEST

CASTLE HARBOR

GREAT SOUND

BERMUDAS

Somerset Point

Harrington Sound

Heathers;
IMPROVED CHART OF
THE
BERMUDAS,
DRAWN
FROM THE BEST
Surveys
By J.W. NORIE, Hydrographer.

Prologue

A JOURNAL FOUND
AT ST. DAVID'S ISLAND, BERMUDA

Having been requested by Messrs. Langdale, Beauchamp, and others to record the particulars of the recent and extraordinary voyage of the C.S.S. *Galveston*, I take up my pen on this the first day of June, in the year of our Lord 1863, to describe the voyage of the *Galveston*, from England via Bermuda to the Carolina coast.

The C.S.S. *Galveston* put to sea from Liverpool on March 12, 1863. Destination: Bermuda. The ship weighed anchor at dawn and cruised with the current down the River Mersey. We anchored near the bank at the river's mouth to avoid detection from Union ships lying in wait in neutral waters. At night, under cover of darkness, the *Galveston* hoisted sail and quietly rode the waves into the Irish Sea. Before dawn, we had sailed into the Atlantic without sighting an enemy ship, and the captain ordered steam to gain speed.

The voyage was arduous. A strong, cold gale blew across the ocean, and the skill and perseverance of the captain and the navigator were taxed to the utmost. With little rest, Captain Varner, the helmsmen at the wheel, and the navigator with sextant in hand manned the bridge. A mere glimpse of the sun, moon, or the north star was all the awful weather afforded.

After nine days of hard sailing, we reached the tepid waters of the Azores and anchored. We had arrived in Santa Cruz, a port town on the island of Flores — one of nine in the Azores. Santa Cruz lies at the foot of a mountain rising from the depths of the sea. The island is covered with dense greenery and flowering white hydrangeas, among houses perched on slopes, and gives the appearance of a garden floating on the ocean waves.

Upon our arrival, the Portuguese government dispatched an envoy to our ship. He handed the captain a writ signed by the governor ordering us to depart immediately. The Confederate States bear no diplomatic recognition, and, absent an emergency, no ship of the Confederacy is welcomed in an international port. Nevertheless, Captain Varner, fluent in many languages and knowledgeable in diplomatic matters, evaded the order to depart for five days, thankfully giving the crew a respite from the cold and blustery weather of the North Atlantic.

I state without reservation that I have grown to admire the Captain. He is absolutely devoid of fear, is careful, daring and cool in emergencies. The success of ships such as ours to run the blockade and to defeat enemy ships depends, in large measure, upon the skill of our captain — commander of the ship.

Captain Varner is not a big man, but he is long-waisted and appears tall on the bridge — impressive to all who observe him. A professional seaman from Louisiana and a graduate of the Naval Academy, he wears his sword, cap, and uniform bearing epaulets and a triple row of brass buttons down the coat strictly according to protocol. He is a disciplinarian but with a kind heart, absolutely just. The captain, as you will see, is a man of iron nerve. He is a splendid, handsome gentleman of about 35. Friendly and engaging, he maintains good rapport with the officers and crew.

When we sailed from the harbour, several cannon shots from the harbour fortress soared overhead in honor of the *Galveston* and her crew. Doubtless, the shore cannon were fired without orders by private soldiers acting independently. All our crew understood the meaning: The soldiers firing from the shore batteries recognized the *Galveston* was sailing into certain violence and deadly encounters. Soldiers or sailors of all nationalities, regardless of politics, salute bravery and valor. The captain ordered us to return fire, acknowledging the honor. We waved our hats and cheered the gallantry of the cannoneers on shore.

The six-day voyage westward from the Azores was uneventful until we neared Bermuda. At dawn on April 1, Captain Varner called all hands on deck. A literate man, he regularly delivers speeches to the crew.

The captain told us he expected to encounter U.S. warships that very day. Bermuda is a British colony, neutral in the war, but the Union is aware that blockade runners have commenced using Bermuda as a base for the run to Confederate ports. Within one marine league or three nautical miles of Bermuda, U.S. ships may not attack. Outside the three-mile limit, we are fair game. The captain expected U.S. ships to be patrolling Bermuda in international waters to intercept us. He ordered the watch doubled. As an incentive to vigilant watch, he decreed that the first man to see a Yankee ship would receive a ten-dollar gold coin.

The *Galveston* would be difficult to catch. Constructed in Birkenhead, she is a sight to behold on the high seas. Long-hulled and narrow, 205 feet by 27 with a powerful screw propeller, she deftly skims the waves at fifteen knots under full sail and steam. Her smooth, wooden hull covered with copper sheathing slices through swells like a sword filed to a keen edge. The sea air itself seems to fuel her, and only the fastest Union ships can match her pace. Carrying little cargo on this voyage, she rides high in the water, making top speed.

Since her christening eight months ago, the *Galveston* has

barely been seen by a federal vessel. Invisibility, care, and preparation are the secrets of her success. When the captain expects an encounter, he orders everything aloft taken down, until nothing is standing but the two lower masts. The rowboats are lowered to the level of the ship's rails. The whole ship is painted a dull white color, a precise shade of white that is absolutely indiscernible from afar. Captain Varner requires the crew to wear white uniforms when we are in danger of detection. All these precautions and more were taken as we approached Bermuda.

At two o'clock in the afternoon, the lookout on the mast sang out, "Sail ho!" The captain asked the usual question, "Where away?"

"Dead ahead, sir."

The captain ordered the crew to pass the word, "Absolute silence."

Captain Varner virtually whispered orders to the sailor at the wheel to turn the ship away from our enemy, "Hard-a-starboard." Not a soul stirred, hoping the ship on the horizon flying the stars and stripes had not discovered us.

At once, smoke billowed from the cannon on the Union ship, the sound of the firing delayed. The shell plunged into the sea 100 yards away from us.

Captain Varner shouted, "General Quarters!" The crew, having eight months training and sharp as a serpent's teeth hurried to their guns and appointed posts. The first shell from the enemy ship was intended to find our range. Successive enemy shots splashed into the water closer and closer.

The Union ship, which the Captain identified as the frigate *Chicago*, outgunned and outmanned the *Galveston*. Speed was the *Galveston*'s forte, and Captain Varner ordered full sail and full steam away from the *Chicago*. The engineers furiously stoked the boiler furnace, and the *Galveston* gradually gained speed. All the while, enemy cannon shells rained in the water around us.

Although outgunned, we returned the *Chicago's* fire. Our biggest cannon, two sixty-four pounders, lobbed shells at the *Chicago*. One shell struck a porthole and exploded in smoke and flame dismantling one of the enemy guns. But for the danger, the scene would have been dramatic — two powerful ships a mile apart, firing high-arcing cannon shots. Enemy shells fell so closely that they sprayed seawater onto the deck.

The afternoon began to pass as the *Galveston* slowly drew away from the *Chicago*. Nighttime would bring safety. I glanced at the sun, praying for the veil of darkness to fall. The yellow ball seemed to hang motionless in the sky. One shot hit us — a hundred-pound solid shot as large as a pumpkin crashed through the railings and into the water, splintering wood across the deck. Water sprayed twenty feet into the air, drenching sailors starboard. To our good fortune, there were no injuries.

Slowly, interminably, nighttime fell. The silhouette of the *Chicago* was barely visible far in the distance. Only orange fire balls from the cannon identified her location. Captain Varner ordered the officers from our posts to the bridge. He was hoarse from shouting orders through his trumpet.

He said that in precisely one minute, we would cease firing, cut the engines, blacken all lights, and immediately change direction. The captain, an athletic man, climbed the rigging, and beheld the *Chicago* through his telescope. At the appointed second, he shot his fist in the air, signaling "lights out" and silence. In the darkness, we turned ninety degrees from our course. The maneuver worked perfectly and the Union ship's shots fell harmlessly far away. The *Chicago* ceased firing and eventually disappeared from sight. We were safe.

After an hour of silent sailing, a dazzling beacon, brighter than any star in the night sky, appeared in the distance. The charts showed it to be a lighthouse — Gibbs Hill Lighthouse. We had reached Bermuda.

The reefs around the Island are notoriously dangerous and we took soundings to determine the depth. Assured that the *Galveston* was within the three-mile limit, we anchored to wait for dawn to enter St. George's Harbour.

Called *"Atlantic Gibraltar,"* Bermuda is an armed fortress, guarded by a string of forts covering the island. The Yanks would never attack in Bermudian waters. Not only would they risk a diplomatic incident, but also the force of Bermuda's heavy guns. Dead tired, I slept soundly.

When dawn broke, I learned we were anchored a mile off the eastern shore. The islands were lush with greenery and vegetation — more like the tropics than the North Atlantic. Tall, majestic cedars rose on the hills above a profusion of orange and red in the plants beneath. The waters around the island rapidly change colors varying from a delicate green to a deep green and from a sapphire blue to a deep blue.

Late in the morning, after breakfast, we sailed around the island and entered the picturesque harbour of St. George's. Five Confederate blockade runners flying the Confederate "Stars and Bars" were anchored in the harbour among scores of merchant ships.

The St. George's Harbour was alive with activity. Wharves were piled high with cotton, and the streets thronged with busy life. Captain Varner called a conference of the ship's officers. He warned us to avoid mischief onshore. Wartime Bermuda was reputed to be filled with all sorts of rogues, foreigners ready to kill or steal on a moment's notice.

The officers were rowed ashore in a dinghy and landed at the St. George's wharf. We paid our respects to government officials and met Major Norman Walker from Richmond and Mr. Sol Haas from Wilmington, the Confederate agents. The Major would arrange for the loading of cargo on the *Galveston*. Our destination would be Wilmington — our task to carry supplies through the Union blockade. Every day for a week, the other officers and I met with Major Walker to arrange the loading of the cargo and prepare for the dangerous voyage.

The officers lodged at a small whitewashed hotel on the market square of St. George's. The town is a maze of crooked alleyways, bordered by high walls and gardens with flowering shrubs and towering date palms. The market square and government buildings of cedar and whitewashed limestone lend stateliness and dignity to the town.

There was, however, no dignity in the behavior of those who now inhabited the town. St. George's seemed to be on an orgy. Wild, reckless men of all sorts — privateers, pirates, merchant mariners from foreign ports — roamed the streets. Their chronic thirst seemed to be assuaged only by rum and whiskey. Sailors crowded into saloons and pubs seeking bounties for their services. The men who commanded many of the blockade runners — vessels from England, France, Spain — received thousands in gold for a single return trip through the blockade. Cotton prices had exploded. A bale delivered to Bermuda brought a dollar per pound. Prior to the war, sailors who probably never before in their lives received more than ten dollars a month for their services could earn hundreds of dollars — paid in gold — for a single voyage.

Influential firms from Britain and the South established offices at St. George's or the capital Hamilton. Fraser, Trenholm and Co. of Charleston alone owned a fleet with more ships than whole countries. Every day vessels left the harbour to try their luck running the blockade.

To my surprise, the Confederates were greeted as heroes. One night, I attended the theater in St. George's, where a troupe presented Sheridan's *The Rivals*. Actually, it was a Masons' lodge house called Sessions House, converted to a theatre by the troupe. As soon as my gray uniform was noticed, a whisper went through the audience that an officer of a Confederate ship had joined them. Before the play, a distinguished-looking gentleman rose and proposed three cheers for the Confederacy, and the crowd lustily joined in. The theater director elbowed his way to my chair and escorted me to a special box. When the curtain dropped after the first act, the audience cheered, not the actors, but me, the officer in gray sitting in the box. The director insisted that I stand and bow, acknowledging the compliments. After the show, perfect strangers introduced themselves and invited me to supper. The director declined all invitations for me and took me to dine with the leading actors and actresses. I felt like a hero — at least for an evening. I recommended the play to my fellow officers.

I do not purport to explain the astonishing sympathy of the Bermudians for the Southern cause. The British abolished slavery years ago, and I doubt they prefer to re-establish the peculiar institution. Perhaps the natives view Confederates as cavaliers in arms waging the honorable war. Certainly the South, more so than the North, shares with Bermuda the bond of a common mother-land in the British Isles. Perhaps they view us as Arthurian knights fighting the powerful dragon, the North.

I hope the gentlemanly behavior of Confederate officers has caused the natives to display such kindness, but I would be naive to believe greed is not a factor. Like everybody, the Bermudians are elated by the gold and silver flowing like rainwater into their island country.

Whatever the cause, I for one, am grateful.

As the week progressed, the *Galveston* was loaded with cargo for the Confederate army — cannon, rifles, medicines, cloth for uniforms, paper for cartridges, boots and shoes, iron, lead, saltpe-ter to manufacture gun powder, and blankets. We took on several small barrels of oil which the crew scattered about in the ship's hull with a fuse connected to each barrel. In case of capture, the ship could be run aground and burned to keep the cargo from the enemy.

On April 7, 1863, the seventh day in port, we were ready to sail. Three passengers — Messrs. Pemberton and Marshall of the Confederate government, Mrs. Earl Barrett of Richmond — came aboard and were provided a cabin below. During the early after-noon, Major Walker came aboard for inspection. A Bermudian shipping merchant, James Beauchamp, accompanied the Major. Mr. Beauchamp carried under his arm a long metal tube sealed tightly with a metal cap with "Waterloo Bank of Bermuda, Ltd. For delivery to Fraser, Trenholm and Co., Wilmington, N.C." printed in bold letters on the side. He requested me to sign a receipt and personally deliver the tube to his agent in Wilmington. I told Beauchamp the obvious — that the voyage would be hazard-ous. He said he accepted the risk. The tube contained important material, and its delivery was crucial. The Major handed me a more important item — a leather satchel containing a packet of letters from Confederate sailors for delivery to the postal clerk in Wilmington, 690 miles to the west. With the captain's permission, I stashed Beauchamp's tube and the postal satchel with the ship's papers inside a strongbox in the captain's cabin.

In the early afternoon, before our departure, Captain Varner invited the three civilians to dine with him and the ship's officers. During dinner the captain described the danger of the voyage. The passengers seemed surprised — no, appalled — to learn that the captain would, if necessary, cast overboard their wooden chests to lighten the ship in the event of detection.

After dinner, he called all hands on deck. He climbed to the bridge and began to speak. I record his stirring oratory as precisely as my memory allows. "Gentlemen of the Confederacy, we sail tonight for God and country. I call upon you to do your duty. Your brothers in the field fight desperately. Hooker and the federals have invaded Virginia. General Lee's army awaits them. In the West, Rosecrans advances on Chattanooga and Grant down the Mississippi. Our troops, brave and committed to the cause, are lacking. They march without shoes and fight without proper weapons. We carry in the ship's hold cannon, guns, medicine, clothing and shoes for delivery to Wilmington.

"Be aware of our difficult position. When we leave Bermuda, we will be in danger from a Union squadron just outside the international boundary. From now until we arrive under the guns of Fort Fisher, we must be alert and disciplined.

"Lookouts, keep a sharp watch for enemy ships. We live or die by your vigilance.

"We have been entrusted this vessel by your Confederate government. We do not take the responsibility lightly. Our people have limited resources. Major Walker informs me we carry cannon manufactured in England with the highest skill — cannon more accurate than anything in the Union army.

"By delivering our cargo, we shall strike a blow against the ruthless industrial hordes. We strike against mercenaries sent to subjugate and despoil you of your liberty. We strike for Southern civility. We strike for our homes and property. We strike for our loved ones. We strike for honor. Remember the precious stakes. Remember the broad, abounding lands that will be desolated by defeat. We strike! The prayers of your mothers, wives, and sweethearts are with you. May God go with us as we strike a blow."

The first mate, Mr. Pierce, led three lusty, vigorous cheers from the crew and passengers. We weighed anchor and steamed toward the harbour entrance. The cannon from the battery at Fort Cunningham honored us with a volley.

The weather was favorable. The evening turned to a misty, rainy night, the moon shrouded by dark clouds. To avoid a Union ship outside St. George's Harbour, Captain Varner edged the *Galveston* just beyond the reefs after we cleared the harbour. A native Bermudian pilot, an aged man named Gabriel Johnston, with knowledge of the dangerous reefs, guided us in a southerly direction away from the Union ship. In dead silence, except for the muffled sounds of the ship's engines, we crept through the murky night.

The captain's plan was simple — sail past the Union naval squadron during the night. By dawn we would be far from Bermuda in the vast expanse of the Atlantic Ocean ready for the dash to Wilmington. The *Galveston* crept along to the south of the island carefully avoiding the sharp coral. All lights were out, except the light in the binnacle protecting the compass. At about midnight, I saw a dim ray of light through the mist. Although dulled by the weather, the light was the beacon from Gibbs Hill Lighthouse. We had cleared the westernmost point of Bermuda. The vastness of the Atlantic Ocean with no Yankee gunboats lay before us.

The *Galveston* sailed westward in the calm morning seas. The U.S. blockade is actually two blockades. The first blockade, the "Gulf Squadron," or "outer blockade," is a cordon of fast steamers stationed ten or fifteen miles apart inside the Gulf Stream about 200 miles off the American coast. The second blockade, the "inner blockade," patrols the coast near Confederate ports. The Gulf Squadron in the open sea is the most dangerous for blockade runners. As soon as a Union cruiser discovers a blockade runner, it signals others to take up the chase. The cruisers have great speed and chase blockade runners for miles. The Union ships in the inner blockade are slower, makeshift vessels more easily avoided and outrun for short distances to safe waters.

Around noon, approaching the Gulf Squadron, the "outer blockade," the weather changed for the worse. By late afternoon, a fearful storm was upon us. The rains increased to a torrent. High seas dashed over the ship. The captain kept the ship's bow into the wind. To keep from being washed overboard, sailors on deck lashed themselves in the rigging. The terrible storm prevented our detection by the enemy, but the fight with the storm was as dangerous as any fight with Union warships. The sea became a mass of seething foam. All hatches were battened down to keep the water out. No one could leave the wardroom and cabins below. The crew on deck fought the raging storm for hours. With daylight, fortunately, both wind and sea subsided. The crew had been on deck since six o'clock the previous evening.

More exhausted men can hardly be imagined.

Dragging myself to my quarters, I rolled into my hammock to sleep. When I arose in the afternoon, the indefatigable Captain, still on the bridge, informed me we had passed the "outer blockade" during the storm, our position being 100 miles off the Southern coast. With the ship out of immediate danger, we persuaded the Captain to return to his quarters for rest.

The weather was clear and the sea smooth the next day, and the *Galveston* approached the safety of the Carolina coast. No sail of enemy ships appeared — until late in the afternoon. The solemnity of the day was interrupted with the cry from the crow's nest, "Sail ho!, enemy warship to the north."

I volunteered to go aloft to observe the ship. I beheld a vessel rising rapidly on the horizon. Her flag lay limp, indiscernible, but she was definitely a U.S. ship. The vessel made little smoke — a certain sign of U.S. ships, which burn anthracite coal. She was steaming in our direction, but there was no sign she had discovered us.

The captain determined to outrun her to the coast. The danger had just begun. During the next hour, three ships appeared in quick succession along the coast, all flying the Stars and Stripes. We continued the run to the coast, hoping our camouflage prevented our detection.

By dusk, we had approached the Union ships closely enough to see the silhouettes of sailors on the ships in the squadron. The captain cut the engines. In dead silence we drifted toward the Union squadron ahead — still followed by the enemy ship bearing down on us. The captain's face never changed expression, even in the face of danger. He hoped to pass through the coastal squadron undetected in the growing darkness.

A single rocket, then a second rocket flashed into the air above the ship following us. The *Galveston* had been discovered. Captain Varner shouted, "Let her go. Full speed ahead." The engineer threw the throttle wide open and the *Galveston* leaped ahead.

We steered for the opening between their ships. Every whistle in the Union fleet was screaming, drums were beating, rockets were whistling through the air. There was the devil to pay.

The three ships before us opened a furious bombardment. At

first, their aim was bad in the dusky light. But in time, their shells began pelting us.

Shells exploded everywhere — high on the mast, on the deck, and against the sides of the ship. It was like a fearful storm. The shot, shell, grape, and canister tore through hull timbers. Union cannon belched forth fire, death, and destruction. Bullets from Yankee rifles whistled past. Missiles of death flew in every direction.

Captain Varner recognized running past the squadron in our front was certain suicide — like crossing a "T" of fire. He ordered the engineer to reverse course to head southeast to open sea, away from the coastline.

Enemy shells burst around us in blinding orange and red balls of flame. The concussion of exploding shells was overpowering. Within ten steps of me, an ammunition chest burst. It tore the clothes off two poor fellows and blackened their faces. For an hour a barrage of Union shells thundered from the sky, crashing into the ship's deck, spraying splintered wood through the air. Everywhere, sailors fell like leaves. The screams of the wounded and dying created a mournful roar. The captain himself took two musket balls through his clothes, and a third hit him in the leg drawing blood. I was uninjured, except for a deck splinter that struck me in the jaw.

The decks below looked like a slaughterhouse. The sides and ceiling overhead, and the ropes and guns were splattered with blood and lumps of flesh. Pools of half-coagulated blood, and fragments of shells, arms, legs, hands, pieces of flesh and iron, and splinters of wood, mixed in one confused, horrible mass covered the decks. The air was foul with the stench of blood and death. The casualties — at least nine dead and twenty wounded.

In the midst of the somber scene, the crew's training was invaluable. The survivors remained at their posts — loading the cannon, then firing, reloading, and firing. To our good fortune, the rudder and steering mechanism, sheathed in iron, remained undamaged. We began to pull away from the Union fleet.

The shelling slowed. Then a random solid shot suddenly struck us just above the waterline. The shot staggered the ship, crashing through the hull timbers and copper sheathing. The captain called the first lieutenant and officers to the scene. Seawater rushed like a mill stream through the hole. The blow seemed fatal. Captain Varner climbed below to observe the damage. Several of the crew held lanterns for light.

The first lieutenant said nothing, but the look on his face was one of hopelessness and surrender. For a moment, the captain stood silent, watching the gushing stream of water.

Finally, he raised a lantern and announced that the ship was ours and we would make it through. We would man the pumps, and all hands would collect blankets, nails, wooden planks and heavy poles to stop the leak.

The captain climbed down in the ship's hold, deep in the fast-rising water. The pumps hardly slowed the surging sea. When the blankets arrived, he ordered the strongest to stretch the blankets across the gaping hole.

The blankets covered the hole and carpenters nailed the blankets to the wooden hull. Crewmen, using long solid poles, forced planks against the ship's sides. The carpenters worked in concert lashing and nailing the wooden planks across the hole. The leak slowed, the pumps operated furiously, and the water level receded.

Up on deck, things were manageable. We threw cargo — crates of steel bars, cases of artillery harnesses, and the trunks of the male civilians — overboard to lighten the ship. The engineer kept her going southeastward at a decent speed.

The captain seemed everywhere at once — on the quarterdeck, in the shell rooms and magazine — encouraging the crew, comforting the wounded. He had the presence of mind to order the steward, young Finlay, to the captain's cabin to retrieve papers from the strongbox to protect them from water rising in different compartments.

High waves in the open sea made the *Galveston* a difficult target for enemy gunners, and few cannon shots threatened us. The deep darkness of the night and the speed gained by pumping out seawater allowed us to distance ourselves from slower enemy ships. They stopped firing.

At four o'clock in the morning, we were far ahead of our pursuers to the west, and the captain called the officers to the bridge. He told us what we already knew — the Galveston remained in a precarious position. The damage below had been only temporarily repaired, and a serious leak remained. The water had not been completely removed by our pumps, and only by constantly manning the pumps could we remove the water. The three enemy ships had ceased firing, probably awaiting first light to finish us off, and the cruiser that discovered us maneuvered to the east of us blocking our escape.

Fortunately our steering mechanism and our engines were workable, and our cannon were unscathed. In the face of our predicament, the captain announced a bold strategy. We would attempt to outrun the ships following us and, at dawn, attack the Federal cruiser lying in our path to the east. The cruiser outgunned and outmanned us, but an attack might catch her unprepared. By defeating her, we could probably make Bermuda and safety. The captain's coolness and iron will inspired us.

When dawn broke, the federal fleet of three ships following us was visible on the horizon to the west. The enemy cruiser in the other direction steamed about two miles away off our bow.

During the night, the terrible leak was almost completely stopped. Passenger Mrs. Earl Barrett gallantly volunteered to assist in the repair work. The captain graciously accepted her assistance, and Mrs. Barrett skillfully used the naval needle and thread designed for sewing torn sails to sew the blankets plugging the hole below.

I digress to say that I marvel at the Captain's ingenuity in using the combination of wool blankets and wooden planks to stem the flood of water and repair the leak caused by enemy fire. I never learned such ship construction techniques at Annapolis. The wool blankets pulled taut and nailed against the sides of the ship with sturdy planks behind them acted as a fine seal, blocking most of the seawater. During the night, with Mrs. Barrett's heroic assistance, more blankets sewn tightly together covered the damaged area. It was quite apparent, however, that another blast to the hull could be fatal.

In the morning dawn, we approached the enemy cruiser. The captain did not raise the Stars and Bars of the Confederacy, but instead raised a variety of signal flags to confuse the enemy. Doubtless, Captain Varner hoped the federal cruiser before us, identified as U.S.S. *Annapolis*, would confuse the *Galveston* with the federal ships following us and hold her fire.

I digress. The mind travels at bullet speed. As we approached the cruiser *Annapolis*, I confess that my mind was filled with happier scenes from my years as a midshipman at the academy — quiet moments in the chapel, dress parade along the banks of the Severn River, and Saturday night celebrations in Annapolis taverns hoisting rum and whisky with bands of thirsty seaman. Nevertheless, I confess that I would without hesitation strike down any classmate in Union blue for our cause.

The *Annapolis* failed to fire upon us as we steamed toward her. The distance closed quickly between the two warships. All hands, manning the ship's cannon or armed with muskets, rifles, and even pistols, stood silently, awaiting the signal to commence firing on the *Annapolis*.

At a distance of 200 yards, the captain yelled the order, "Fire!" Like a serpent breathing flame, our cannon erupted with all of hell's fury. All four pieces fired simultaneously at virtually point blank range. The *Annapolis* quivered from the blows. We closed on the enemy ship, and the crew with small arms rose from the railing and fired a deadly volley raking the deck of the enemy ship with miniballs and bullets. Even the captain aimed and repeatedly fired his Navy six-shooter. Our riflemen in the rigging picked off Yankee gun crews, making life perilous for anyone showing himself. Bullets crashed through the bulwarks of the *Annapolis*.

Our cannon scored direct hits on the enemy ship. One shot blasted the main mast of the *Annapolis*, setting her main sail ablaze. The fire produced dense clouds of smoke. High in the rigging, the first lieutenant yelled "Keep it hot. Fire on the scoundrels, boys!" The *Annapolis* returned our fire, but her volley was weak and harmless. Our relentless attack continued unabated. The *Annapolis* took hits of solid shot below the water line. When the main mast split from a direct hit, the men burst into jubilant cheers of triumph that rang across the waves like a concert of trumpets. The fire on board the *Annapolis* quickly spread, the flames leaping about her sails and rigging. Black smoke rolled out of her hatches. In a matter of minutes, the *Annapolis* was engulfed in flames.

Any man would be moved by the sight of sailors battling such a furious fire storm, and the captain ordered us to cease fire. The *Galveston* steamed past the fiery wreck of a warship, passing within twenty yards of the *Annapolis*. Fortunately, her crew lowered the boats and abandoned ship before casualties mounted and the ship sank. The bad fortune of the *Annapolis* was the good fortune of the *Galveston*. We had demolished our only barrier to safety, and we sailed eastward in front of the pursuing fleet.

The crew and passengers of the *Galveston* breathed freely. The *Annapolis* burned and sank in a cloud of steam, and the three ships in the pursuing fleet were mere specks on the horizon. Captain Varner ordered the starred cross of St. Andrews, the Confederate flag, hoisted and the crew cheered in honor of our naval victory over the *Annapolis*. The approaching night would be like a comfortable blanket, bringing us safety and escape.

The celebration, however, would be short-lived. During the afternoon, the ship's speed reduced perceptively. The engineer reported the cause — the large volume of water which almost inundated the *Galveston* during the past evening had soaked the ship's coal supply. The dry coal was burned up and the wet coal was slow to burn and ineffectual. Captain Varner ordered the crew to shovel coal onto the deck to dry. Then he ordered the engineer to stoke the fire with wooden planks. Still, the ship's speed failed to increase. The situation became dire. The navigator announced the federal fleet had gained a whole mile on us during a single hour. We would be captured or forced to fight, just as nightfall arrived.

The captain and crew desperately chucked anything that would burn into the belly of the steam engines. Nothing worked. I thought we would be forced to give battle. As a last resort, Captain Varner ordered large turpentine jugs brought to the deck. Then he ordered pieces of wood soaked with turpentine. The turpentine burned with fury when thrown into the stove, and the ship began to gain speed. The *Galveston* again lurched ahead of its pursuers.

At dusk, the captain used his ploy of making a 90-degree turn, perpendicular to the course of the enemy ships. The darkness was indeed a blanket of safety. We sailed the entire night without sighting an enemy ship. The C.S.S. *Galveston* was clear to return to Bermuda.

The next morning, we reached the tepid water of the Gulf Stream, and sailed through the steamy protective fog where the warm Stream meets the cold waters of the Atlantic. When the fog lifted, not a Yankee ship or vessel could be seen, and we made directly for Bermuda. After all we had endured in the last few days, the lush greenery, the rocky hills and the rose-tinted coral beaches were a sight to behold. In the *Galveston's* crippled condition, the narrow passage between the Atlantic and St. George's Harbour became tortuous. Despite the pilot's best efforts, the ship struck the rocky coral causing more damage to the hull. But when we finally passed into St. George's Harbour late in the afternoon, the Harbour was wrapped in the golden splendors of the most gorgeous sunset it has ever been my good fortune to behold.

Upon returning to St. George's, there were no noisy hurrahs, no stirring speeches, and no celebratory artillery salvos. After enduring a great sea battle, observing horrible sights of gore and deaths of brave men, precious life was plenty to celebrate.

We had failed to deliver the valuable cargo, but had survived.

The final casualty toll was high. Of a crew of one hundred five and twenty officers, there were fourteen dead and twenty-six severely wounded. Such was the butcher's bill from the voyage.

Before we anchored in the harbour, a whaling boat rowed by four stout black men, bending hard to the task with their long ashen oars, approached us from St. George's. The good fellows loaded the wounded onto soft pallets for the short trip to the dock. For two hours the whaleboat leaped through the waters shuttling the wounded to shore under the powerful strokes of the oarsmen.

James Beauchamp and a banker, introduced as Langdale, arrived by dinghy soon after the whaling boat. They inquired about their papers handed to me for which I had signed a receipt. I called for Finlay, the Captain's steward, who during battle had been ordered to the captain's cabin to save the ship's papers. Finlay, a young Scot, told the gentlemen and me the unfortunate news that the papers — ship's commission, captain's orders, and sailors' letters — bundled inside a leather satchel had become soaked with seawater and were worthless. Finlay produced the leather satchel. Sure enough, the contents were thoroughly drenched. The ink had faded away, and nothing was legible.

I then recalled that the papers handed me by Messrs. Beauchamp and Langdale were encased inside a metal tube. I requested young Finlay to again search the captain's cabin for a long metal tube with printing on its side. In a minute, Finlay returned clutching the tube. The document sealed inside remained safe and dry, which pleased the gentlemen to no end. To their credit, the men offered a shilling to Finlay and me, which we refused. The gentlemen's document, which consisted of several pages of parchment, was the only paper to survive our journey.

Only after all the wounded were safely ashore did the captain order an inspection. The *Galveston* was a wreck of a ship. Only the

Galveston's solid construction saved her. She rode low in the water from the weight of her cargo and the gallons of remaining seawater. Dozens of pockmarks scarred the hull. In several places, the hull was actually punctured. One shot had even entered the ship on the starboard side and exited the portside. Deck timbers straining to hold back rising water had bulked like warts. Other timbers had been ripped for fuel the day before leaving the frame of the hull visible. The masts, yards, sails, and rigging were disfigured and useless. To be serviceable for duty, the *Galveston* would have to be repaired and refitted in local shipyards.

I have nothing but good to say about the crew. They are first-rate fellows and acted in perfect union under the most trying conditions. Over the next week, the crew, mostly British, would be assigned to other Confederate ships — the *Florida* and the *Lady Davis*. The heroine of the voyage, Mrs. Barrett took passage on a Royal Mail steamer to Halifax, Nova Scotia, with plans to reenter the Confederacy in a less adventuresome manner. Within a month, the two government officials, Pemberton and Marshall, entered the Confederacy through a private blockade runner, the *Banshee*.

It was evening before I set foot on the darkened dock by the town square of St. George's. I purchased an English newspaper in the town square. On page two was a cartoon. It depicted two graves — on one headstone was the word "North." On the other headstone was the word "South." The caption to the cartoon read, "The End of the American Dream."

Finally, I sought the solace of a church — St. Peters — just off the square. I knelt on both knees before a three-decked pulpit, and thanked God that I dwelt in the land of the living.

I have remained in Bermuda for two months now supervising some of the reconstruction, and the native cedar is an ideal replacement for damaged timbers. I have traveled by horse or carriage over most of the island. I find this island to be the perfect tonic for body and soul from the rigors of the sea and troubled homeland. With its quiet beauty, its tidy solid cottages with white roofs, its rose-colored beaches, I could stay forever. I travel by carriage most days from St. George's to Hamilton. Every trip is pleasurable — the sedative sound of horses' hoofs along curving white coral roads flanked by aged stone walls or brightly colored hedges. Hardly anywhere can you see ahead on the road beyond a quarter of a mile. The road twists, dips, rises, and meanders past mansions and farmhouses, gardens and marshes with the sea never far away.

I enjoy the seafaring culture of the place. Most houses are built close to the water, and each household seems to own a rowing boat. A colored boy will row you across Hamilton Harbour to the Salt Kettle for a half-penny. It's a perfect place to view the yacht races on Sunday afternoons.

The solitude of the island makes a man ponder his future, his fate, and the ways of the Almighty. Like Napoleon, I do not believe that the bullet that will kill me has yet been cast. I do believe I have survived for a purpose.

I have thought from time to time about that curious little metal tube that survived the voyage. Of all the ship's papers, it was the sole survivor. Like a note in a sealed bottle tossed into the sea, might it tell a story or perhaps reveal some mighty secret?

I beg your pardon. I have diverted my attention from the voyage you requested me to describe. I now end the journal.

I remain,
Your obedient servant

Rivers Black,
Lieutenant

I

THE American courthouse is a temple of justice, a theater where every phase of human society, every form of human character, and every attribute of human life is played out. All human emotions — honor and shame, courage and fear, love and hatred — are on public display.

A trial like a play is often a tragedy, but a tragedy in a life, a crisis where details of a life are revealed. A play has a script. A trial has a transcript. A drama student reads the masters of the theatre — Shakespeare, George Bernard Shaw, Tennessee Williams. A law student can study the masters of the courtroom — Clarence Darrow cross-examining William Jennings Bryan at the Scopes "monkey trial," Justice Robert Jackson's opening argument at the Nuremburg War Crime Trials, F. Lee Bailey's relentless representation of "the fugitive" Sam Shepherd, or Gerry Spence's defense of Imelda Marcos and Randy Weaver.

In a trial, a lawyer applies his intellect, common sense, and knowledge to real-life situations. A lawyer's work is a challenge. That is why I chose the legal profession for my life's work. That is also why I became a judge.

After twenty years on the bench, I appreciate a lawyer who

possesses the tools to understand more than just the black letter law from the books. A good lawyer understands science, business, history, and particularly psychology. That is why a good lawyer needs a classical education — and experience to go with it. A lawyer better be a private detective, too.

I want to tell you about a case, a recent case I heard during the fall court term of '95.

Like all cases, it is a story, and I am going to tell it like a story. This case involves criminal law, property law, the laws of evidence. And big money. There are powerful people and exotic settings. I was lucky to hear the case. I've supplied some minor facts to make this a story, but the principal facts are solid. I know. I heard the evidence. I'm no Freud and the human mind is too complex to understand, but observing hundreds of witnesses, jurors, and lawyers has perhaps given me insight into people's thinking and motivations. In the story, I've taken the liberty to speculate about the thoughts of some of the characters. You need to know, also, that I am no expert in geography, but I am smart enough to look up facts that I don't know. So I've studied the places where this case developed — like Bermuda, Hong Kong, New Orleans. I didn't need to research Choctaw County. That's part of my circuit.

The story starts in the fall of '94.

Listen —

I COUNT Zack Whitcomb as a friend. He and his wife live in Butler in a rambling, old, wooden house four blocks from the courthouse square. Zack's about seventy. He's been practicing law in some shape or fashion since the late forties. He's a World War II veteran. I fought in Korea. We've exchanged a few war stories in our time over a bottle of bourbon or gin mixed with a little Vermouth. For the uninitiated, bourbon plus Vermouth equals a Manhattan, gin plus vermouth, a martini.

Neither of us was a war hero. The heroes were the ones who didn't come home.

Zack was *circuit solicitor* back in the fifties and sixties. That's called *district attorney* now. Zack did a fine job. People respected him. He won two elections and then decided not to run. I've heard that he didn't run for a third term because people said he had a little drinking problem. I never asked and I'm not gonna ask him about it.

Zack has slowed down, but he's still pretty sharp.

After you get to know him, you realize Zack's well-read. He writes as well as anybody I know — clear, logical sentences, no spelling or grammar errors. I think it's the Latin — Caesar, Cicero — people used to study.

Zack and Ann, his wife, are regulars at the little Presbyterian church north of town. He is not a holier-than-thou type, but can add Presbyterian doctrine to a religious debate. It's hard to argue with a five-hundred-year-old answer to age-old issues like "What is God?" or "What is the chief end of man?"

Zack was a good athlete, too. He played left halfback for the Butler Tigers. Back then everybody ran the Notre Dame box and the left halfback was the quarterback. Zack played baseball at Alabama under Happy Campbell. They won the Southeastern Conference. He's proud of that, and I don't blame him.

There's a tough side to Zack. To stay in shape, he did some amateur boxing in college. He never actually trained, but he knocked down the team captain, George Wallace, in a bout in Foster Auditorium. Yeah, that's the same George Wallace, the "fightin' judge" who stood in front of Foster Auditorium twenty years later fightin' off integration and the federal government.

ZACK WHITCOMB wheeled his fifty-five Chevrolet out of his driveway into the street. He pressed hard on the clutch pedal and shifted the three-speed gear shift on the steering column from first to second. He gave her gas. The engine roared, and the heavy black sedan lurched up the hill.

The cool autumn air blowing through the driver's vent window whipped his shirt. Instinctively, he pulled his wide-brimmed hat down tighter on his head and buttoned his overcoat just below the starched white button-down collar.

The Chevrolet cruised past the grammar school and cemetery and coasted into a service station. A young black man, wearing faded blue jeans and khaki shirt with a patch on the sleeve reading "Dixie Gas" trotted from the painted metal shed toward the self-serve pump. Whitcomb opened the heavy car door and walked toward the pump.

"Mister Zack, gimme that hose. My lawyer ain't gonna pump gas." He offered his hand and the men shook. "Mister Zack, why you keep this old bomb of a car? Got no power steering, no power brakes, no radio, nothing."

The lawyer — six feet in height and slim with a narrow face, high cheekbones and a chiseled nose — leaned against the hood and smiled. "Two reasons, Luther. One — it's paid for. Two — it works."

Luther Hawkins finished pumping, screwed on the gas cap and then pounded his fist on the hard top. "I got a third reason, Mister Zack. This is the baddest bugger on the road. This baby could meet a Mack truck head on and roll out without a scratch. She's tough as a twenty-five cent steak."

Hawkins accepted a credit card. "Gimme a while and I'll change the oil."

Whitcomb changed the subject.

"How's your grandmother, Luther?"

"She all right, as long as I keep repayin' that five thousand I owe her. Every time she come in here, she checks out the cash register and complain. She say 'Luther, I know you stay busy, but there's too much diggin' and not enough dirt flyin'.'"

Whitcomb chuckled. He hadn't heard the phrase in years.

"Okay, Luther, I'll leave the car and walk to work. Need the exercise." Whitcomb's youthful eyes and athletic movements contrasted with his wrinkled skin and thin, light gray hair. He left the car keys with young Hawkins then strolled down the street. He cupped his hands in front of his mouth and blew warm air.

What's on my office schedule today? Hell, I can't remember. My memory's still fading. I forget details of a telephone discussion yesterday, but remember details from decades ago.

It's the first cool day of fall. The breeze flowing through my cuffs. These gold cuff links Ann gave me. Through the distance of fifty years, I can see my war years as a clear memory. It seems it is not myself, but a different man entirely who lived through those years of excitement.

Nineteen forty-five. The war's over. My first date with Ann to a football game. A year before we got married. Alabama's playing Tennessee in Legion Field. Crimson and burnt orange jerseys. Lineups broadcast from the public address speakers. Echoes, sipping bourbon — straight. Ann's laughing, squeezing my hand with her red leather gloves, an elegant era — ladies with hats and gloves. Coach Tommy and the staff calm on the sidelines — in three-piece suits. Wild cheering, 'We'll all get drunk and burn Woods Hall,' Harry Gilmer's fifty-yard jump pass to Grant for a touchdown. The warm crowded train from Birmingham to the depot on Greensboro Avenue.

Whitcomb strolled in front of the grammar school building and then disappeared down a long flight of concrete steps into a pedestrian tunnel beneath the street. He walked slowly through the tunnel — built by the WPA during the Depression. Each step echoed against the walls of corrugated steel. He heard no sound and felt no movement — absolute peace.

I wonder how many times I walked through this old tunnel to eat at the school lunchroom. Twice a day from first to six grade. A hundred and sixty days a year. For six years. That's almost two thousand times. Often during the war, I thought about this little pedestrian tunnel and its serenity. I came and stood in this tunnel the day I returned from war.

It's been a half a century since the war ended for me. But looking back, it hardly seems a day has passed. The memory of those war years is as fresh as a breath of cold winter air.

20 September 1945 — my last day of the war. I hopped on the

Southerner at Pennsylvania Station in Manhattan, the world's busiest city, at 800 hours and hopped off the next day at 1300 hours in Meridian, Mississippi, in another world — the Deep South.

Daddy and Louise, our maid, hugged me like a little boy at the depot.

Strange how one chapter of life can end and another one start so abruptly.

Daddy drove across the state line to Butler, and I was home, in one piece. The war had taken two years out of my life. But I was safe, thank God, with my whole life ahead of me. I was on my way.

The war came too damned fast. I'm sitting in a college class in Tuscaloosa taking a final in June of '43. A week later, I'm at Fort Monroe, Virginia, at Officer's Candidate School — brutal competition and the war won't wait for slackers. General Clark's fighting up the Italian boot, and Ike's gonna invade France. Six hours of academics, six hours of training, Fort Monroe is tough — lights out at 2200 hours. My Alabama buddies — Drew Redden, Harry Riddick — pull me through the math courses. The class graduates from OCS in October.

By December '43, I'm a nineteen-year-old second lieutenant, and we're sailing the rough churning waters of the North Atlantic. There are hundreds of soldiers crammed like cattle on board the Liberty ship. Half are seasick and can't eat. I can't eat either, not because I'm seasick; I'm scared to death of the wolfpack — the U-Boats. Thanks be to God, destroyers, and sonar. I never saw a prettier sight than the port of Southampton — even with gray skies and a cold drizzle.

It's Christmas time 1943, and I have shore leave in London — hot tea at the Vicarage Hotel, the picture shows — cinemas they call 'em — at Leicester Square, walking Picadilly Circus, prayer service at Westminster Abbey.

It's overwhelming. I'd never left the South, never been in a city bigger than Birmingham, never heard a shot fired in anger, never been in church with over a hundred people. And there I sat in the grandest cathedral in the English-speaking world with a thousand in the pews, in the midst of a world war, in London — the center of the British empire.

I copied a prayer from their prayer book in my diary and memorized it — Defend us, thy humble servants, in all assaults of our enemies, that we, surely trusting in thy defense, may not fear the power of any adversaries, through the might of Jesus Christ, our Lord.

I closed my eyes tight and beheld only deep blackness. The congregation in the church seemed lifeless. The cold rose from the stone floor of the Abbey, and my feet felt numb in the leather army boots.

Watching Movietone newsreels at the picture show, listening to Roosevelt's fireside chats and Edward R. Murrow's radio broadcasts from London, it seemed perfectly reasonable for American soldiers to be fighting in Europe.

But now I wondered. The evidence of a brutal world war was everywhere in London — bombed-out shells of buildings, claxon warning horns, antiaircraft gun emplacements surrounded by sandbags on top of buildings and on street corners, drab green army convoys plodding through the city, war posters plastered on walls.

I'd seen London's face of war. Now I was a participant in their war. I wondered why I was here. My body shook beyond control. My pulse raced. My muscles tightened. I didn't know whether from cold or fear. Beads of sweat oozed down my forehead.

I covered my eyes with my hands, and prayed as hard as I could pray for relief.

Immediately, I beheld a blazing orange light in the darkness. The light grew. I felt the shaking stop. My pulse subsided. I felt a presence like a blanket around me. I was bathed in warm air. The light filled my vision. My muscles relaxed.

I opened my eyes. A hundred feet above, immense monastic flying buttresses, centuries old, supported the roof like ribs of stone. Warm beams of light pierced the rose window at the end of the sanctuary. The priest, high in the pulpit, uttered comforting words from the worship book. A song from the boys' choir resounded off the ancient stone walls. I'd never experienced such comfort as I did that Sunday morning at Westminster Abbey.

I'm lucky. I survived. Duty as an army supply officer aboard mer-

chant and Navy ships moving material and German prisoners across the ocean beats combat. German subs lurk in the dark waters, but the Allied convoys are winning the Atlantic battle. And duty at sea means hot meals and a warm place to sleep.

By all rights, Marley Ashe deserved to survive. Good, brave men ought to survive, but bombs and bullets don't know courage from cowardice. Marley Ashe — losing him, my best friend, takes a chunk out of a man. Strange — I'm hauling German prisoners across the ocean in February '45. The Axis surrender is only four months away. Italy's already surrendered. I'm in port in Southampton. Suddenly my blood runs icy cold. Around the world, a Jap kamikaze pilot drunk on propaganda flying a human guided missile slams into Marley's ship off Iwo Jima. His life is snuffed out as quickly as a winter wind blows out a blazing campfire.

I try to understand — to create meaning. But it's like a torpedo exploding underneath, blasting shrapnel straight through your mind. Pieces of your own body seem to disintegrate like the flowers of a goldenrod.

You cling to memories — Marley's a hell-of-a-guy. He has everything. Good looks and good-looking dates. Natural athletic ability. He beats me in tennis, ping pong, even horseshoes — everything but arm wrestling. But you don't mind. He's older and he never gloats. We hunt together squirrels, quail, turkey, deer, and those wild hogs along the Tombigbee.

I miss those carefree days — long drives to pick up dates and go to parties in little Black Belt prairie towns; conversations about juvenile matters, knowing you could reveal everything with perfect confidence that your words will never be turned against you; shared secrets he took to a watery grave.

Marley, you were smarter, too. You got the appointment to the Naval Academy. But buddy, there's one thing I beat you out on. I married the loveliest, brightest girl in the world, a magnificent beauty who matches your favorite Ava Gardner, a beauty whose dark hair, blue eyes, lips, long legs, and female hips still excite me. I married Ann — your sister.

I remember, yeah, I remember now. Bea scheduled the oilmen this morning.

He left the tunnel, walked quickly to his office four blocks away, and entered through the back door. His secretary had heard the door shut and was hurrying down the hall. She was an open, unpretentious woman who enjoyed her working relationship with her boss. She loved talking to clients — sometimes too much, he thought. She wore beautifully tailored but not stylish clothes that she made herself. Today she wore a straight navy blue dress with a white blouse.

He tossed his dark gray, wide-brimmed hat on the conference table in the library. "Are the oilmen here yet?" He shed the coat of his Glen plaid suit and hung it on the rack.

"Yeah, they been here for a while. They got an oil and gas case for you — one of those big title opinions you love to work on. They're nervous, really anxious to talk with you."

In anticipation, he raised his bushy eyebrows revealing bright hazel eyes. "Bea, we got a busy schedule today? We need to make plenty of time for those fellows."

"Not bad — a will and a timber deed to be signed."

Whitcomb combed his hair and fixed the knot of his tie in front of a small wall mirror.

He opened a file cabinet door in the library and pulled out a fresh legal pad, gathering his thoughts before meeting the oilmen. *Shanks and Elder. Good boys. Texans without the brass. You never hear complaints about 'em. They follow the rule book. No safety problems. No oil spills. They run a clean, low-budget operation. It's a Dodge, not a Cadillac operation. Intelligent guys. Professionals from A&M. Shanks is outgoing and enthusiastic. Colorful. Elder's more introverted and pensive. Both have a sense of humor. Neither takes life too seriously. No big egos, just two guys making a living. That's probably why they're able to raise investors and keep drilling.*

Whitcomb jotted notes. "Conference, 20 September 1994

E&S Exploration Company." Whitcomb carried the pad into the waiting room. The oilmen were chatting with his secretary over coffee.

"Lawyer Whitcomb, where you been?" asked Shanks. He stood and offered a moist hand. His thick neck and broad shoulders strained the seams of his black cotton tee shirt.

"You're late, Zack. It's 8:30. The sun's been up for three hours."

Shanks spoke quickly, his face glowing with enthusiasm and good humor. His large mud-brown eyes flickered. He sounded like a football coach delivering a pregame speech. "Jess and I already been turkey huntin' this morning. Your wonderful secretary's been typing, word processin' and faxing. The oil market's booming. The stock markets are rocking."

Shanks glanced at his watch, "The Texas Aggies football team hit the practice field in College Stadium two hours ago. The log trucks are rollin'. The school teachers are teachin'. Jess and I are ready to drill an oil well. Young man, you better get cracking!"

Whitcomb enjoyed the Shanks monologue, especially the playful lie about his youth. He slapped Shanks on the back and smiled. "Jim, sounds like you fellows been hittin' the bottle — a little too early. I hope y'all drill this county like a pin cushion. I'll lease my land cheap. Just drill me a gusher and I'll retire.

"Let's talk business. Y'all must be ready for action." The lawyer motioned the oilmen, and they followed Whitcomb down the hall past a gallery of photographs into the library, his inner sanctum.

The three men sat at a heavy oak table — the grain of the wood barely visible on the table top beneath a glass cover and years of polish. Whitcomb took a fountain pen from his shirt pocket.

"Zack, we got a problem." Shanks rubbed his sweaty hands together. "We gotta spud a well in thirty days — a month from today. We ain't done nothing, except drive out here from Texas last night. We stayed in Meridian."

Shanks, wearing cowboy boots, looked taller than his six-four.

He stood up and paced the room. "Jess, you're calmer than me. You explain."

Elder, half a foot shorter than Shanks, wore gray work pants and a dark green flannel shirt under a khaki army jacket. He folded his hands on the table and focused his droopy bloodhound eyes on the lawyer. "Zack, you've helped us get wells drilled before. We need help — your help — again. We gotta move as soon as possible," Elder smiled, "if not quicker."

The lawyer leaned forward in the chair. "I'm the doctor. You're the patient. Whatever the ailment, we'll cure it. Fire away."

Elder and Shanks exchanged a momentary glance. They read each other's minds. The lawyer's simple response reassured them. In the past, whenever the oilmen drilled here, they hired Whitcomb. He delivered his work product — title opinions and legal advice — timely at a fair price. He answered questions clearly and directly — a straight shooter. An expert in property law, he knew oil and gas law cold. He knew everybody in the county — politicians, land-owners, public officials — and fixed problems. On the drive from Texas, Shanks and Elder discussed hiring Whitcomb. They wondered whether the aging lawyer could handle the job. His strong, direct response to Elder reassured them.

"We've had short fuses on contracts before but this situation tops it all." Elder snapped open his briefcase and pulled a file folder from the leather pocket.

He opened up the file folder and a single sheet of paper fell out onto the conference table.

The lawyer looked up at the oilmen and started laughing. "Jess, that's pitiful, fellow. One file folder in that big briefcase with just one piece of paper in the file folder."

Elder shook his head and joined in the laughter. "Jim, this *is* pitiful. We call ourselves an oil company — an independent oil company and we're pulling into town with one month to drill a million dollar oil well, and all we got is a big leather briefcase with one sheet of paper. Pathetic, isn't it?"

Shanks started chuckling. "We travel light." His chuckle grew into a couple of laughs, then a roar. The humor of the situation relaxed Shanks.

Whitcomb turned to face the oilmen. "Gentlemen, let's fix the problem."

Shanks sat down at the end of the conference table and picked up the single sheet of paper from the glass top. "Standard Petroleum gave this farmout agreement to Jess and me."

Shanks waved the paper, with tiny single-spaced printing. "Under its terms, we got one month to drill the first well on a tract of land or the agreement expires. The good news — all we need to do to comply with the agreement is spud one well. Just break the dirt with a drill bit. The bad news — we've already said — we ain't done nothing. I mean nothin'."

Whitcomb smiled and shook his head. "Jim, you know what I like about you fellows? You're honest. Y'all ever heard the army engineers' motto? We used to say, 'The difficult, we do immediately, the impossible takes a little longer.'"

"Never heard it, but I like it," said Shanks. "That's inspiring, but where do we fit in — difficult or impossible?"

Whitcomb didn't answer, and Shanks continued.

"Zack, we wanna hire you to check the title on the mineral rights covered by the farmout agreement."

Elder pointed at the document. "We got a good deal here. Standard Petroleum, like other majors, is leaving the U.S. to drill overseas. They believe it's too expensive to drill — too many environmental laws, legal liabilities, and not enough oil and gas in America. So Standard's selling off its domestic holdings."

"Naw, Jess. It's guts," Shanks interrupted. Whitcomb put down his pen to listen. He detected a wild diatribe emerging. "That's the real problem. Those majors ain't got any guts. It takes two things to drill oil wells — money and guts. They got the cash, but forget the other."

"They fired all their oilmen. They wait for real oilmen to find it, then they buy 'em out. Majors got financial men — CPAs and corporate lawyers — runnin' everything. Anybody willin' to risk some money gets clipped outta the hierarchy."

"Almost all the wildcatters are gone. And those corporate financial types runnin' the majors ain't gonna take any risks. It's those institutional stockholders — pension funds and all."

"Those jacklegs runnin' the company wouldn't invest in a wildcat well if they saw an oil seep."

"If you ever meet the head of a major company, check him between his thighs. He's smooth as glass."

Elder smiled and slapped Shanks on the back. "Jim, don't sugarcoat it. Besides, if they were drillin' the prospect, we wouldn't be here."

Elder nodded toward Whitcomb to refocus the conference.

Whitcomb picked up his pen. "Tell me about the contract."

Shanks calmed himself down. "We cut a deal with Standard on the Durant lease here in Choctaw County. If we can spud a well in thirty days, we get the right to drill as many wells as we want on 64,000 acres. And that's without paying any cash. Standard keeps an overriding royalty of one percent of any oil we find."

"Standard has leased the mineral rights from the Durant family for years, but they never drilled a well. Jess and I talked 'em into giving us this farmout agreement. The deal is simple — if the first well is a good one, we own the Durant lease. Then we can drill as many wells as we want on the lease. Standard retains only the override. The thirty-day provision is onerous, but the deal was too good to pass up. Jess has studied the Alabama geology for years. He's confident we can make a good well. I'll handle the engineering — the drilling operations." Shanks looked at his partner.

Elder pulled a piece of heavy rock from a pocket in his jacket. He held the rock between his thumb and index finger. "This is a core from the Smackover formation in Choctaw County. This core came out of a well just west of our proposed well site. The company that drilled the well plugged it as a dry hole, but they encountered oil, sure enough. This core proves there's oil. They plugged the well because they encountered too much water in the well." Elder's voice became impassioned. "If we can hit the Smackover formation just to the east, I believe we'll get the oil without encountering water. We'll make some money — real money." Elder curled his fingers around the rock core and squeezed.

Whitcomb put his pen down. "Sounds so simple. Why hasn't another company drilled on the location?"

Elder answered. "I dunno. Learned long ago you can't worry about competitors. You accumulate the data, evaluate the data, and make your own independent decision. I believe we got an excellent opportunity here, but it's still just a theory, an opinion — my opinion. Besides, most good ideas are simple, but somebody's just lucky enough to be first to have the idea."

Shanks leaned forward in his chair. "We were first to ask Standard for the farmout and we raised the drilling money. We happened to be firstest with the mostest, and we got the deal. It's that simple."

Elder dropped the rock core back into his coat pocket. "Zack, we need a title opinion on the Durant lease to verify the ownership. We need it right now."

"I'll do it," Whitcomb said. "64,000 acres is a big tract, but don't worry. We'll write the title opinion in no-time flat. Worry about something else — surveys, clearing the well site — but don't worry about the title work. I'm the doctor here. Consider it done."

Whitcomb glanced at a calendar hanging from the wall. "A week. Give me a week. I'll have it."

2

REAL estate title opinions reminded Whitcomb of the jigsaw puzzles he and his mother worked together. Every Christmas she bought a puzzle. After everybody opened their presents, she would dump it on the floor in the den. For weeks during long, dark winter nights, hundreds of pieces jigsawed into twisted forms lay on the floor in front of the fireplace.

Zack's mother bought landscapes. They were the toughest and most time-consuming. Piecing together hundreds of shades of blue sky was tedious. But with his chin resting on his hand, Zack would pore over the pieces in deep concentration. He never quit. His mother and he reveled in the simplest of feats — piecing a segment of the sky, building the border with edge pieces, or finishing a corner. The puzzle might sit for weeks as a jumbled maze in hundreds of pieces — a challenge before them. But mother and son were relentless. Piece-by-laborious piece, a picture would take form. The work could be agonizingly slow.

Then — an epiphany. The scene would crystallize before their eyes. In ten minutes a puzzle worked off and on for a month would rush to its quick conclusion. Patience and concentration had conquered again. A shape had been formed from chaos. A sliver of order had been imposed on a complex world.

Title work, detailed and intricate, rewarded such patience and concentration.

WHITCOMB OPENED his office at seven the next morning. The challenge put forth by the oilmen excited him. Other lawyers couldn't understand his penchant for oil and gas title work, but Whitcomb relished the task.

His face glowed. He walked faster, talked quicker, slept better, and dressed neater. He couldn't conceal his pleasure, and everybody noticed.

His was a simple thrill — the thrill of solving the ownership puzzle and producing a work product worthy of compensation and of contributing to the discovery of energy.

Zack recognized his good fortune in choosing as a teenager to be a lawyer, and in oil companies retaining him. His personality, his mind, his conscious emphasis on a thorough, logical work product, his accuracy, and his clarity of thought conveyed in written word fit perfectly into the needs of oil companies. They wanted accuracy — in determining ownership of mineral rights — at any cost. He delivered.

He charged oil companies well for his services and they paid. He read every deed and wrote every word of every title opinion. His accuracy was legendary. Once, when a Louisiana oilman challenged his conclusions, Whitcomb wrote a biting response. Zack's letter made the rounds among the members of the bar.

Mr. Ronald G. Akin, President
Akin Energy, Inc.
1010 Lamar
Houston, TX 77001

RE: Zinn Well, Catahoula Parish, Louisiana

Dear Mr. Akin:

I have received your letter in which you requested more information about the ownership of the Zinn Well. Ronnie, I am surprised that you thought my report to be incomplete. In examining the ownership, I reviewed the Louisiana records from 1804 to the current time. I understand from your letter you want to take the report as far back into the past as possible. Okay, Ronnie, here we go.

Lafayette Rackley bought the land in 1804 from the United States of America.

The United States bought the land from Napoleon Bonaparte and the French in 1803 in the Louisiana Purchase, a treaty with which I am sure you are familiar.

The French received all of Louisiana by treaty from the Spanish early in 1800 in the Treaty of San Ildefonso.

The Spanish received Louisiana from Louis XIV of France by the Louisiana Treaty in 1762.

Our buddy Louis XIV claimed Louisiana in 1682 through the French discoverer LaSalle. Louis XIV derived authority from God, and the Pope as agent of God recognized Louis's authority as being derived from God.

And Ronnie, old boy, if you need to go back farther than God, you better hire yourself another lawyer.

Very truly yours,

Zack Whitcomb

IN ALABAMA, circuit judges run for reelection every six years. I've won three elections in the First Judicial Circuit, which covers Washington, Clarke, and Choctaw Counties. If you wanna win the elections, you better know your constituents. And you better know the counties in your circuit.

Choctaw County is a sparsely populated piece of rolling land on the coastal plain in the southwest corner of Alabama. A line of rugged hills crosses the county in the center, and two dozen creeks — mostly with long Indian names like Tallawampa and Okatuppa — braid their way through the countryside.

Broad forests of longleaf, shortleaf, and loblolly pine, cedar, poplar, sweet gum, red maple, willow, hackberry, and water and white oak trees cover most of the land. Except for a few thousand acres of cotton grown on bottomlands along the Tombigbee River, the antebellum days of King Cotton are long gone. It's the fruits of those forests — timber, lumber, pulpwood, and paper — that provide the jobs and money for most of the citizenry.

Like rural life everywhere, life marches at a slow pace — plodding log trucks with busted brake lights on near-empty farm-to-market roads, simple houses on forty-acre quarter plots with fertile vegetable gardens, dirty lumber mills with boards stacked high, small barns of weathered wood with rusty tin roofs.

The people — black and white — charm visitors with a soft accent called *coastal Southern*, the inhabitants preserving Elizabethan words like *reckon* and *yonder*. The county seat is Butler — named for Colonel Pierce Butler, a governor of South Carolina who died a hero's death in the Mexican War. The name of the county and several communities (Pushmataha, Naheola, and Yantley) and most of the creeks (Tuscahoma, Souwilpa, and Puss Cuss, for example) memorialize the Choctaw Indian tribe who lived in this part of the country. The Choctaws were a peaceful people, master farmers and traders, and military allies to the Americans. Perhaps that's why they were one of the last tribes to be "resettled" out west — by President Andrew Jackson.

When the red man left, the white man arrived — some with black men in tow. By 1847, the land had been populated enough for the Alabama legislature to create a new county. The legislature established Choctaw County, taking lands from Sumter to the north and Washington to the south.

Nevertheless, the courthouse records don't go back that far. An arsonist, probably anxious to destroy incriminating evidence, burned the courthouse and the probate records just before the Civil War. A dozen years later, somebody again burned down an outbuilding that held the land records. Obviously, arson's not a new crime.

But you can research all real estate records since 1871. That gives a pretty good idea who owns the property. And through the years, some documents dated prior to 1871, particularly patent deeds from the U. S. government, have been recorded.

Courthouses tell you a lot about the citizens. The courthouse in Butler is a fine two-story yellow brick building with archways, stone floors and a set of four Corinthian columns on the second story. The courtroom itself sits on the second floor. With a long balcony built for Negroes it recollects the days of segregation. Although it's been modernized with bland additions, the original building, a turn-of-the-century structure, presides with dignity over the town square.

THE HEAVY DEED books and will books lay stacked on rollers in metal shelves in a windowless steel vault inside the probate office. The steel door to the vault hadn't been locked in years. Nobody knew the combination.

Zack Whitcomb kept a key to the front door of the courthouse on his keyring. By 7:30 a.m., the day after he met the oilmen, he was alone in the vault pulling deed books off the shelves researching title to the Durant property. Without interruption, he worked quickly. In two days he had copied what he needed — deeds, affidavits, wills and leases.

Unlike most lawyers, who rely on a clerk to compile an abstract of the recorded documents affecting a piece of land, Whitcomb prepares his own abstract.

Whitcomb and his secretary have a method for thorough, error-free title work. He dictates every word to her, face-to-face.

She checks him. He trusts her. She knows grammar and even property law almost as well as he does.

BEA LOOKED up over her word processor when he opened the office door. "Zack, how's it coming?"

He remembered hiring Bea — almost thirty years ago. She married just before she graduated from high school and couldn't afford college. She walked into his office to apply for the job holding her high school report card. Every grade was an A or A-plus. The lady who taught business courses at the high school — typing and stenography — had written a simple note on the back: "Best student I ever taught, bar none." After a five-minute interview he knew Bea was perfect. She asked about the Supreme Court decisions of the Warren Court. They talked about the Scottsboro trials. He hired her on the spot. In all the years, her enthusiasm never waned. One trait, perhaps, marred her professionalism.

Bea was known to be a gossip. And in a law office, a secretary revealing facts about cases is a serious hindrance. Facts seemingly inconsequential — the date of a deposition, the name of a witness, the location of the lawyer — can be vital to an opponent. Whitcomb knew of his secretary's habit. But he was too good-natured to stop it, so he just ignored it.

He answered her question. "I found these papers on the Durant property." He motioned for her to join him in the library. He relaxed into a leather chair, pulled a pair of reading glasses from his shirt pocket, and balanced them on the tip of his nose.

"Bea, this is strange. We've written hundreds of title opinions. And I hardly ever saw ownership so simple — not with so much land involved and so many generations involved." He stacked the papers in chronological order, cleared his throat and dictated in monotone. She scribbled on her pad.

"By patent deed executed in 1844, President John Tyler conveyed 64,000 acres in Choctaw County, Alabama, from the United States to Raymond Herbert Durant."

Whitcomb turned to the next document. "By deed dated 1880, Raymond Herbert Durant conveyed the surface rights in the property." Whitcomb ran his finger across the paper, and his eyes followed. "A handwritten clause in the deed states 'Grantor Raymond Herbert Durant reserves the mineral rights in perpetuity to himself and his heirs.'"

He continued. "Under Alabama law, where the mineral rights have been severed from the ownership of the surface, acts of adverse possession of the surface rights do not constitute adverse possession of the mineral rights. This rule of law means that if a person obtains the mineral rights separate and apart from the rights to the surface, then the owner of the mineral rights and his heirs continue to own those rights forever. No matter what type of activity the owner of the surface rights engages in, the owner of the mineral rights does not lose his mineral rights."

Whitcomb continued, "An Affidavit signed by Peyton W. Durant provides the details of the Durant family lineage. In the Affidavit, Durant states: Raymond Herbert Durant was born in New Orleans, Louisiana in 1822. By Patent Deed, Raymond Herbert Durant purchased 64,000 acres, formerly Choctaw Indian lands, from the United States of America in 1844. In 1850, Raymond Herbert Durant married Michelle Bondurant. The couple had no children. Raymond Herbert Durant died in 1895. The land records of Orleans Parish, Louisiana, indicate Raymond Herbert Durant died without a will. Raymond Herbert Durant had one sibling, a younger brother, LeMoyne A. Durant, who inherited Raymond Herbert Durant's Alabama lands under Alabama intestate succession laws. LeMoyne A. Durant died in 1905 and willed the property to his oldest son, Paul B. Durant. Paul B. Durant died in 1940, and willed the property to his two children, Joseph L. Durant and Barbara Durant Hardee. Joseph L. Durant died in 1985 and willed his interest in the property to his son, Peyton W. Durant. Barbara Durant died in 1986, and willed her interest to her nephew Peyton W. Durant, the current owner.

"By oil and gas lease dated 9 January 1992, Peyton W. Durant leased the property to Standard Petroleum Corp. The lease contained a five-year primary term."

Eyes transfixed with concentration, Whitcomb passed methodically through the stack of papers. He liberally dictated comments. The papers — deeds, wills, mortgages — were like a journey through time in the life of a family. The generations passed as the lawyer moved through the stack of papers. Whitcomb finished the stack and stopped dictating. He started to dictate his conclusion, then hesitated. He rifled through the stack, pulled the *Affidavit* signed by Peyton Durant, and studied the document again. He sat motionless, engrossed in thought. He looked down at the diagram of the ownership on his legal pad. Whitcomb shook his head. Then he stood and paced the room.

The lawyer had examined so many titles that he instinctively recognized questionable ownership. He had learned to be wary of even his own suspicions, but it was hardly possible to practice property law and write title opinions off-and-on for forty years without knowing when an affidavit seemed to be a fabrication. Still, he understood better than anyone that title opinions are based on the records — not on suspicions. He poured out his thoughts to his secretary.

"The real issue in this chain of title to the Durant property is pure and simple — 'Is Peyton Durant the heir of Raymond Herbert Durant?'"

"The answer — yes. According to the affidavit."

"The affidavit of Peyton Durant is straightforward, but could the person that signed the affidavit know those facts about Raymond Herbert Durant?"

Bea answered his question. "Of course not. That's over a hundred years ago."

Whitcomb's voice rose. "Exactly. Peyton Durant's affidavit is self-serving. Shanks says Peyton Durant got a cool quarter of a million bucks from Standard just to sign the lease. Peyton Durant, or anybody else, might sign an affidavit if they stood to gain that kind of money."

Bea cocked her head. "Your suspicions are usually right on target. If the affidavit turns out to be erroneous, then who wins?"

"I don't know. But it's sure not Peyton Durant." Whitcomb continued. "There's one other thing that's suspicious. Durant struck through the warranty clause in his lease to Standard. Cute lawyering. That means he gets to keep the two hundred fifty thousand even if it turns out he doesn't own the mineral rights." The lawyer stated the issue again. "Is Peyton W. Durant the heir of Raymond Herbert Durant? According to record title, the answer is yes, and, if Peyton Durant is the heir, no problem with the ownership to the mineral rights. The recorded documents unequivocally support ownership by Peyton W. Durant. Suspicions are not what count. Hardcore evidence counts, and the evidence supports the claim of Peyton W. Durant to the mineral rights. By law, by practice, we gotta follow record title. So Peyton Durant owns the mineral rights. Closed case. He signed an oil and gas lease to Standard Petroleum, and Standard Petroleum has assigned the oil and gas lease to Elder and Shanks. Therefore Elder and Shanks have good title to the oil and gas lease."

Whitcomb delicately removed a Cross fountain pen from his shirt pocket. He slowly drew a thick circle of ink on his pad around the name — *Peyton W. Durant*, then shoved the entire stack of papers into a file folder. He shook his head. "Don't feel good about this. But, here's my conclusion. Take it down. 'Based upon the records filed in the probate office of Choctaw County, I conclude that Peyton W. Durant owns record title to the mineral rights in 64,000 acres in Choctaw County known as the Durant Place.'"

1844	United States	Patent Deed from United States to Raymond Herbert Durant
1880	Raymond Herbert Durant	Durant Reserves Mineral Rights to Himself in Deed
1895	Raymond H. Durant to LeMoyne A. Durant	R. H. Durant dies without a will, LeMoyne A. Durant, brother of R. H. Durant, inherits
1905	Paul B. Durant	LeMoyne A. Durant wills to son, Paul B. Durant
1940	Joseph L. Durant and Lydia Durant Hardee	Paul B. Durant wills to son, Joseph L Durant and daughter, Lydia Durant Hardee
1985	Peyton W. Durant	Joseph wills to son, Peyton W. Durant. Lydia Durant Hardee wills to nephew Peyton W. Durant.
1990	Standard Petroleum	Peyton W. Durant leases oil and gas rights to Standard Petroleum Corp.
1994	Elder and Shanks	Standard Petroleum enters Farmout agreement with Elder and Shanks

Diagram prepared by Zack Whitcomb on September 23, 1994.

3

O N the same autumn day the two oilmen were discussing their woes with lawyer Whitcomb, halfway around the globe a British Airways jet was banking hard in preparation for landing at Hong Kong. The sole first-class passenger on the port side saw thousands of specks of light outlining the islands against a blanket of darkness. Mountain peaks rose sharply on the islands like spires above the waters. The plane dropped low to find the narrow runway protruding into the harbour.

Peyton Durant closed his briefcase and stuffed it under his seat for the landing. He tightened the Windsor knot on his silk tie, sipped the last taste of brandy from the tumbler, and then continued reading a column from *The Financial Times*.

COTTON PRICES SMASHED

Cotton buyers were raked over the coals again. Prices dropped a third straight day on London and American markets. Analysts forecast weak demand as designers see a return to artificial fibres for spring fashions. Traders in the pits are, however, dubious of a fundamental shift in demand. They claim the drop is simple: bountiful harvests in China, Texas and the Mississippi Delta.

A firm double tap on the shoulder broke his concentration. "Buckle up." The stewardess spoke with a soft feminine British accent. "Landing in Hong Kong can be — exciting."

Durant tore the newspaper page in two and stuffed the clipping in his pants pocket. Then he snapped the buckle and peered out the window again. The lights from small boats in the harbour flickered like stars. Reflections from the glass and steel skyscrapers sparkled on the harbour waters. The 747 whipped at a harrowing low height past apartment buildings.

Bright lights beamed along the runway. The wheels screeched, bounced, then screeched again. The stewardess unbuckled and reached for the microphone, "Welcome. Local time is 10:40 p.m. I trust you enjoyed the flight from Delhi aboard British Airways."

Durant traveled light — one carry-on suitcase and a leather briefcase. He booked the front row of first class whenever possible to depart the plane first.

The stewardess pulled his jacket from a hanger compartment and helped Durant slip it on. His indigo blue double-breasted jacket blended perfectly with his gray trousers and black turtleneck. Meticulously he combed his blonde hair and brushed lint from his clothes.

In fifteen minutes, Durant had hailed a cab and was resting in the back seat of a Vauxhall taxi. In another quarter of an hour, he was checking into the Prince Albert Hotel two blocks from the American Embassy.

TWO ORIENTAL women in uniform standing in front of a floor-to-ceiling American flag at the entrance to the American Consulate motioned the man in a blue Austin Reed suit, white shirt and a shiny solid maroon silk tie to lay his briefcase on the conveyor belt at the security checkpoint. He emptied his pockets and marched through the metal detector. A somber Marine watched the operation from a glass bulletproof booth and saluted. Another oriental woman dressed in gray emerged and escorted Durant into a spartan conference room. The room seemed consciously uncluttered and functional. It smelled of disinfectant from the morning's cleaning. A long, narrow table with a modest wood veneer was lined with metal folding chairs. The shelves of a bookcase held a set of the United States Code and the Acts of Parliament. Outdated Venetian blinds hung from the only window in the room.

At nine a.m., a short, balding man wearing a brown suit joined Durant and four other men at the conference table.

"Gentlemen, I'm Harvey Kruk, agricultural attaché at the consulate." Durant had heard the same opening line the year before. "The ambassador regrets he is unable to meet you personally, but extends the warmest welcome to his fellow Americans."

"At the ambassador's request, I have prepared a report on the cotton harvest . . ."

Durant popped the latch on his briefcase, pulled a handful of business cards from an inside pocket and laid one in front of Kruk at the end of the table, "Peyton Durant, New Orleans Cotton Exchange Building, Suite 200, Carondelet St., New Orleans, Louisiana 70001. Cotton broker."

Durant looked at the business card. The words "Cotton Broker" seemed archaic. He thought to himself, *Hell, I'm a speculator — a cotton speculator. But 'broker' is okay. 'Speculator' sounds so mercenary.*

For the past three years Durant had visited the American consulate during his annual data-gathering trip through the Far East. Each year Kruk had briefed Durant and a handful of businessmen on Chinese cotton production.

Kruk knows the ag numbers, but he doesn't know shit about clothes. He's worn a brown suit every year. Probably the same damned suit. Shiny polyester. A Goddamned plastic suit. Never underestimate the taste of Americans.

But Kruk gave a razor-sharp presentation. Same the year before — slides, overhead, and graphs.

Kruk's no rookie. A gray-hair. Seasoned pro. Serious data. Impressive.

The meeting ended just before 12:00 — when a blast from the naval cannon signaled the noon hour.

After the presentation, Durant bought Kruk's lunch at the Prince Albert. Durant enjoyed his guest's company. Kruk was intelligent and well-spoken. They talked China, cotton, and crops. Durant asked Kruk to spend the evening out. Kruk accepted, said it would be a good excuse for a night away from home.

THE VAUXHALL TAXI stopped outside a high-rise apartment building, and Kruk, still wearing the brown polyester, slid inside.

"Harvey, you want a bite?" asked Durant.

Kruk loosened his tie. "Hell, no. I wanna gamble. And I'm sick of Chinese food. Five years of chopsticks and rice."

"Then let's go to Macao. But find me a market for pearls. I need to buy a strand or two of freshwater pearls."

Durant motioned the driver. The taxi whizzed through the narrow streets, the endless market place of Hong Kong. Tiny shops and stalls sold everything — electronics, western-made suits, perfumes, jewelry, and shellfish. Bright neon beckoned customers into elegant off-street shopping centers.

The cab driver stopped on the street curb, and Durant trotted to an all-night newsstand displaying hundreds of newspapers and magazines. He bought *The Asian Wall Street Journal* and jumped back inside. The cab sped away before the door slammed shut. The men continued their talk of cotton prices and trading markets. The car stopped again.

"The jade market, man. We're at the jade market. Best place for pearls. Hop out. If you're lucky twenty dollars will buy you a ten-strand necklace."

Durant trotted away. In ten minutes, he returned holding three tiny boxes, and the cab sped away again.

Trolleys rambled past. Taxicabs honked in the traffic and

construction workers in hard hats pounded metal a thousand feet high on a new building. Capitalism roared in the world's freest market.

The taxi braked to a stop at the ferry port. Durant pulled a fifty-dollar bill from his billfold to pay the fare. The driver opened a metal box and stared for a moment at varying currencies clipped together — American dollars, British pounds, Hong Kong dollars, and Macao *patacas*. The driver squinted his eyes and raised his shoulders in mock confusion.

Durant smirked, "Listen, buddy. I know you speak English, and I know you've seen a fifty-dollar bill before. And you sure know that I ain't leaving a thirty-dollar tip on a twenty-dollar fare."

The driver counted out thirty dollars in Hong Kong dollars from the cash box.

Durant sneered and laughed at the same time. "And you damn sure know I ain't taking Hong Kong dollars as equal to American dollars — not when they're worth half as much."

The driver slapped a Jackson-twenty and a Grant-ten in Durant's palm, motioned his passengers to leave, and sped away cursing in his native tongue.

The ferry plowed through Hong Kong Harbour past bobbing junks, oil tankers, and freighters in the harbour flying flags from Greece to Australia, India to Panama. Durant and Kruk sat on the bow of the ferry watching the rows of Hong Kong skyscrapers and the energetic activity in the markets and bazaars on the streets. The British colony was like one giant trading floor. Every commodity in the world seemed for sale — from diamonds, pearls, and ivory to carpets, computers, and clothing — every citizen trying to become richer the next day than the day before.

In an hour and a half the ferry arrived at Macao — the Portuguese colony. A cab at the Macao ferry terminal whipped the men to the casino district.

Kruk led Durant into the Lisbon Casino past the guards and

the doorman. The doorman nodded. Kruk was a regular. He played every game of blackjack like it was the last hand dealt. Like a pro, he watched the cards from the end chair, played two and three hands on a deal, and often doubled down. Durant played the minimum bet on the table.

Kruk bet with only fifty-dollar chips — *patacas* in local currency. His stack of chips rose and fell like ocean waves.

After an hour's gambling at the blackjack table, Durant suspected a problem. Kruk had lost four hundred bucks and simply whipped a casino club card from his billfold and withdrew another four hundred in chips from the cashier — high stakes for a government employee drawing sixty thousand max, plus a cost-of-living stipend.

Durant and Kruk played the fifty-dollar roulette table — Durant for fun, Kruk to feed his fever. Durant played low risk, betting *even* or *odd*. Kruk bet wildly on long shots. He'd bet fifty dollars on a thirty-to-one bet and lose — every time.

Durant was glad when the night was over. Kruk had complained about everything — cards, dice, child support payments, high cost of living, low government pay. Kruk was a mess. Hell, he wanted to play the Hong Kong Jockey Club — the horsetrack — the next night.

4

BERMUDA is an isolated group of about 150 small islands in the western Atlantic. Bridges and causeways connect the principal islands, which stretch for twenty-two miles. The islands are hilly, the highest point rising 260 feet above the Atlantic. The Gulf Stream warms the chain of islands so that they are the northernmost in the world with coral reefs. The nearest land to Bermuda is Cape Hatteras, North Carolina, 600 miles to the west.

You might think Bermuda would lie routinely in the track of frightful hurricanes. Wrong. Generally, hurricanes in the North Atlantic miss Bermuda, passing between Bermuda and the North American mainland.

But some find the mark.

On the afternoon of September 28, 1994, Hurricane Beatrix hit Bermuda head-on with 125 mile-per-hour winds. At sunrise the police had already ordered the beaches evacuated. No one needed prompting. Television broadcasts of satellite pictures, hurricane coordinates, wind-speeds, and computer models had alarmed the islanders. On a tiny island, the residents cannot escape a hurricane, only endure her force.

For four hours Beatrix unleashed her fury on the tiny Atlantic archipelago. Her winds wreaked havoc — uprooting trees, demolishing acres of onions and Easter lilies, overturning cars and sending debris flying through the air at shattering speeds. The swirling winds scattered motorcycles — the islanders' favorite transportation — like plastic toys. High storm waters smashed boats to pieces against the rocky coral coastline and flooded low-lying areas of Front Street in Hamilton and the town square at St. George's.

Streaks of jagged lightning ripped into power wires causing flashes like New Year's fireworks. Broken voltage lines whipped back and forth in midair. Electrical transformers exploded. Wailing sirens cut through howling winds.

Ian Langdale felt like the last man out. He reached for his key to lock the front door to the bank. The rains blew horizontally, and he covered his eyes for protection. Gripping the key with both hands, he rammed it in the lock.

In his mind he recited his checklist — steel shutters bolted, power off, safe secured, and now front doors locked. He ran to his car a block away. All alone on the street, he leaned into the wind, tasting salty rainwater on his lips. Waves from Hamilton Harbour crashed over the seawall into the car park on Front Street. Water sloshed up to his ankles. He forced the car door open and climbed into the driver's seat.

The engine roared, and he threw her in gear. The Peugeot dodged uprooted palms scattered across the street. The sign at Trimingham's department store buckled from the force of the winds. Anything not lashed down — trash cans, canvas umbrellas, and plastic chairs from the row of balcony bars along the harbor — spun in whirlwinds through the air at racecar speeds. Hailstones pelted the Peugeot like chopped ice. Langdale drove toward high ground out of the rising water and sped out of Hamilton — a lonely car on the road.

His hand trembled as he turned on the radio. One lone station was broadcasting. "Weather bureau predicts a ten-foot tidal surge. That's ten feet. And wind gusts of a hundred forty miles an hour. Take cover immediately." Langdale headed home. A flying timber from a boatyard crashed into the passenger window shattering the glass. Icy hailstones pounded dents in the Peugeot. Langdale passed through the Crow Lane Roundabout outside Hamilton. The center signpost fought the winds, then blew into pieces. The winds grew in intensity. His ears popped from air pressure. In a minute, he was home pulling into his driveway.

Ian Langdale's house sat on the crest of Bostock Hill in Paget Parish overlooking Hamilton Harbor and the city. In its one hundred years, the two-story stucco house had survived dozens of hurricanes. Surely the house would survive one more.

From his second floor bedroom window Langdale watched the storm battle the city across the harbor.

Skies of purple, gray and green attacked the eighteenth century town. The church steeple of the Anglican Cathedral, the twin towers of the old Sessions Building, and the spire above City Hall, rising like pointed fingers high above the Harbor, taunted the stormy skies. Sloops and yachts in the harbor bobbed and dipped, heaving and straining to survive.

Langdale glimpsed the bank, owned by the Langdale family for four generations, rising three stories along the harbor. The bank, constructed of stone from Bermuda's quarries, could take it. He hoped. He'd done all he could to protect her, including sandbagging the basement. He could do no more, except endure the long night and wait for daylight.

FOG IS RARE in Bermuda. But the island woke up the next morning in a rare soupy vapor. The hurricane had passed. By 8 o'clock the fog had barely thinned. With Langdale watching from his residence on Bostock Hill, the fog rapidly rolled away and the city became exposed. It was like the lifting of a curtain above a stage. The rising fog revealed all — the Cathedral steeple, then the towers of the Sessions house, the City Hall spire and white-washed rooftops, and finally the Waterloo Bank on the harbor.

The Bank had survived. It took thirty minutes for Langdale to drive his sports car through the mile of broken limbs into Hamilton. The water had receded from Front Street, but in the wake of the surge, boats from the harbor were deposited in piles along the seawall. Barr's Bay Park, adjoining the bank building, was a mass of uprooted trees and crushed motorboats.

He parked outside the front steps. The building survived the storm intact, but not without damage. Cracks in the walls and missing chunks of limestone on the roof gave the building the appearance of having been shaken like a toy by a giant hand.

The interior was powerless and dark except for streams of natural light through floor-to-ceiling windows. All seemed normal and undisturbed in the lobby.

Langdale stopped in his tracks. There was a man-sized hole in the wall. The breach was shaped roughly in the form of a doorway. Puzzled, he switched on his flashlight and approached the hole. With heightened interest, he shined the beam into the dark space. A staircase! A descending stone staircase. A passageway. A tunnel of arched masonry roof barely high enough for a man to stand.

He stepped over stone and rubble and entered the passage. Obviously, the hurricane had shaken the foundations and loosened the blocks. It looked like an explosion had blown out stone and plaster. Dust floated thick in the flashlight beam.

Slowly, desperately slowly, he descended into the blank space. Fifteen steps. His mind wandered. He'd heard the story of a lost vault and a secret passageway to the harbor. Cobwebs and damp moss hung from the arched ceiling. Water dripped through cracks. He smelled the pungent musty odor of a hundred lost years.

Langdale halted. His foot hit a flat cobblestone landing. The beam from the flashlight revealed an iron door. A faded seal — *Waterloo Bank of Bermuda, Ltd.* — was painted on the metal door. He lit a candle and set it on the bottom step. He twisted the door handle. The lock popped. He pulled hard. The steel door didn't budge. With both hands, he jerked on the door. The hinges creaked and the door moved. A tiny breach.

He pulled at the door. He slid the flashlight into the crack and peered inside. Air escaping from the chamber made the candle flicker. His eyes grew accustomed to the light. Details of the room emerged. He froze staring through the opening in the vault door.

He felt the urge to drink in the moment. He wiped the sweat off his face.

A century had passed since another man walked and breathed in the chamber. But it seemed like yesterday. A black felt hat with a ribbon around the brim hung from a brass hook near the entrance. The ceiling was arched brickwork. The vault reminded him of a large oven for baking bread.

The banker gasped — a pile of glistening gold and silver coins lay on the shelf opposite the door. The heap of brilliant, dazzling treasure dominated the room. This was indeed a vault — sealed for over a hundred years.

He stepped inside. The scene grew clearer. Shelves on the side walls were stacked high with paper money and bank notes. A blackened lantern hung from the low ceiling. A double-faced clock rested on the top shelf beside the piles of coins. Langdale felt like an intruder in time. It seemed like the banker — possibly his ancestor — had, merely a moment ago, blown out the light in the whale oil lantern and locked the door.

In the center of the room resting on the cobblestone floor stood a wooden table with a slanted top — a plantation desk. A dried-up inkwell and a wooden writing pen fit into a slot on the desk. Langdale lifted the top of the desk. It was empty, except for one item. A long metal tube, its length as long as an umbrella, its diameter the size of a Coke can, lay inside. The label bore an inscription in bold handwritten letters — "Waterloo Bank of Bermuda, Ltd., for delivery to Fraser, Trenholm and Co., Wilmington, N.C."

Langdale pulled the rusted metal cap off the end of the tube and shook out a roll of pages. He untied the faded red ribbon that bound them and spread out the pages on the table. The paper was thicker than modern paper, more like parchment. Protected from the elements by the metal tube, the pages were a creamy white color, like new. Smooth handwritten strokes of black ink covered the pages, the product of a gifted calligrapher. The first two words of the document, in tall capital letters an inch high, jumped off the page — *This Indenture*. Langdale trained the flashlight on the document and scanned the pages.

It was a bank mortgage, an extraordinary one. The collateral for the loan was 64,000 acres of land in Alabama — a massive piece of property. The debt was 100,000 pounds — a remarkable sum of money for 1860, the equivalent of perhaps ten million in today's dollars. The Indenture was signed by powerful men — the gover-

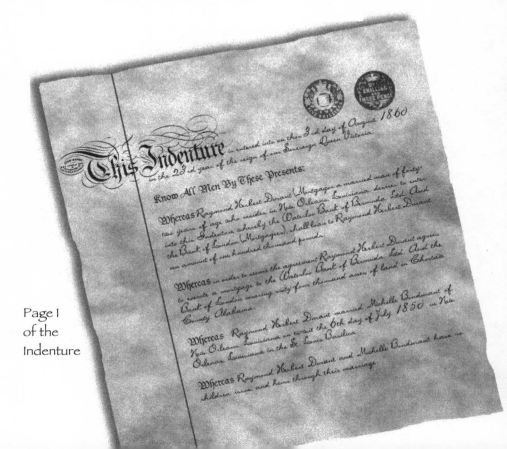

Page 1
of the
Indenture

nor of Louisiana, and Disraeli, a future British prime minister. Two separate banks, Waterloo Bank and the Bank of London, loaned the money.

The contents involved a strange family matter — a husband and wife recognizing an illegitimate boy as their lawful son.

Debtors — foreign debtors, residents of faraway New Orleans — had signed the mortgage. Wax seals and ribbons were affixed to the parchment, beside the debtors' signatures.

Clearly, the mortgage embodied a momentous loan for the Waterloo Bank of Bermuda — possibly the largest loan ever. Powerful people. An enormous sum of money. An imposing document.

Langdale read the Indenture again, more carefully this time.

Preparer: Chas. Hardie
              32 Furnival St.
              London

STATE OF ALABAMA   )(

                                                    INDENTURE

COUNTY OF CHOCTAW   )(

THIS INDENTURE, is entered into on this 3rd day of August, 1860, in the 23rd year of the reign of our Sovereign Queen Victoria.

KNOW ALL MEN BY THESE PRESENTS:

WHEREAS Raymond Herbert Durant (Mortgagor), a married man of forty-two years of age who resides in New Orleans, Louisiana, desires to enter into this Indenture whereby the Waterloo Bank of Bermuda, Ltd. and the Bank of London (Mortgagees), shall loan to Raymond Herbert Durant an amount of one hundred thousand pounds.

WHEREAS in order to secure the agreement Raymond Herbert Durant agrees to execute a mortgage to the Waterloo Bank of Bermuda, Ltd. and the Bank of London covering sixty-four thousand acres of land in Choctaw County, Alabama.

WHEREAS Raymond Herbert Durant married Michelle Bondurant of New Orleans, Louisiana on to-wit the 6th day of July, 1850, in New Orleans, Louisiana in the St. Louis Basilica.

WHEREAS Raymond Herbert Durant and Michelle Bondurant have no children, issue, and heirs through their marriage.

WHEREAS on or about the year 1840 Raymond Herbert Durant, became acquainted with a free Negro, quadroon woman, known as Eugenie, at New Orleans, Louisiana.

WHEREAS Raymond Herbert Durant and Eugenie consummated their relationship and she bore him a son, whose name is Robert Durant.

WHEREAS, since their marriage Raymond Herbert Durant and Michelle Bondurant have treated and accepted Robert Durant as their son and have held out Robert Durant to the public, as their lawful son.

WHEREAS, Raymond Herbert Durant and his wife Michelle desire that Robert Durant inherit all their lands.

WHEREAS Raymond Herbert Durant and his wife Michelle do acknowledge Robert Durant as their son and heir to all their lands.

NOW, THEREFORE, in consideration of the premises, Mortgagors, RAYMOND HERBERT DURANT and his wife, MICHELLE BONDURANT DURANT and their son ROBERT DURANT do hereby GRANT, BARGAIN, SELL and CONVEY unto Mortgagees, WATERLOO BANK OF BERMUDA, LTD., and BANK OF LONDON, the lands described on Exhibit A, which is attached hereto and made a part hereof.

TO HAVE AND TO HOLD unto said Mortgagees. If said Mortgagors pay the indebtedness of one hundred thousand pounds sterling, then this Mortgage shall become null and void.

IN WITNESS WHEREOF, the undersigned Mortgagors have set their signatures and seals this 3rd day of August, 1860 A.D.

Executed in the presence of:

Thomas Moore	**Raymond Herbert Durant**
Governor of Louisiana	**Mortgagor**

Michelle Bondurant Durant

Wife of Raymond Herbert Durant and Mortgagor

Robert Durant

Son of Raymond Herbert Durant and Mortgagor

James Langdale

President, Waterloo Bank of Bermuda, Ltd.

Benjamin Disraeli

President, Bank of London

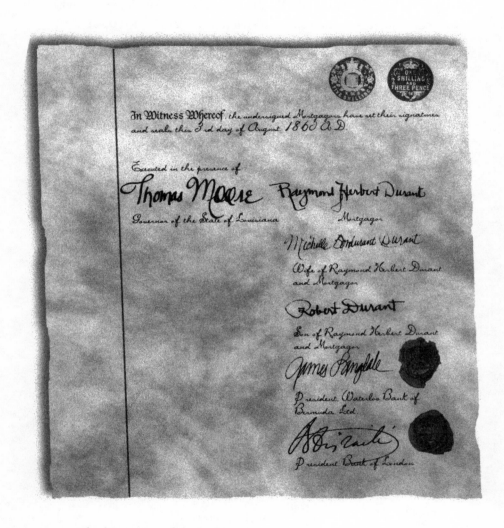

The last page of the Indenture

5

S HANKS's white Ford pickup truck bounced along the narrow road, leaving behind billowing clouds of dust. "Dammit, this road's rough — rough as a corn cob."

The two oilmen drove in anticipation through a sunbathed countryside. The winding dirt road passed through varying Choctaw County landscapes — a towering forest of emerald green pine and cedar, a treeless pasture filled with cattle feeding on waves of grass, a field of knee-high cotton ready for picking, and the jumbled remains of a timber forest recently mowed down in a clear-cutting operation. Shanks switched on the radio and touched the *scan* button next to the digital clock. The tuner tracked the *AM* channels in search of a radio station, but raced through the entire spectrum without finding a single station. Shanks raised his voice over the drone from the engine. "Jess, we're in the country, sure 'nough. The radio can't pick up a station." He punched *FM* and *scan*. The tuner located one station, blaring Travis Tritt.

"Good choice," Elder said sarcastically. He rolled his eyes. "Country music ain't been the same since Ferlin Husky left the Grand Ole Opry. Ain't nothin' better than Conway Twitty singin' 'Hello Darlin'.'"

Shanks shook his head and laughed. "I miss the radios with the hand dials. You could hunt 'til you found a station — static and all. We'll catch the LSU-A&M tonight on that big New Orleans station."

"Jim, I wonder if we took on too much with this Alabama project. We got such a tight schedule," said Elder.

"We're okay. Let's take it one step at a time. Once we settle surface damages with the Hawkins woman, we'll be rollin'."

Elder leaned against the door. "Heck, Jim, we don't have a decent place to stay, much less an office."

"Don't worry so much," replied Shanks. "We're like the cavalry. Our headquarters is in the saddle — in the truck."

Shanks shifted gears. "We'll get it done. I guaran-damn-tee."

Elder laughed. "God, you got a good attitude."

Several minutes passed in silence. "Jim, the damned thing about the oil business is you work your rear off to drill a well — buy leases, work deals like this farmout agreement, raise funds, try to keep investors happy, hire an outfit to build the drill site, hire a drilling contractor. All that, and nine times out of ten, you get a duster."

Elder shook his head. "Wish I hadn't said that. It's kinda discouraging. I'm 'bout to convince myself it's stupid to drill this Durant well."

Shanks smiled and interrupted, "Aw heck, you gotta do something with your life. Might as well drill oil wells. Don't complain. The barn's clean when all the horses are gone. Besides, if drilling wells were easy, everybody would be drilling. Get a grip."

Shanks turned toward Elder and raised his voice. "I been readin' some old lectures from A&M. I found a copy of the commencement address. It got me fired up."

Elder sounded sarcastic. "All that stuff about puncturing rocks to glimpse the puzzle of the earth's geology. The grand search for oil, for energy — the quest."

Elder's voice faded. "That's a long time ago. And that college rah-rah, it doesn't pay the bills." Elder continued, "I do miss College Station. The twelfth man and all that stuff. The corps. A&M football's on a roll. We've beat Texas eight outta the last nine."

Elder's voice faded again. "Dammit, I still feel like a one-legged man in an ass-kickin' contest — trying to drill this well in thirty days." With his right hand, he pulled the fingers of his left until they cracked.

"Take it one thing at a time. We'll make it," said Shanks.

Elder cracked his fingers again. "I just hope this woman — this Miz Hawkins who owns the surface — is easy to deal with."

"Durant owns the mineral rights. Correct?" Shanks asked.

Elder opened the flap of a manila envelope, pulled out a twenty-page title opinion and turned to the last page. "That's right. A fellow from New Orleans named Peyton Durant owns the minerals."

"You got those forms to settle with landowners for using the surface?" Shanks asked.

"Right here in my brief case. I got some checks with me, too. If we make a deal with Miz Hawkins, we'll cut her a check on the spot. Jim, you got an idea what the surface rights are worth in Choctaw County?"

Shanks shifted between third and fourth gear on the winding dirt road. "Couple of people at the courthouse told me five hundred to a thousand bucks per acre." Shanks responded. He thought a moment. "Let's split those estimates and offer her seven-fifty. We'll need two acres. So that's fifteen hundred dollars. An oilman's gotta get along with landowners. Gotta keep 'em happy. If they ain't happy, they gripe about everything — traffic, noise, dust. Drive you crazy complaining. Remember the gal in north Louisiana who sicced her goats on us?"

Elder laughed. "Oh, yeah, I remember. They gnawed and chewed every piece of paper on the drill site — maps, well logs, drilling reports. The boss held back our wages to buy a steel safe."

Shanks smiled.

"Jess, on second thought, let's offer her a thousand."

"Okay. Least we're honest. We can sleep at night," said Elder.

"Speak for yourself," replied Shanks. "I'm honest, but I still can't sleep. I worry too much."

"What you worry about?" asked Elder.

"Everything. Making a living, the price of oil. Thank God for late night TV and CNN. I used to worry about whether I was going to heaven, but I don't worry about that anymore."

Elder leaned against the door. "Is that cause you're sure you're saved?"

"Not really. I just don't worry 'bout that anymore."

Shanks turned off the radio. "I see her house up ahead. Let's be smart. She owns all the surface rights around here. Wherever we drill, we're gonna be on her land. So let's get along with her. Whatever she wants to talk about, we'll talk about. Whitcomb said to mention his name. It might get a foot in the door."

Elder unbuckled his seatbelt. "Okay by me. We'll talk all night if she wants to."

MELVINA HAWKINS lifted the front brim of her straw hat to look down the road when she heard the truck approach. She straightened herself in the garden and leaned against the wooden handle of the hoe. She raised her hand to acknowledge Shanks, who waved at her out the driver's window. The truck slowed to a stop by the side of the house.

The light-skinned black woman pulled the straw hat back on her head. She walked with a slight stoop toward the truck. She pointed east down the road, "Follow this road for a couple of minutes. You'll get to Bladon Springs. Turn left. It's a straight shot to highway eighty-four."

"Ma'am, you think we're lost?" Elder asked from the passenger seat.

"You got Texas tags. You're not hunting doves 'cause you got no guns. Mine's the only house on this road, and I'm not expecting anybody."

"Miz Hawkins," Shanks started to speak.

"How'd you know my name?" she interrupted abruptly.

"Looked it up in the courthouse — the land records." Shanks responded.

Shanks sized her up. Elderly woman, but bright, quick — and suspicious. Hard sell.

"Miz Hawkins, I'm Jim Shanks. This is Jess Elder. We're not lost. We came here to visit with you." He spoke quickly. "We're oilmen from Texas. We wanna drill a well around here. Could we have a minute of your time?"

Shanks didn't give her time to answer. He opened the truck door and pointed to the garden. "What you growing, turnips?"

She appreciated his interest. "You can't get greens like these in the grocery store. Y'all like turnips?"

"Yes'm, with cornbread."

She dropped the hoe to the ground. "I'm Melvina Hawkins." She offered her hand and Shanks accepted.

The woman wore a light blue cotton dress with a simple white collar. Tall and handsome with peaceful brown eyes, she wore her gray hair braided in sections around her head. The deep lines on her bronze face showed her seventy-four years.

"You've got a nice place here ma'am. I'd trade my house in two seconds to live here."

She smiled. She didn't believe him. The house was worn. It had a rusted tin roof, and the walls of graying lumber had not been painted or whitewashed in years. Raised three feet above the ground, the house sat on heavy rock pedestals making an open crawl space beneath. An open-air hall ran down the middle — a dog trot. Once, these houses were everywhere in the South, but time and house trailers changed things.

Mrs. Hawkins motioned for Elder and Shanks to join her on the porch. The oilmen sat in two homemade oak rocking chairs.

She sat down on a wooden swing at the end of the porch. The rusty hinges squeaked. The late September breeze cooled the porch.

Elder spoke. "Feels like fall Miz Hawkins."

"Autumnal equinox was last week. It *is* fall." Mrs. Hawkins said abruptly.

The woman's reply surprised Elder. "I haven't heard *autumnal equinox* since school — in my earth science class."

"I oughta know science. Taught school thirty years."

"Where?"

"Place called Choctaw Training School. It's in Lisman — west of Butler, toward Meridian."

For the moment, Shanks avoided business conversation. *She's wary of us — those curt answers. At least she's cordial. Maybe she'll relax.*

"When was this house built?"

"Daddy built this house. He started building in eighteen-ninety and finished it — like you see it now — in ought-four. That's nineteen four."

Shanks learned long ago that Southern blacks and whites, despite their differences, shared a common history and culture. Southerners, regardless of race, enjoyed gardening and eating. He motioned toward the setting sun. "Do your pecan trees still bear?"

"About one out of three years."

"Did those camellias bloom this past winter?"

"Yes sir. Beautiful."

"Do you get many pears off that pear tree?"

"I fill up so many washtubs that I give pears away. I make enough pear preserves from that one pear tree to last me a year."

She understood the oilmen's tactic. *They make casual conversation to gain my confidence, and then spring a business deal. No matter. We both understand each other. Sure, it's two fast-talking Texas oilmen, but it's nice having company visit.*

"She's a pretty lady — white blossoms in the spring and gold leaves in the fall."

Shanks caught the reference to the pear tree. He detected an opportunity for a compliment.

"You got quite a place." He stood, walked to the end of the porch, and looked across the fields. "It's like a botanical gardens — pecan trees, pear trees, a forest of hardwood and pines, and camellia bushes, flowers. Did you plant everything yourself?"

If he's trying to con me, he's doing a good job. "Daddy planted the pear and pecan trees. The forest is natural, of course. I hire somebody to clear out the underbrush. Yeah, I planted all the bushes and flowers." She rocked far back in the swing. "I got a lot more ideas. Gardening keeps me busy."

"Probably keeps you healthy," said Elder.

"Gentlemen, let's take a walk."

Shanks helped her rise from the swing. She stepped tentatively down the porch steps, one step at a time. She led her captive audience to a half-acre garden inside a barbed-wire fence. Sounding like a teacher in class, she dominated the conversation. "I love growing flowers." She pointed toward the bright orange salvia and chrysanthemums.

"Y'all know what this is?" She didn't wait for an answer. "It's a scuppernong arbor." She clutched one of four wooden poles supporting a wooden structure with a latticework top, covered with scuppernong vines.

"Vegetables are my specialty, especially beans. I got lots of beans."

"What kind of beans?" Shanks asked, stepping high across the neat garden rows.

Anticipating the question, she flashed a grin and sang the answer. "Well sir, I got pole beans, snap beans, white beans, string beans, red beans, navy beans, pinto beans, butter beans, kidney beans, and lima beans."

A smile slid onto Shanks's face. "Ma'am, you got everything but baked beans and jelly beans." With obvious satisfaction, Melvina broke into a happy laugh, and Elder and Shanks chuckled.

The barriers tumbling, Shanks felt everyone at ease. "It's gonna get dark on us if we don't get down to business. We wanna talk about using your land to drill a well."

She nodded and they returned to their places on the porch.

Shanks and Elder told the details of their drilling plans. The oilmen would bring a drilling rig down the dirt road a quarter of a mile from the house and begin drilling in a week. The drilling operation would last about a month. They needed access over her property to reach the well site. The oilmen offered to pay her a thousand dollars for the easement. Melvina told the men she would consider the offer and let them know tomorrow.

"By the way, our lawyer, Zack Whitcomb, said to say hello." Shanks almost forgot to drop the lawyer's name.

"You shoulda told me, I know Zack junior well. He's a good lawyer, especially on deeds and stuff. Knew his Momma, Katie, and his Daddy, Zack Senior before him. It's nice he said to tell me hello. He used to be my husband's lawyer. When my husband — that's Abe — died in an accident a few years ago, the children and I didn't use Zack. I heard it upset him."

Shanks avoided a serious subject, "How many children you got?"

"Seven."

"That's a bunch."

"After the first two, havin' babies is like shellin' peas. Six boys — they played a lot of baseball out in my pecan orchard. Matter of fact I used to watch Zack play baseball out there at Fowler Field in Butler. After the soldiers came back from the war — World War II — he played for the baseball team here. The colored people use to say Zack was a 'singles and triples man.'"

Jim interrupted. He knew he'd struck a sweet chord. "I've never heard anybody called a 'singles and triples' man."

"Zack hit line drives. They didn't have fences in the outfield in those days, so if an outfielder caught the line drive on the bounce, there was a single. If the outfielder couldn't make the catch, it was a triple. Everybody liked watchin' Zack play. He was smooth as silk at shortstop. Probably helped him win the race for circuit solicitor. Y'all ask him about Demopolis — Butler playin' Demopolis. I was sad about that one."

"Miz Hawkins, how do you know so much about baseball?" Elder asked and then leaned forward to listen.

Melvina laughed. "Everybody enjoyed baseball — young and old, black and white, male and female — didn't matter. No TV back then. Colored folks went to white folks' games and whites went to our games. Funny thing is, there was a big chalkboard sign by the gate entrance to the ball field. The sign said, 'adults one dollar, children fifty cents, and colored twenty-five cents.'" Melvina howled.

Elder spoke his words carefully. "Times change. Why you figure they charged colored people only twenty-five cents and adults and children paid more?"

"Cause the colored folks sat way out along the foul lines. Although black and white all went to the games, there was still segregation — sort of. The white people sat behind home and the teams' benches. Guess somebody figured colored shouldn't pay as much 'cause their seats were not as good. Made sense to me."

Shanks asked, "How big were the crowds?"

"Several hundred, maybe a thousand. They could raise a ruckus when the local boys did well. And you should have seen the betting that went on. Fans sitting and standing around the field bet good money on everything — who would win, the score, whether the batter would strike out. Money changed hands like a hot potato. I saw a colored man bet a white man five dollars, even money, that on the next pitch, the batter would hit either a single or a triple. Darned if he didn't get a single on the next pitch, and the white man paid off the bet."

Melvina leaned back in the swing. "Everybody, black and white, had a lot of fun — back then. Still, things are a lot better now for black folks and, I suppose, white folks too." She vastly under-stated the momentous social changes since those days of segregation.

"There were a lot of good white people back then." Her voice trailed off, "Maybe just not enough."

Shanks arose from his rocking chair and Elder took the cue. They shook her hand and started down the porch steps. "It's been a true pleasure to meet you, talk with you, and do business with you. I wish you owned some of the mineral rights in the Durant lease. If we get lucky and hit a barn burner of a well, you'd make a ton of money," Shanks said.

Mrs. Hawkins looked Shanks straight in the eye. Her face had suddenly changed from a happy countenance to discontent, and the peace had left her eyes. "I do own the mineral rights. I'm a Durant."

Startled, Shanks stopped on the bottom step. He cocked his head and faced her. He spoke slowly and distinctly. "Miz Hawkins, I'm gonna be straight with you. We got a deal with Standard Petroleum. Standard has a report naming the owners. The report says you're not the owner. We got a title opinion from Whitcomb. He's a fine oil and gas title lawyer. The title opinion also says you're not one of the owners. According to the records, a man named Peyton Durant owns the minerals."

Shanks climbed the stairs to the porch and leaned against a post. "Tell us how you claim the mineral rights to the Durant property."

Her face beamed. "Gentlemen, y'all get in the kitchen. I'll fix some supper and iced tea, and I'll tell you how I own the Durant property."

Elder and Shanks followed Mrs. Hawkins into the kitchen.

"Sit yourselves down."

The oil men scanned the kitchen and adjoining bedroom through the open door. A spotless linoleum canvas covered the kitchen floor. A 1950s Frigidaire hummed loudly. Copper pots and pans and an iron skillet hung from iron hooks on the kitchen walls. Through the bedroom door, he saw a set of outdated encyclopedias in a bookcase. A framed certificate hung on the wall above a sturdy roll-top desk. The certificate confirmed her degree, a Bachelor of Arts from Stillman College, class of '38.

Mrs. Hawkins poured three glasses of iced tea from a pitcher kept in the refrigerator. She handed each man a long sleek silver tablespoon. Shanks noticed an engraved "D" on the handle and the hallmark "WH" on the back.

"Miz Hawkins," said Shanks, relaxing in a chair at the table. "Tell us how you're kin to the Durants."

"Okay, first thing. I am a Durant. My maiden name is Melvina Durant. My granddaddy was Robert Durant. Granddaddy was the son of Raymond Durant who got this property way back in time."

Melvina delicately dropped a sprig of mint leaves in her tea and sipped from the glass. "Now, Raymond Durant met this woman, named Eugenie, at one of those *droon* balls down in New Orleans. They loved each other and she bore him a baby boy — my grandfather. Granddaddy was their only child. He left the place to my father, Calloway. And my father left it to me. So the way I got it figured, all that Durant property belongs to me as heir property."

Elder and Shanks looked at each other across the kitchen table. They were stunned by Mrs. Hawkins's clear understanding of her claim. She sounded convincing, but surely some knowledgeable person had checked out these facts. What about the Standard Petroleum report? What about lawyer Whitcomb's title opinion?

"I'd like to ask you some questions about your claim," Elder said.

"Sure."

"Was the man who bought this property — you called him Raymond Durant — a white man or a colored man?"

"He was white, but he had his only child by a colored woman, my great-grandmother."

"Do you know Peyton Durant, a white man from New Orleans,

and how he claims the Durant property?"

"I never met him. Don't know how he is kin because Raymond Durant only had one child, my grandfather."

"Was your grandfather a slave?" Elder knew his history. If Melvina's father were a slave, he could not inherit property.

"No, he was a free man."

"What's a *droon*?"

"Don't know. I just always heard Raymond Durant met my great-grandmother at a *droon* ball."

"One more question, Miz Hawkins." Elder raised the crucial issue, "Do you have any proof of your story?"

She sipped her tea and thought for a moment in silence. "Don't reckon I do. It's all in my head — just family history handed down by word of mouth."

Shanks lightened the conversation. "Miz Hawkins, you will get a kick out of this. A famous oil man, John Paul Getty, once said, 'The meek shall inherit the earth, but as for the mineral rights, it's every man for himself.'"

Melvina pointed to a Bible by the kitchen sink. "I got the King James Version. I never heard your version of the Beatitudes."

Shanks chuckled. Then he spoke seriously. "To inherit these mineral rights, your claim will have to be proved. You and your family been livin' here, keeping this place for a hundred years. It's your homestead. In all fairness, you oughta own any oil that we discover under the land."

The woman nodded in agreement.

Shanks continued. "Miz Hawkins, you don't mind if Jess and I talk privately? We'll just step outside on the porch."

"Y'all ever had Alabama gumbo?"

Shanks kidded her. "Ain't no such dish."

"Trust me. Here's what's in it." She opened a drawer and reached for a deep black pot. Then she began to sing — in rhyme. "Start with okra and chicken and bacon to fry. Add tomatoes to peel and stew. With a nice bit of lamb, a slice of ham, maybe a squab or two. You grate fresh corn, sure as you're born, it'll thicken your soup just right. Sage leaves prime, and a bit of thyme. These can be gathered overnight. Then an onion round, fried a neat brown. And butterbeans stirred in between. If your pot's boilin' hot, then you'll cook a gumbo that hits the spot. Served with a crisp green pepper beside, and a plate of rice, cooked dry and nice. It'll be the best eating you ever tried."

Elder clapped. And Shanks threw up his hands in mock-surrender. "I stand corrected."

She turned on the water in the sink. "Y'all talk. I'll cook."

The oil men excused themselves to the front porch. The day drew to a close in the growing darkness. "Jess, I've heard wilder tales than this woman's. She's sincere and believes her story."

"Yeah, I know," said Elder, "but she needs proof. Whitcomb's title opinion is based on recorded documents. Her claim is based on family legend, at best. Still, it's plausible. What we gonna do?"

"Jess, why don't we offer to lease this land from her? By leasing her land, we protect ourselves in case the facts ultimately prove she's the correct owner. By buying the lease from her and recording it in the land records, I suppose we give a modicum of support to Miz Hawkins's claim," said Shanks.

"I agree," said Elder. " Let's make her an offer. Maybe offer her a thousand dollars and one-sixth royalty."

"Okay," said Shanks, "but no more."

Elder nodded in agreement. "One big issue remains. How's she gonna prove her claim?"

"Beats me. First things first. Let's buy the lease from her. Besides, you know what they say in the oil business," Shanks started back inside. "A dry hole cures all the title problems."

Elder followed. "I'm tired of business. I'm ready to eat."

The oilmen joined Melvina in the kitchen and sat down to supper. They made their offer to Melvina, and she accepted. They ate supper then departed into the darkness of the Alabama countryside.

The miles passed in silence except for the truck's engine.

Elder broke the silence. "I admire that woman's independence, Jim. She's lived a hard life, but she's lived with dignity."

Shanks looked up at the stars, bright and undimmed by the city lights. The chilly air free of pollutants seemed like a window to a universe of constellations. "Yeah, and I feel some responsibility — some kind of bond with her."

"Jim, they say profit, financial success, and material wealth are fleeting, but friendships are forever."

"Yeah, I've learned that through the years. You remember the people you deal with." Shanks smiled. "But right now, I'd damn sure take some of that financial success."

Elder laughed. Then switched on the radio and found the *LSU* football station.

6

A WOMAN's voice resonated down the hall and through the law office. "Is there a lawyer in the house?" Whitcomb took a sip of iced tea from a Dixie cup and opened the door. He called out. "Depends. Who's asking?" With a sense of humor in his voice, he sang out, "I'm looking for payin' customers only."

"Zack Junior, I drove clear from the other side of the county to get your advice."

"Come on back, Melvina. You caught me on my lunch break. But if you want legal advice, that's what I'm sellin'."

He was resting in his high-backed office chair with his feet crossed on the edge of his desk, but he rose and shook her hand.

The light-skinned woman was dressed in a flowing navy print skirt, a white cotton blouse, and white heels. He drew back a leather chair for her to sit. Then he seated himself on the opposite side of the desk.

The sweet scent from her perfume mingled with the smell of aged law books lining the shelves.

"I sure miss your husband. Abe was a fine man. We liked to kid each other. One time I tried to talk him into voting for Ronald

Reagan. He said he'd do it if I'd promise to write-in Jesse Jackson."

Melvina chuckled. "Abe Hawkins and I had fifty years together. He was fond of you, Zack. He said you were an honest lawyer and to come see you if I needed help. Well, sir, I need help."

"What you got?" His pointed question surprised her.

"You're as good as there is at wills and deeds. I need your help."

He nodded faintly signaling her to continue.

"Two oil men came by my house last night. Said they wanted to use my land to drill."

The lawyer cleared his throat. "Let me interrupt you, Melvina. It's Elder and Shanks, isn't it? They're clients of mine."

She continued, "The oilmen said they hired you to figure out the land ownership around my property — all around Bladon Springs."

"That's right. They're trying to drill down there. Unfortunately for you, the mineral rights were severed — reserved — years ago. Based on the courthouse records, you only own the surface rights out there, not the minerals. That's why they were seeing you — to negotiate for use of your property — your surface rights."

The black woman reached down for her purse, set it on the edge of the desk, and pulled out several pages of neatly folded stationery.

"I spent last night and this whole morning writing down everything about my property."

She unfolded the stationery and handed it to the lawyer. Names, addresses, and dates were neatly written on sheets of thin, white paper.

"I wanna hire you to represent me. To prove the mineral rights are mine. Zack Junior, I want you to take my case."

Whitcomb took a big sip of tea. Then he opened the brown cover of a legal-sized folder bound at the top. "Melvina, this is an abstract of all the records in the courthouse covering the old Durant place. Here's an affidavit. It appears to defeat your claim to the mineral rights. The affidavit is recorded in the courthouse. It says Raymond Herbert Durant sold the surface rights, but reserved the mineral rights."

Whitcomb heard the front door open and he looked at his wrist watch — one o'clock.

"That's Bea back from lunch. I'll have her copy the affidavit for you."

The lawyer glanced at the sheets the woman had given him. "I'm gonna read your material. Give me a minute."

For five minutes he read and jotted notes. His eyes grew wide under bushy gray eyelashes. She sat silently shifting from side-to-side in her chair. Then he tapped on the desk using a pencil as a gavel.

"Melvina, if you're correct in saying that your grandfather was the lawful son of Raymond Herbert Durant, then you *are* the lawful owner of the mineral rights. In this affidavit it says Raymond Herbert Durant had no children. That's incorrect according to your notes. Your grandfather was their child. The affidavit says LeMoyne A. Durant was the sole heir to the estate of Raymond Herbert Durant. You dispute that. I've been researching title — ownership to property — for years. I've found that lots of times, family history handed down by word of mouth — oral history — is accurate. What you know is oral history. It's not admissible in court. It's record title and documentary evidence that counts."

Her eyes brightened.

"Your problem is simple — there's no written proof that your grandfather is the lawful heir of the Durant estate." The lawyer looked down at the notes on the stationery. "You've done a good job in explaining your claim. Tell me, what's all this about a *droon* ball?"

She leaned forward in her chair. "I don't know, Zack. My mother always said my great-grandmother met my great-grandfather at a *droon* ball in New Orleans. Even though she was colored and he was white, they were bonded together. That's what the family always said, 'they were bonded together'. I never knew granddaddy, but he was a real dandy — a good-looking man. He died young. Wish I knew more about him."

"Who is this woman with the New Orleans address — Doll?" Whitcomb asked.

"I wrote Doll's name because she's a cousin who keeps the family history. Nothing's written. She's got a gift. She's the seventh child of a seventh child — they say. She knows kinfolks way back in time. She can tell stories about people who died a hundred years ago like they were flesh and bones."

"What's Doll's real name?" Whitcomb asked.

"Don't know. Everybody knows her as 'Doll.' Years ago, Doll told me the story about the *droon* balls in New Orleans, about my great-grandparents meeting and fallin' in love."

Whitcomb leaned back in his swivel chair. "No use sugar coating it, Melvina. There's no doubt you got a claim to the mineral rights on the Bladon Springs property. But you got a problem — proof. You can't prove it in court. And this fellow who signed the affidavit and oil and gas lease — Peyton Durant — can prove he's the owner."

"Does just signing a piece prove anything?" she asked.

"In court it does. There's a standing joke among lawyers. 'You can prove hell itself froze over with an affidavit if you can get somebody to sign it.' I don't wanna hurt your feelings, Melvina, but I'm gonna talk straight, just like I'd tell Abe if he were here."

His voice was gentler than his words.

"Your grandfather was probably illegitimate. You know as well as I that blacks and whites didn't marry. Back then, they couldn't marry. It was illegal. So your grandfather was probably illegitimate." He paused, then continued.

"Melvina, I hate to be so blunt, but under the old law a bastard child could not inherit property. Under the old law, in order for a bastard child to inherit from his father, there must be a clear and unambiguous recognition of the child by the father. The father had to recognize the bastard son as his heir. So, you got a tough row to hoe. You gotta prove that your grandfather was the son of Durant. Also, you gotta prove his father actually recognized him as his son. Tough, but who knows?" He shrugged his shoulders. "In the end truth usually prevails." He didn't sound convincing.

"Zack Junior, you gonna take my case, or not?" Melvina asked.

"Don't expect miracles."

"What you gonna charge me?" she asked.

"Do they still mill sugar cane and make sorghum on your place?" he asked.

"Every year, Zack Junior. If you want a pitcher, you got it."

"Thanks, that'll be my retainer."

"Please be serious. Will you take the case?"

His question was stone cold, "Why didn't y'all let me handle Abe's case?" He spoke quickly. "You disappointed me. For years, I did Abe's work for next-to-nothing. Then that truck runs over him. And y'all hire somebody else."

She stood to leave, but before she walked out the door, she stopped. She twisted her head, unsure what to say. She stared at the ceiling so her eyes would not meet his. "I let the children talk me into using that other lawyer. They heard you were having — problems."

"I'm disappointed. Y'all let that other lawyer talk you outta hiring me."

She muttered, "The other lawyer told me . . ." She stopped herself.

"I gave the money to the children. They spent it all." She spoke softly, but clearly. "I didn't do you right. Zack Junior, I just hope you'll handle this case."

He nodded. "I said I'd take it. Twenty percent is customary in an oil and gas case. I'll take it on a twenty percent contingency. Bea will type up a contract and send it to you. If I decide I can't help, I'll tear up the contract so you can hire somebody else."

"Thanks."

When she left, Whitcomb typed the name *Melvina Durant*

Hawkins on a label and pasted the label on a manila file folder. He handwrote her address and phone number on the inside cover.

A new case still excited him. For a moment he felt a feeling of happy anticipation. *Somebody's trying to beat her out of these mineral rights. A man always needs a new challenge. This could be fun — piecing together facts from a hundred fifty years ago. Now that's quite a challenge. Maybe I'll get a New Orleans trip out of this to research records in Orleans Parish.*

And I'll meet this Doll — this seventh child of the seventh child. People used to say they had special powers. The seventh child of the seventh child knows secrets that beguile — that's the saying. There's no such thing anymore. Families are so small.

Ann and I haven't been there in a while. The French Quarter. The Absinthe House on Bourbon where we listened to the piano man on the honeymoon. And Antoine's Restaurant. And Diamond Jim's place. Maybe I'll catch the train.

But — but do I want to fool with Melvina Hawkins? The woman's a little too self-righteous. She showed no appreciation for my friendship with Abe and all that legal work I did. She hired that other lawyer without even talkin' with me. That wrongful death case was simple. The trucker admitted liability to the cop right after he flattened Abe's car. A third-year law student could've won it. I hear he paid off a cop with a big kickback to get the referral. Cop and lawyer ought to be investigated. The lawyer probably made a fee of a quarter million.

Why should I represent Melvina Hawkins? Even if I could resurrect some ancient evidence — and that might take divine intervention — the well still may be dry. Am I a social worker? Her chances are nil. I don't have to take every case that shows up at the door like a solo practitioner right out of law school. I owe this woman nothing.

Aw, heck, Abe would help me if he were here. I'll send her a contract, try to help her out, and hope for a good well.

ANN WHITCOMB, Zack's wife, grew up in a prominent, well-to-do family in Greensboro — in the heart of the Black Belt. She graduated from high school at sixteen, and her family sent her to Stephens College, a "finishing school," in Columbia, Missouri.

Ann's older brother, Marley, was a top-notch athlete in high school — just like Zack Whitcomb — and Zack and Marley played football, baseball, and basketball against each other and became good friends.

Marley earned an appointment to the U.S. Naval Academy at Annapolis — no small task during the war. And Zack headed to the University of Alabama. But he and Marley stayed in touch. In fact, the army assigned Zack to Officers' Candidate School at Fort Monroe, Virginia, at Norfolk, only two hundred miles from Annapolis. Zack and Marley spent a few weekends together.

Zack and Ann knew each other, but they truly met as Marley's guests at the Naval Academy's Farewell Ball in '44. Ann still has her dance card from that evening. It's a little white book with black and gold binding and the academy seal on the front with Zack's name and eight other guys' names written in the slots.

Zack and Ann wouldn't have occasion to see each other for over a year after the ball, and when they met, it was the saddest of occasions. The forties were war years, and Zack Whitcomb and Marley Ashe were young warriors. Marley was killed in action in February 1945 as a lieutenant junior grade aboard the U.S.S. *Saratoga* off Iwo Jima in the Pacific.

Two weeks later, the Ashe family received the telegram from the War Department. In Marley's honor, the family erected a marble monument, a cenotaph, with an anchor beside it in the cemetery and invited close friends to a memorial ceremony. Zack caught the train to Greensboro and stayed with the Ashe family for a few days. By then, the war had ended and Ann was flying for Trans World Airlines as a stewardess. Zack was beginning his law practice in Butler. They started dating. Two years later, they married.

Grief had been transformed into joy.

ANN WHITCOMB has an inquisitive mind and a good memory for details. She keeps an unabridged dictionary and a set of encyclopedias in her den. She reads regularly and subscribes to the *New Yorker* and solves the *New York Times* crossword puzzles. She's a lively lady with a lively curiosity, which Zack loved about her.

Zack tilted his wife's head against the back of the sofa and kissed her gently — as soft as satin. Her face was wrinkled but still regal. He stroked the side of her face, trailing his fingers along her cheeks and jaw. Then he kissed her again.

Her thick black hair, streaked with natural gray, was brushed back and held in place with a barrette. She wore a pleated gray skirt and a black cardigan sweater. Ann had been a marvelous beauty as a young woman. Age had worn but not taken her attractive features, blue eyes, graceful chin and nose, high cheekbones and a slightly mischievous smile.

"Aren't you in high spirits," she remarked. "A good day at work?"

"Dance with me," he said.

Zack switched off the television, then spun an album onto the stereo — Sinatra backed by a big band. "Just in time. I found you just in time. I was lost. The losing dice were tossed." He pulled her from the chair, and the couple danced a fast-paced jitterbug. Even in her sixties, Ann remained a luminous beauty. She moved her arms and legs gracefully and conveyed high excitement. His right hand gripped her left tightly and they moved gracefully, twirling around the den furniture. When the first song ended, he pulled her arms onto his shoulders. "You ever danced at a droon ball? You ever *heard* of a droon ball?

She gazed at him.

"Droon ball? Nope. Means nothing to me."

Sinatra began again — more tender and nostalgic — this time. Zack sang along. "The way you dance 'til dawn. You can't take that away from me."

The fingers on his left hand intertwined comfortably with those on her right. His other hand gently caressed her below her long swan-like neck.

"I'm a lucky man. Not every guy gets to dance with the best lookin', the brightest girl in the world."

She smiled — as softly as the Mona Lisa — then ran her hand through his hair. "Those college lines are a little dated, don't you think?"

"Never." He picked up the pace with the music.

"Give me some details — about those droon balls."

"Melvina Hawkins, from Bladon Springs, came by my office. She believes she owns a big tract of mineral rights. And she wants me to represent her. Says she's the heir of a Louisiana land baron. It sounds far-fetched but she knows a lot of facts. She says her grandparents met at a droon ball in New Orleans. Droon ball. They met at a droon ball. Still doesn't mean anything to you?" The second song ended. She raised her eyebrows as if to see better with eager blue eyes.

In a strong voice, Ann declared, "Keyes. Frances Parkinson Keyes." She winked at him as if to say, *you're one lucky fellow to have me along for the ride*. "She's a novelist. Lived in New Orleans. She wrote about quadroon women meeting white men. Quadroon. That's it — a quadroon ball. Maybe Melvina's ancestors met at a quadroon ball. Time's right for her grandparents. The nineteenth century. The balls were in the nineteenth century."

Zack laughed. "You never cease to amaze me."

7

THEY say oil exploration is seductive. The risks and rewards can be intoxicating. A man named Lee DeGolyer drilled a well in Mexico in 1943 that produced 110,000 barrels a day. In Alabama a typical oil well produces half a million barrels over ten years. That's one well bringing in ten million dollars. It's that kind of money that keeps the drill bits turning.

The romance of the oil business is exploring for oil. And exploration begins with wildcat wells drilled in search of oil where it has never been discovered. The success rate for wildcat wells is dismal — about one in ten hits oil. But the financial rewards can be astonishing.

Everett Eaves of Shreveport, Louisiana, and Zack Brooks of El Dorado, Arkansas, drilled the wildcat well at Citronelle, Alabama, in 1955. Since then, the reservoir has produced 159 million barrels, worth over two billion dollars.

Oil exploration involves varied occupations — geologists to study rocks and pick drill sites, landmen to buy leases, engineers to drill wells, financiers, and lawyers. Oilmen have created colorful names: toolpushers, roustabouts, mudmen. It can be tough, rugged work, but it's a noble profession.

THREE WEEKS after they met with Melvina Hawkins, Shanks and Elder pulled their truck into the parallel parking space across the street from Whitcomb's law office. Red clay clung to the fenders of the pickup. The oilmen climbed out of the truck and waited for a log truck to pass. The heat felt good on the brisk October day.

Bea looked up from her word processor. "Ye gods, y'all got mud all over yourselves." She glanced down at their mud-spattered boots and trousers. The oilmen wiped their boots and shed their jackets. Shanks hung his maroon A&M cap on the hat rack.

"We got news, Bea, big news. Is the lawyer in?" Shanks's strong voice carried throughout the small building. An office door opened, and Whitcomb appeared in the hall, "What news?"

Shanks spoke with enthusiasm. He slapped his hands together, producing one loud clap. "An hour ago at three o'clock, we spudded the well — started drilling the Durant well."

Whitcomb nodded, "Congratulations gentlemen. Come in. We'll have a cup of coffee, maybe something stronger, and celebrate."

Bea gave the lawyer a disapproving look, and Whitcomb turned his head away. "Come on back."

"It's satisfying, very satisfying," said Elder, "to bring this off on time, to drill the well with two days to spare on the thirty-day clock." The oilmen followed Whitcomb to the conference room.

The lawyer pulled three coffee cups from the cabinet. "Y'all want a drink? I got a bottle of bourbon."

Shanks reached down to pull beggar's lice off his pant's leg. "I'll take the whiskey."

Whitcomb reached into a cabinet, grasped a quart bottle of Rebel Yell and twisted off the cap. The smell of whisky overpowered the room. Whitcomb closed the library door, afraid that it would permeate the whole office.

The three sat at the conference table. "My brother-in-law fought in the navy under Admiral Hulsey. The admiral believed,

'You can't trust a fightin' man who doesn't drink.'"

"I guess I'll take the hard stuff, too." said Elder. But before I drink anything, I'm faxing the investors. And Standard Petroleum."

> DATE: 10-14-94
> FROM: J. Elder
> Permit No. 11050, E&S Exploration Co., Durant 20-14 Well.
> Bladon Springs, Choctaw County, Alabama.
> Spudded well at 3:00 p.m. Set 2,500' of surface casing.

The lawyer poured three coffee cups full of bourbon.

"Zack, we saved the farmout by spudding the well," said Shanks.

Whitcomb lifted his cup. "I raise a toast to E & S Exploration's spudding the Durant well. To success."

The three coffee cups converged above the table.

"How long will it take to drill the well?" Whitcomb loosened his tie.

Shanks answered. "About four weeks. Drilling goes on night and day until we reach total depth. Come to the well site. Brother, it's in the middle of nowhere. One big forest for miles. Takes a team of mules or a four-wheel drive to get in there. Site's between Collumburg and Bladon Springs. Ground was so wet we built a plank road."

Shanks drank some bourbon, "By the way, if we get lucky, who's gonna get the royalty — Miz Hawkins or Durant?"

"Melvina's case — it's a dog. No proof, yet. But y'all are okay since you got both sides leased."

Elder pulled a pint-sized plastic bottle from the pocket in his khaki army jacket. "I been drinking your mineral water from Bladon Springs. In this day and time, I didn't expect the springs to still be flowing. The well's a mile west. The spring water tastes awful," he smiled. "But it grows on you."

Elder took a swig from the water bottle. "What's the story on Bladon Springs, Zack?"

"Bladon Springs was a resort for the wealthy before the Civil War. Mineral springs were attractions in the 1800s. Travelers came from the Black Belt, Mobile, as far as New Orleans. The big hotel at Bladon burned years ago. Beauregard spent time recuperating at the resort during the Civil War."

Whitcomb's voice ebbed. "The heyday of Bladon Springs passed long ago. The resort hotel burned in the twenties. There's a park and a few stately homes down there. That's all."

Elder swigged the water again, then passed it to Shanks.

Shanks sipped the water and rolled his eyes. "Boy, this stuff would gag a gnat. I'll stick with the whiskey."

"Try it with whiskey, Jim." Elder helped himself to another cup of bourbon, filling the cup to the brim. Shanks looked at Elder funny, but took a sip.

"Not too bad, if your concoction won't kill me. Tennessee bourbon and Bladon Springs water."

Shanks lifted his cup triumphantly. "To a new drink — B and B — Bourbon and Bladon."

Again the cups converged above the table.

Shanks finished his cup, then filled it again. "Baseball. We heard about your baseball exploits, about this Black Belt league. Miz Hawkins said ask you about some big game — Demopolis I believe."

Thoroughly relaxed, Whitcomb's face glowed. His voice rose.

"We were in the playoffs with Demopolis in '52. They hired a pitcher off Alabama's SEC champion baseball team — Frank Lary — for the game. And Frank Lary could breeze that fast ball. It looked like an aspirin tablet coming at you." He held the bottle in his hand.

"The Town of Butler and half of Choctaw County shut down and everybody went to Demopolis to see us play against Frank Lary. The mayor of Butler, Bob Locke, bet five hundred bucks on us. The team itself put up another five hundred on the game. Stupidest bet I ever made. How we gonna get a run off Lary? The man is an All-American. Alabama just returned from the college World Series, and Lary is a shoo-in for the major leagues. He pitched for Detroit for years. They called him the 'Yankee Killer' because he whipped Mantle, Maris, and Yogi so much. Plus, we gotta deal with their home crowd and home cookin' from the umpires.

"I still can't believe I bet on that game. And, to boot, we'd never seen a slider, and Frank Lary threw a slider. A slider was a new pitch in '52.

"We warmed up and visited with the Demopolis players. Competition was hot in those leagues, but the players always visited with each other before the game — tradition. When the umpires called the teams to exchange line-ups, Hugh Sloan, the manager, and Mr. Hannah, a coach, and I walked to homeplate to meet with the umpires.

"Beautiful setting in Demopolis. The ballfield is across the street from a lovely antebellum home called *Gaineswood*.

"While we're talking at home, Frank Lary is warming up on the mound. Mr. Hannah's not worried about the game. We get half the gate receipts, and he's worried about the ticket takers. Mr. Hannah tells the Demopolis owner, 'Ain't nobody, except the ticket takers, gonna make any money unless you put a pair of bathing trunks on those guys at the ticket booth.'

"I'm watching Lary. He walks over to the catcher. They're having an argument. Lary says to the catcher, 'I throw a mean knuckleball five or six times a game.' The catcher says 'Not today. I ain't getting killed by no knuckler.' Lary says, 'Y'all are payin' me a hundred bucks to win, and I'm using the knuckler.' Finally I overhear Lary and the catcher work out a deal. Lary agrees to use the knuckleball just one time, just one pitch during the entire game. So that's the deal between Lary and the catcher. Lary will throw the knuckleball when he gives the catcher a signal. The signal is a clenched fist. I'm the only one to overhear the conversation, and I'm not forgetting.

"The game starts. Nobody scores. Demopolis isn't too strong without Lary on the mound. Cecil Tew, my cousin, is pitching for us. We got a fine defensive team and Demopolis can't score. It's a good, tough ballgame.

"Well, I come up to bat in the fourth. Demopolis has a short right field fence — only about two hundred fifty feet from home. I hit right-handed. I choke up on the bat trying to get a piece of Lary's fastball. I've never hit the long ball. I usually hit line drives. Damn, if on the second pitch, I get a fastball from Lary and hit a blue darter — a shot — that just clears the short rightfield fence for a homerun. Butler leads one to nothing. First hit off Frank Lary.

"In time, Demopolis scratches out a couple of runs and leads going into the top of the eighth. We probably get three hits, tops, off Lary. But we know he's going the distance because Demopolis paid a hundred bucks for his services. Lary's getting hot and tired. It's a Saturday afternoon in July. Probably ninety-five degrees and not a leaf is stirring. Lary's wool uniform is sopping wet.

"In the eighth, he walks the first batter. They mess up a sacrifice bunt and we got two men on with nobody out. The next guy pops a Texas Leaguer into left for a single but nobody scores. So now we got the bases loaded and no outs. Well, Mister Frank Lary gets his dander up. He breezes fastballs right by our eight and nine hitters and fans both. So it's two outs, bases loaded, and I'm up.

"We didn't wear batting helmets in that league and with a big guy like Lary on the mound, fear becomes a factor. The mound in Demopolis seems four feet high. Lary looks seven feet tall, and when he strides toward home plate during his wind-up, he was standing on top of the batter.

"I manage to foul a couple off and work a full count. I step out of the batter's box. I look down the third base line to the coach. It's Mr. Hannah. Strange sight, even for 1952. Mr. Hannah's wearing a shirt and tie, baggy pants and a hat — like Connie Mack I suppose. I decide to have a talk. So I call time out and walk down the third base line to the coach's box. Our manager, Hugh Sloan, walks to the third base box. We have a big pow-wow with the runners from second and third. Meantime, Frank Lary is talking with the catcher and the Demopolis coach in a meeting on the mound. Hugh and I agree on the strategy. We substitute Jimmy 'Flea Powder' McCary, our team's fastest man, for our slowest runner, Garfield Plowman, who's on second base. The umpire — he's circuit solicitor — that means DA, for that part of Alabama — grows tired of all this high-level strategy. He hollers 'Play ball.'"

Whitcomb put down the whisky bottle he was holding.

"I step in the box with the three-two count to face Lary again. Sure enough, as I figured, Lary gives the clenched fist signal to the catcher — the signal meaning he's throwing the knuckleball. He takes a full wind-up, and our runners get a big jump.

"I remember the pitch like yesterday. Unlike Lary's fast ball and slider, the pitch coming at me looks like a big grapefruit. I could read the trademark — *Spalding*. For an instant, I almost swing. The knuckler can entice you to swing — that's it's beauty. But I hold the swing and wait for the ball to drop. Finally, just in front of home the ball darts down and away, hard. I couldn't have hit the pitch with a bass fiddle, but I'm not trying to hit it. I swing the bat down in front of the catcher's face to distract him. The ball skips through the dirt in the left hander's batting box. I didn't have a prayer to hit the pitch. But the Demopolis catcher didn't have a prayer to *catch* it either. The ball bounces to the backstop. Must have rolled twenty yards before the ball hit the bottom of the chicken wire backstop.

"I strike out, but since it's the third strike and the catcher misses the ball, I run safely down to first base. Our runner from third scores tying the game and 'Flea Powder' McCary, who could pick 'em up and put 'em down, is running on the full count. Frank Lary was well trained. He covers home on the passed ball, but the catcher is slow running to the backstop. The catcher obviously doesn't expect 'Flea Powder' to keep going at third. 'Flea Powder' runs like a scalded dog, never slows at third, slides into home head first like Pepper Martin and beats the throw to Lary covering home.

"Butler three, Demopolis two, after seven and a half innings. Harry Moore comes on to pitch and shuts out Demopolis in the eighth and ninth."

"Smartest play I ever made. I struck out, but we won the game. I've got the box score on my wall."

"Hell, Zack, I thought y'all lost. Melvina Hawkins said it was a sad day."

"She's from south end of the county. They always pull against Butler."

8

PEYTON Durant whipped his bright red Mercedes convertible down St. Charles Avenue toward the New Orleans Central Business District past slow-moving traffic. The tops of the skyscrapers up ahead looked strangely mystical above the dense early morning fog. He gripped the steering wheel tightly, leaned forward, pushed the accelerator, and sped down the tree-lined boulevard. He glanced at the warm-colored mansions and neatly manicured lawns along St. Charles.

Durant stopped at a red light at Lee circle, reached for a pad in his briefcase, and read the notes he'd written last night. "10-15-94: On the opening, buy 1000 contracts, December at 64 cents or below. Target — 70 cents. Potential profit — $3 million."

An idea had sifted through his mind since his return from the Far East. Six days in the Orient observing the cotton crop in Islamabad and Hong Kong convinced Durant the cotton market was ripe for a strong upward move. Harvey Kruk's charts at the American embassy predicted the harvest would be weak. Last week's bearish market — straight down for five days — was illogical. The cotton price was approaching a four-year low.

Durant's floor broker, Hunter Morris, had sensed panic selling on the floor yesterday.

The bearish market played perfectly into Durant's key trading principle: When there is panic buying or selling, trade in the opposite direction from the panic. Time after time, when virtually all traders were caught in a selling fever, driving the price down, Durant would patiently buy cotton, and when the market reversed, ride a wave of buying and return big profits.

The traffic signal's green light sliced through the fog, and Durant raced around the traffic circle beneath the imposing statue of Robert E. Lee. In the distance down Poydras, the Dome's gold exterior sparkled in the morning light.

Durant's mind raced as he pondered the day's trading possibilities. *Demand for cotton remains strong.* He'd seen, firsthand, the busy textile mills in Hong Kong.

Durant laughed out loud when he thought of the wild rumor making the rounds in the cotton pits driving the price down — somebody developed an artificial fiber that would cut into the cotton market. *How often have I heard that one? Never anything to it. Damn plastic clothes.*

Durant turned off La Salle Street into the Joliet Garage and parked in his private space.

Buying at this price is the deal of a lifetime. I'm buying at sixty-four cents with a target of seventy, maybe even seventy-five.

He walked at a fast pace the block to the New Orleans Cotton Exchange Building. He pushed hard on the polished brass revolving door, nodded politely to the guard and trotted up the marble staircase to the second floor.

His secretary sitting at her desk in the foyer nodded. "G'morning, Mister Durant." By the look of concentration on his face — narrow eyes, lips tightly together — she knew to be brief. "You got several messages."

Durant hung up the coat to the custom-made suit he'd bought in Hong Kong. "Who called?"

"Couple of traders from the Mississippi Delta. You got a call from Senator Ratliff's office about another fund-raiser. Plus, you've had a call every day from the same man. The caller wouldn't leave a message. Just said tell you 'Hong Kong called.'"

Durant hit the switch by his desk. Two computers, the laser printer, and the fax came to life. He stared hard for several minutes at charts, clippings, and reports pinned to the cork-paneled wall.

"Hong Kong's on the line again."

Durant put on his telephone headset with the tiny wire speaker to take the call.

Durant answered curtly, "Yeah."

"Mister Durant. This is Kruk in Hong Kong."

Durant was silent.

"This is Harvey Kruk. At the embassy in Hong Kong."

Durant's mind was blank. Then he remembered the man in the brown suit. The gambler. The agricultural attaché.

"Talk, Kruk. I'm busy."

"I wanna help you. And you can help me. You can make money. And I can make money. I've got access to crucial cotton information. You know that I'm the guru when it comes to the cotton crop. If you want the stuff — if you want some market-moving cotton information — call me. At the Prince Albert Hotel in Hong Kong." Click.

Durant understood. Kruk had carefully wordsmithed his offer. On the surface, the words constituted no offer of insider information, but the implication was clear. *Kruk provides me critical inside information before it's public. In return, I compensate him.*

Durant rolled his eyes.

Cheap-ass, low-life government bureaucrat. He's probably still wearing the same brown plastic suit.

Again Durant studied the charts. Then he punched the phone button, automatically dialing his floor broker.

At thirty-five, Hunter Morris was only five years younger than Durant. The two communicated well. Hunter Morris knew the trading business as well as anyone. Like most floor brokers in commodities markets, Hunter was a young man. Trading commodities is a quick bucks, fast-paced, high-decibel game. The stress can be unbearable. Commissions are great for traders — averaging fifty dollars per trade for each contract, but the *real* money lies in the floor traders' personal trading — trading for your own account. Every trading day covers five hours of fast-paced action — hand signals, yells across the pit, trades and contracts being executed constantly among buyers and sellers.

Morris and Durant had thrived together in the trading pits in New York, Chicago, and New Orleans. Durant looked down from his office window over the trading floor. From his office window, he could view the entire trading floor — the size of a basketball court.

"Hunter, I'm trading today, man. I wanna buy a thousand *Decs* of cotton. On the opening."

Morris bounced up from his chair at his telephone desk — one of many traders' cubicles along the walls of the floor. When Hunter heard Durant's order for a thousand cotton contracts, he gripped the phone tightly, and calmly cleared his throat, "All right, Peyton. That's big, mighty big. Let me repeat your order for confirmation. Buy a thousand cotton contracts at the market, December delivery. That's one thousand *Decs*. I'll buy on the opening at 8:30. Okay?"

"Right. Do it, Hunter."

Durant hung up, twisted the lever to open the blinds more widely. The floor of the exchange was coming to life. Traders wearing jackets of bright blues, reds, and yellows woven in strange designs emerged from the cloakroom, having swapped conventional suit coats for the colorful jackets identifying the different trading companies. The hall filled quickly — traders, clerks, and regulators moving along the narrow aisles connecting the twelve trading pits — one for each commodity traded in the hall. In the nineteenth century only cotton was traded, but other farm products (rice, corn, wheat) and the metals were added to compete with bigger commodities exchanges in New York and Chicago.

Anxious traders mounted the narrow raised platforms of the trading pits. The platforms, a yard wide and two steps high, formed a ring seven or eight steps across — the circular design allowing traders to view all the action while they traded. Inside the ring, exchange clerks carrying hand-held computers acted like referees recording deals consummated. The floor of the entire hall was covered with a dark green carpet, which rose and fell over the twelve pits on the floor, giving the appearance of swells on an emerald sea. At 8:30, the gavel sounded and trading commenced. Traders screamed offers, bids, and acceptances at each other across the pits — hundreds of contracts being traded every minute. Thirty seconds after the market opened, Hunter Morris marched from his telephone desk toward the cotton pit, dodging traders in the aisles and ducking telephone lines hung like Christmas garlands around the hall. Durant watched Morris enter the pit and join in the trading.

Durant balled his hands into fists. He felt a rush of energy through his body. It was always this way for Durant — a fierce surge of nervousness overwhelmed him when he entered a large order and trading started. Durant closed his eyes, rolled his head, and waited for the rush to subside.

Durant watched Morris buying the thousand contracts for Peyton Durant's account. He traded feverishly, taking notes, giving hand signals, hollering in traders' lingo at other brokers in the cotton pit, and glancing up at the electronic board from time to time.

The huge trading initiated by Morris began to draw the attention of rival cotton brokers. When Morris started buying, there were only four traders around the pit. But cotton traders rushed to the pit as Morris continued to buy. Soon there were twenty-five brokers trading in the cotton pit with Morris.

The trading quickened to a frenzied pace, thousands of dollars being made and lost in moments. Morris continued to bark out orders, buying more and more cotton. The downward trend from the past three days continued. The electronic board high above the floor told the numbers on the price of cotton — *64, 63.50, 63, 62.50.*

After an hour of trading, Hunter Morris turned and walked away from the pit to his cubicle off the trading floor. He slumped into his chair like a puppet whose strings were clipped. He wiped the sweat from his face with his shirt sleeve and dialed Durant. "This is to confirm that I have bought a thousand cotton contracts for your account at varying prices below sixty-four cents." Morris pointed at his stomach. "Guts, brother. You got guts. And some big ones between those legs."

The order had been entered. Satisfied and confident about the huge trade, Durant sat down and relaxed in his high-backed leather chair. All factors were favorable, particularly Durant's tried and true theory of trading against a panic. Sure enough, as the minutes passed, the falling cotton price began to stabilize, and then slowly rise — *64, 64.50, 65, 65.50.* Each upward tick of the market brought a profit. By eleven-thirty, the cotton price was at 66 cents — the high for the day. In just three hours of trading, Durant's profit was already hundreds of thousands, with the promise of more.

Durant dialed Morris. "Hunter, when the price reaches seventy, I'll take the profit."

"Yes, sir. I'll repeat. On your December cotton contracts, I'll take you out of the market at seventy cents."

Durant watched the flashing numbers on his computer screen and charted the price. His secretary interrupted his concentration. "Mr. Durant, you got a call. Want it?"

"Who is it?"

"A lady — Mimi Mitchell."

He nodded, shoved the office door shut, and pushed a button to take the call over his headset.

"Mimi. How you doing? Can't talk much. I got a big-time position on in cotton. Lot at stake."

"You sound really harried, Peyton."

"Well, just trying to make a living."

She hesitated for effect.

"Peyton, I need you here with me, baby. I'm at Galatoire's. I'm sitting all alone at a table for two. I waited outside thirty minutes to get in. I already got hot bread, and just opened a bottle of Chardonnay."

"That's enticing, but I gotta watch the market. Maybe later. Tonight."

"Come on, Peyton. I already ordered you an entree."

He laughed, "What is it?"

"Trout marguery — the poached trout with shrimp and crab meat sauce."

"Don't tempt me. I got a question, Mimi. You always look great in hats. Are you wearing a hat today?"

"Yeah, the black one with the veil. I wore it to the party at the track, out at the Fairgrounds."

"Never seen it, Mimi. Musta been another guy."

She hesitated for a moment. "You've pulled that one on me before. And I'm wearing that short black dress you bought me at Saks. Now, Peyton, you straighten your tie. Put on your jacket. Take a stroll. And I'll see you in five minutes."

He closed his eyes. He saw her thick black hair under the hat, her gorgeous legs crossed at the knee, sitting at a corner table. Probably half the men in the restaurant were glancing at her.

"Pour me a glass of wine. I'll be there in five minutes."

9

IN THE fall of the year, New Orleans' permanent residents join the tourists walking the streets of the French Quarter. The city's autumn air is clean and crisp, and the streets lose their unpleasant summertime smell — a combination of steamy stagnant air, stale booze from the previous night's Bourbon Street celebration, and rotting garbage piled on the narrow eighteenth-century streets awaiting pickup.

Confident and optimistic about his trade, Durant descended the marble steps onto the lobby floor and walked out of the Cotton Exchange Building onto Carondelet. A crowded streetcar rambled past. He walked with the flow of foot traffic three blocks to Canal Street, then crossed Canal to Bourbon Street and his lunch destination.

Galatoire's is a classic old-world Creole restaurant where New Orleanians go to see and be seen. Durant strolled past a dozen customers waiting in line against the marble wall outside the restaurant. The maitre d', a middle-aged man dressed in a dark blue suit, opened the front door, and Durant stuffed a ten in his coat pocket. "Where you been, Mister Durant? Your lady friend's waitin'. To the right, in the corner."

Durant stepped inside and glanced across the restaurant floor. Tuxedoed waiters balanced trays high over their heads. Young busboys in white jackets hustled among the tables on the shiny tile floor. Brass ceiling fans turned high above the business crowd. The smells of hot French bread and spicy creole sauces filled the room.

"Peyton," He barely heard the feminine voice over the chatter and clinking sounds of glasses and silverware. "Over here."

Durant waved to acknowledge a friendly wave from the rear and then joined Mimi at the corner table. Her dress was simple, black, and short with a low vee barely exposing her breasts. A necklace of pearls hung along her neck, and the brim of her black felt hat swooped low just above her eyes.

"Mimi. Love the hat." He kissed her cheek.

She whispered in his ear, "Love your body."

"Mimi, you got an ego, don't you? Waiting in line at Galatoire's, calling me while the market's open, expecting me to drop everything on the spot, and join you. I must be crazy to walk away from the trade I just entered. You got a spell on me."

She filled his wine glass. "Kick back. Relax, Peyton. It's only money."

"God, you look sexy, Mimi."

She pointed to a colorful card lying on the bread and butter plate. "What's this?" He opened the card.

Peyton,
    I've missed you bunches. You entertain me. You buy things for me. You treat me like royalty. And the sex — it's off the Richter scale.
    Love,
    Mimi

A former gymnast at the University of Texas, Mimi still took dance lessons three times a week, stayed trim, and even at twenty-nine — seven years out of college — looked like an athlete.

He had met her last January after work during happy hour at an uptown bar. He was sitting with Hunter, having a drink. She asked Hunter to dance, then grabbed his hand and pulled him out of his chair. They playfully danced a Cajun waltz. Mimi became the center of attention, gracefully twirling around the room in a short skirt and boots. With her lithe dance movements of her arms and legs, she conveyed an erotic excitement.

When the music stopped, he escorted her back to the table to join Durant. The threesome made small talk and drank Coors.

Mimi dominated the conversation, talking about her Pi Phi days at U-T, her year teaching high school economics, her switch to the business world, and her move to New Orleans to take a stockbroker's job. Durant found it all boring, but he couldn't stop gazing at her — long bangs, lively brown eyes, freckled face, black hair pulled back behind her ears, and the sculpted figure.

Hunter understood his place in Durant's hierarchy. He exited the scene leaving the couple alone. He later said he detected "vibrations and raw chemistry" between Mimi and Peyton.

They each drank another Coors. She skillfully pried out the basics about him. He played along — SAE at Tulane, MBA from Harvard, reared on a ten-thousand acre plantation in Catahoula Parish, drove a Mercedes, and owned a mansion in the Garden District.

Mimi wrote her phone number on a napkin before she left.

Mimi was far down a long list of women in the back of his black book. But every time Peyton called her for a date, no matter how late, she was available. He called her at ten o'clock one Thursday night and asked her to fix up dates for two potential clients from Switzerland. Mimi and two of her girlfriends met the men at the Bombay Club in the Quarter. They partied until three in the morning.

Peyton began to call her more often. Three months after they met, he took her to New York for a four-day business trip.

Durant's friends loved Mimi's femininity. He enjoyed being

seen with her. She wore hats, short skirts, short dresses, and high heels.

Meticulously, Durant folded the card from Mimi and slid it into his wallet. He sipped from the wine glass, then reached for Mimi's hand and squeezed it. Resting on the white linen table-cloth, her arms were noticeably tanned.

"Mimi, how's work in the staid and boring world at Merrill Lynch — in the world of leisurely trading and leisurely lunches — where little old ladies go for the big time buying zero-coupon Treasury bills and CDs? Y'all consider it a big risk to buy stock on the NASDAQ."

The waiter slipped a plate of trout covered in a light yellow sauce on the linen tablecloth in front of Durant.

"Don't be so condescending, Peyton. We all don't have the Midas touch. You laugh, Peyton Durant. You gunslingers in commodities live like kings. Those who live by the sword can also die by the sword." She squeezed his hand. "I wanna change the subject. I missed you, Peyton. Where you been?"

Peyton took several bites, then dropped his fork. "Quick trip to check the cotton crop overseas. I gotta know what's going on in the Orient to trade intelligently. China, India, Pakistan — that's where it's at after the U.S."

"Wish you'd asked me to go," she said.

"I'll take you next time. Get a passport."

The waiter refilled his wine glass.

"You still playing tennis, Mimi?" he asked.

"Not since our last lesson."

She winked at him. "Remember the lessons you taught me — where to grip it, how to stroke it, the eastern grip. I like the western grip." She giggled. "You showed me how to hold both balls at the same time."

He smiled and relaxed.

"Last time we played, Peyton, I loved your forehand. Let me know the next tournament you're in, Peyton. I adore your serves

— so hard and deep — in the court. Next time we play, I want you to use a wooden racket. You look so sexy in all white, especially with that white tennis sweater. And holding a wooden racket. And buy some white balls. I love big, fluffy white balls."

The waiter poured them each another glass of wine.

"Mimi, I didn't know tennis was so exotic. I think you like the game."

She tore the end off a loaf of hot bread, buttered it, and fed it to him. "Tradin' cotton. Tradin' futures contracts. A stud on the floor. And a stud off the floor." She kissed him. "I've never asked, how'd you become a trader?"

"My grandfather and his brother helped to start the New Orleans Cotton Exchange after the Civil War. Granddaddy operated a plantation in Catahoula Parish along the Mississippi and another one along the Tombigbee in west Alabama. He sold the plantation in Alabama during Reconstruction and kept the mineral rights. Whenever the family sold property, they kept the mineral rights. Dad always said the minerals might be worth more — more than the surface."

The waiter brought two bowls of bread pudding with a sauce that smelled like a sweet liqueur.

"Anyway, the Durants always owned a seat on the New Orleans Exchange. I used to be a runner on the floor. Back then Daddy didn't speculate. Mostly he traded his own cotton crop. And was damn good at it. Hell, he knew everybody in cotton — like a small fraternity back then. He understood supply and demand. Always quoted Adam Smith."

He leaned back in his chair and fixed his hair with his hand. "I'm not a farmer like Dad. I let the foreman handle the farm. I'm a speculator, pure and simple. It's a zero-sum game. Dog-eat-dog. Kill or be killed. And I'd rather be the killer."

"You've knocked 'em dead. I've seen those trading statements you frame hanging on the walls in your office. Not many guys make those kind of profits."

Durant took a bite from the bowl of bread pudding. He saw the face of his Rolex — 1:00 — and reached for Mimi's hand. "Baby, I gotta move. Gotta go. I'll call."

AFTER TROUT, bread pudding, two glasses of wine and intoxicating conversation, Durant's huge cotton trade entered earlier was the last thing on his mind.

Not for long. When Durant walked through the revolving door of the Cotton Exchange, one of his traders stood in the lobby waiting for him. The trader's face was green, like he was seasick. He grabbed Durant by the arm and told him the unfortunate news.

"Mr. Durant, the cotton market got hit like a train wreck. Price is down ten cents to fifty-four. It's crazy. It's wild. Nobody's buying. You been hammered. That price drop has cost you a fortune. You got a *margin call*. You gotta deposit some big bucks in cash to cover the loss."

The news hit Durant like an Arctic blast. He sobered up quickly. "Why didn't you bastards call me?"

"Hell, we called half the restaurants in the Quarter."

Durant coolly walked up the marble stairs to his office, trying at each step to think clearly about his options.

Identify alternatives first, he told himself. Option one, take huge loss. Option two, raise the money to pay the margin and buy more cotton. Cotton won't stay at fifty-four cents. It can't stay so low for long.

When Durant walked into his office he peered through the office window to the trading board to confirm the price quoted by his trader — *54.00*. December cotton was indeed trading for fifty-four cents. He turned his head away, and closed his eyes hard.

My God — four million dollar loss. There's red ink and blood all over the trading floor today. Unfortunately, it's my blood down there.

Durant sat heavily at his desk and began working his computer. After a few minutes staring at the screen, he concluded he didn't have enough cash and liquid assets to pay the margin requirement necessary to continue trading. Option two was out.

Option one was tough, but he had no choice. Take a huge loss and get out of the market.

He telephoned Hunter Morris downstairs on the trading floor. In a slow, broken voice Durant choked out the words. "Hunter, get me out of all those long positions. I'm taking the loss."

"Yes sir, Sorry about the situation, Peyton. Keep your head up. You'll be back." Hunter dutifully entered the trades taking Durant out of the cotton market.

In one fateful, God-awful day of trading, Durant had lost a quarter of his worth.

The drive home took longer than normal. His arms felt lifeless. He could hardly handle the car. Construction debris covered St. Charles and the traffic snarled. Farther ahead, two police cars with flashing blue and red lights surrounded a gruesome, bloody wreck scene. A faceless cop detoured the traffic through the projects.

He remembered stories about traders losing their fortune in a horrendous trading day and blowing their brains out. A gray-haired trader from Chicago once told him, "If you ever lose half of your net worth in single day, suicide becomes a viable option." Durant used to laugh at the thought. Now perhaps he understood.

Durant arrived home from the Exchange late in the afternoon, numb and weak. He lay on the couch in complete darkness, staring at nothing. He had rolled the dice of the commodities market one time too many. He longed for the day to begin again.

Lord, would I change things. Never put so much money into one deal. I bought a thousand cotton contracts. Ridiculous. What foolishness. Arrogance. Stupidity. Putting all those eggs in a single basket.

How the hell can I get out of this financial disaster? I'll have to pay millions, by God, millions to the Cotton Exchange to cover the loss.

In his mind, he considered ways to raise quick money. He thought through his biggest assets. It looked bleak.

Bean counters — the CPAs — I better call to get the final count on my losses, and how I'm gonna cover.

He fumbled for the telephone receiver on the end table and

listened for the dial tone. The quick beeps told him to listen for a message on voice mail.

"Kruk again. I got important — very important — information. This stuff will rock the market — immediately. I strongly suggest you call. I'm recording this at ten o'clock Hong Kong time. It's four in New Orleans. I'm at the Prince Albert."

Persistent bastard.

Durant hit the light switch and the Waterford chandelier lit up in the dining room. He paced the floor of his mansion, inspecting the furnishings like an insurance appraiser: a Degas original, a gallery of Linda McCartney photographs, antique furniture from the French empire period, a dozen hand-carved dining chairs from England, sterling purchased from the London silver vaults, a wall-sized fourteenth-century tapestry.

He opened his bar, withdrew a bottle of Scotch from a case he'd bought in Edinburgh, filled a crystal tumbler, and swirled the dark liquid. From the bar, he could see the living room, dining room, and through French doors, the deck and fountain in the grounds beyond.

If you follow the rules, you're in a club of one. It's just a little inside information on the Chinese cotton crop. I make a few bucks. The attaché makes a few extra bucks. Nobody gets hurt — just a few dumb mullets. Trading rules are for the mullets in the market. John D. Rockefeller said it right, "Making money is a gift from God." He roughed up his rivals and ran 'em out. Now Rockefeller's name is revered. The Golden Rule? The Golden Rule in this world is simple — The man with all the gold gets to make the rules.

Durant took a deep breath of air like he was diving into bottomless waters. Then he picked up the phone and dialed the Prince Albert Hotel in Hong Kong. The hotel operator answered with a strong oriental accent.

"I'd like to speak with a Mister Kruk. He told me to reach him there." Durant paused to wait for the telephone transfer.

"Yes?"

Durant recognized Kruk's voice.

"Mister Kruk, I'd appreciate it if you would return my call from a pay phone. I'll be waiting by my home phone."

"All right. Give me five minutes." Kruk replied.

Durant poured more Scotch into his glass and waited for the call. The telephone rang only once before Durant grabbed the receiver.

"Hello, Kruk. Where you callin' from?"

"A phone booth on Hennessey Road. It's safe. It's an old-fashioned English phone booth. Enclosed."

"Okay. What you got for me?" asked Durant.

"I got information — straight from Beijing." Kruk spoke slowly and with a trace of nervousness in his voice.

"Here's the deal, Mister Durant. I'll make you some real money, big money with good, very good information. I get ten percent of the profits. Fair enough?" Kruk hesitated to await an answer.

"Fair enough. You got a deal. We'll work out later the details for transfer of the money."

Durant heard the rattle of papers.

"Here's what I got — " Kruk enunciated every word. "The Chinese government is expecting a shortfall in its cotton production. To make up the difference to keep their textile mills going full steam, the Chinese government is buying three million bales on the world market at the market price. It's a one and a half billion dollar deal. I would expect this Chinese deal to bring at least a fifteen cent increase in the cotton price."

"Yeah, I agree," Durant said. "Three million bales will run up the price in a hurry. When do you expect the sale to be consummated?"

"Within the month. You can count on it," replied Kruk.

"Okay, Kruk. But I need something to verify your information. Can you name your source?"

"I dunno. That's dangerous," said Kruk.

"I don't know if I can deal without the name of your source," said Durant.

Kruk hesitated, then blurted out, "Wang Li, Minister of Agriculture. Check it out."

"Okay, Kruk, I'm gonna take a chance. I got blasted hard today, but I still have a little ammunition. If I win, then you win. Ten percent's your cut."

"Before you hang up, Mister Durant, tell me something. Can I trust you with my share — the ten percent?"

"Yes sir," Durant laughed. "You know what they say. There's honor among thieves."

"Fair enough."

Report in *Wall Street Journal*, October 16, 1994.

COTTON COLLAPSES

The cotton market continued its dramatic collapse, closing down 1000 points in heavy trading. Trading experts saw no visible, fundamental reasons for the low price, as sales and domestic consumption numbers have been above last year's. Rumors were rampant on the floor. Unsubstantiated ginning reports indicating bountiful yields in the Mississippi Delta and in California fueled the fire sale of cotton.

One rumor persisted that a large international trader was having difficulty maintaining loans with banks, and he sold his cotton into the market. Spec accounts soon got wind of the rumor and jumped in front of large offers to push sell-stops. A big round of sell-stops was touched off in the Dec 94 contract at 5600 as the December contract was pounded into new low ground. Volume was the highest in six months at 24,984 contracts.

10

IN THE commodities markets, the losers owe the winners. And when you lose, you pay the brokerage house that clears the trades. After the debacle on October 15 — Durant owed four million. That's a bunch of zeros on a check. The brokerage houses give no quarter. They'll lean on you the next day. They expect you to wire the money and pay the debt in full.

Durant called in favors. He had made a lot of money for a lot of people in the markets. He had friends. But even he could only buy himself three days to raise the money.

"Peyton, glad to hear from you." An older, aristocratic voice answered the phone. "I read the Forbes article about you. How's the nation's premier cotton broker doing?" asked Tutt Sanford.

Durant was in no mood for socializing. "Not well. Yesterday was big-time bad. I got my lights knocked out. I gotta liquidate some assets and raise the margin. And I gotta move — fast."

"What you need from your lawyer?" Durant's deceased father was a contemporary of Sanford — also a good friend and client.

"I want you to handle a couple of transactions. You got ten days." Durant hesitated a few seconds. "Sell that place in Gstaad — my chalet. If you can't sell it outright, sell an option on it."

"You're serious, aren't you?" asked Sanford.

Durant didn't answer. "And I wanna sell my share of that shopping arcade in London — that should net a million."

"Peyton, your partners in the U.K. are gonna squeal. There's a gentlemen's agreement not to sell without offering your share to the other partners," said Sanford.

"Screw 'em, Tutt. Have I got the legal right to sell my interest?"

"You certainly do."

"Then sell it. And sell that hick radio station in the Mississippi Delta."

"Peyton, the radio station's a problem. We'll need FCC approval," said Sanford.

"No sweat, I'll call Senator Ratliff and lean on him. I raised half a million for him. He owes me. I need some title work, too. Have one of those hot shot Ivy Leaguers in your firm check the title on my Alabama mineral rights. I been getting reports in the mail that some independent's gonna drill in Choctaw County. If they hit a well, I want the title locked up tight. Dad always said there was something shaky about the title — a nigger in the woodpile."

Sanford ignored Durant's crass talk.

"You got it, boy," said Sanford. "We got a file on the estate."

"And shake it up, Tutt. We'll deal in wire transfers."

RAISING MONEY for three days, at a mercurial pace, Durant, his accountants and high-powered lawyers sold off his assets. CDs, common stock, stock options, corporate bonds, government bonds, treasury notes, then real estate — a beach house at Point Clear and the Swiss chalet. Often complicated trades were consummated on a phone call and a fax. Durant traded — in Shanks's words — like a one-legged man in an ass-kicking contest. The radio station, the London shopping arcade. In three days, he'd raised the cash. His bank wired it all in to the brokerage house — four million.

I I

JESS Elder concentrated hard on a geologic map lying on the card table in his motel room. He stood and reached to focus a lamp directly onto the map. Two cores of rock held down the rolls on each end of the map. *Gotta hit the oil. Gotta do it tomorrow. It's waiting on us under enormous pressure from ten thousand feet of rock, like a caged animal begging to be unleashed. Been lying there fifty million years.*

Elder took a black straight pin and jammed it through the map. *We're drilling in the perfect place. My God, it looks good — the drilling reports, the mud, the cuttings coming out the hole, everything. Right on target. I like these omens — these good omens. Tomorrow, we'll know.*

Elder glanced at his Omega — 10:30 p.m. *I'll be lucky to sleep four hours.*

A piece of stationery, neatly folded on the corner of the card table, caught his attention. The letterhead said Texas Agriculture and Mechanical University.

Jim's copy of the '65 commencement speech.

Graduates:
By that term, I happily address you.

The search for oil will become your quest, your life's work. As it did for Sir Galahad in his quest for the holy grail, this quest may lead you to the ends of the earth. The financial rewards may be great, but other rewards will be greater. To puncture the earth with a well and glimpse at the grand puzzle of the earth's geology is an exhilarating experience.

Wonder at God's creation beneath us. Enjoy the scientific side of your profession. Collect cores; discuss experiences with your peers; make contributions to your profession — an American industry. Be proud of your predecessors — risk-takers, wildcatters, who created a petroleum industry to provide energy for your nation. We live in the hydrocarbon society. Through dedication and scientific curiosity, the quest for oil will reward you for a lifetime.

Oil beneath us is a blessing, a gift from God. Do not allow the naysayers, the pseudo-intellectuals who preach environmentalism to deter you. Yours is a noble task. We have taught you the path. Drill and produce the resources. Beneath our feet is a birthright — a resource more precious than gold. If we fail or forget to share in her bounty, we risk returning to harsher times that mankind has worked to rise above.

The oilman felt a rush of energy. His hands tingled. He closed his fist. *Yes, we'll share in the bounty. Yes, we'll glimpse at the puzzle. I solved the puzzle. We're gonna unleash the earth's energy down yonder in those rocks! We're gonna get it!*

He turned the light out.

THE NEXT MORNING Elder locked the motel door behind him and walked toward the parking lot at Garvis Motor Court. Elder had probably stayed at worse lodgings, but he couldn't remember when.

Pensive, deep in thought, Elder saw his red Ford pickup in the parking lot. At times he regretted the life's work he had chosen.

His career of oil and gas exploration frequently carried him to places far away from his home and family in Tyler, Texas. If he were home in Tyler now, he would be celebrating his fifty-fourth birthday, opening presents at breakfast with his family. Instead of passing the day with his wife, Leslie, and the boys, Jess would *sit a well* in Bladon Springs, Alabama.

When Jess worked for Hunt Oil Company, early in his career, he heard the stories of the Hunts drilling the first oil well in Alabama. During World War II in 1944, with the country in need of oil, H. L. Hunt, an early wildcatter, brought his money and his drilling rig to Alabama. Right here in Butler, Hunt set up operations and bought leases. Whether through good scientific geology, intuition, or bald-faced luck, Hunt hit the first oil discovery in Alabama, in Choctaw County, near Gilbertown. The discovery caused a furor all over Alabama and the country, and made Hunt, already a rich man, a lot richer. In his heyday, no one in America had more money than H. L. Hunt.

Jess laughed to himself. Tales of H. L. Hunt were legend. A sports reporter once interviewed H. L. Hunt after his son, Lamar, lost a pile of money as owner of the Dallas Texans, a football team during the early years of the American Football League. The reporter said, "Your son lost a million dollars this season. How long can these losses continue?" Without batting an eye, the old man responded, "Probably a hundred years."

Jess remembered the day old man Hunt himself taught Jess a lesson — a simple lesson in the difference between the academic world and the practical world. Hunt Oil Company had hired Jess right out of Texas A&M. A month or so after he started working, H. L. Hunt asked Elder to make a geologic presentation to the staff. Elder showed slides, handed out rock samples, and drew on the blackboard. For thirty minutes, Elder droned on about various geologic formations — the Miocene, Eocene, Pleistocene. Then H. L. Hunt abruptly interrupted, "Mr. Elder, I have heard too much about the Miocene, the Eocene. Son, I wanna hear more about some damn kerosene."

Maybe old man Hunt's Alabama luck will rub off on me today, Elder thought. *It's my fifty-fourth birthday, for goodness sakes. Surely that's another good omen.*

He opened the door and saw a large blue envelope on the truck's passenger seat. The name on the envelope was his — *JESS* — in large bold letters. He tore open the envelope and read,

> Baby,
>   Sorry we couldn't be together on your birthday. I probably won't be able to talk with you, but tonight I'm raising a toast to you and to us. I'll be sipping your favorite Scotch whiskey, Babe, single malt.
>   Love,
>   Leslie

The steel derrick rose a hundred feet above the evergreen landscape making it visible from the main highway two miles away. The derrick and the entire drilling rig were painted bright silver and glistened in the mid-morning sun like a shiny bayonet. The Texas Lone-Star flag flew from the top (Clatis Blue, the toolpusher, hailed from Lubbock). When Shanks's pickup drove onto wooden planks laid down on the drillsite, Blue waved, signaling the oilmen to join him on the rig floor. Blue, wearing a work suit and a skull cap, met them at the top of steep steps.

"No problems during the night," said Blue. He handed Shanks the daily drilling log. "We'll be down in another hour. You're fixin' to learn what's in these rocks. I'll tell you this. We had an oil show and a kick a while ago." Shanks and Elder exchanged hopeful glances.

The drilling stopped when the well reached the depth of the rock formation where Elder had calculated that oil should be. A tool was lowered into the six-inch hole, 10,000 feet deep.

The results of this test of the rock formation would prove

whether the well was a success. Elder stood on the rig in silence, leaning against a metal beam on the derrick, watching the operation, and pulling and gnawing on his fingers.

Shanks kept moving, walking around the rig and sometimes climbing up and down the stairs.

In the early days of oil drilling, the driller learned that he had struck oil when the oil would violently blow out of the well. The days of the uncontrolled blowouts are long past. Modern day oilmen drill to a target formation and then cut cores and log the formation with a sonde lowered into the hole. Only after the geologist studies the logs of the formation penetrated are the results of the well actually known.

Blue collected the logs — long strips of paper ten feet long — in a box, climbed down the steps, and handed the box to Elder without saying a word.

Elder carried the box containing the logs into the trailer near the rig. He worked alone in the trailer, studying the long sheets of paper. Shanks stood outside, his hands folded, awaiting the results.

After forty-five minutes, Elder called Shanks into the trailer. Elder turned toward Shanks, a smile starting to grow. Elder's bloodhound eyes twinkled. His face blazed as though from the glare of a bonfire. He couldn't restrain himself. "Jim, my boy, we've done it! This well is the biggest thing I have ever seen. We've hit the mother lode. I figure eight hundred feet of sand. The permeability and porosity of the rock are beyond belief. We hit an oil reservoir like Saudi Arabia!"

For a moment, Shanks sat motionless, then the thrill of success overwhelmed him. The years of labor, study, worry, prayer, failure, determination, culminating in ultimate success were like a tonic.

"Let's go smell it, Jess. Old man Hunt didn't trust paper logs. He liked to smell it."

Shanks sprinted across the red clay to the drill rig, climbed the metal stairs two steps at a time to the floor of the rig. He dropped to a knee beside the top of the pipe, sunk deep into the earth. With his eyes closed, Shanks waved the scent toward his face. His nostrils breathed in the smell. It was oil — like a layer of freshly laid asphalt on a black-topped highway.

Elder joined Shanks on one knee. "To smell it from twelve thousand feet — we got a reservoir — one hell of a reservoir." Shanks offered his hand, and his partner accepted it.

For the next few hours, the oilmen celebrated their victory with bourbon and Bladon Springs mineral water in Dixie cups. Toolpusher Clatis Blue and the four rig hands joined the celebration. Regulators would have shut down the operation if they'd seen it.

Juvenile but jovial, Shanks led the cheers like a yell leader at A&M. The drillers toasted everything — wives, girlfriends, a new five iron, a hunting dog, Ronald Reagan, Bear Bryant, John Wayne, an old high school football game, and life itself. Nobody matched Shanks's toast for passion —

> Boys, here's to rebels, riots, and revolution.
> May prostitutes prosper.
> May whiskey become a household word.
> And may debauchery and decadence flourish in every form.

The celebration peaked when Elder read aloud the report he would file with the investors.

> DATE: 11-13-94
> FROM: J. Elder
> Permit No. 11050, E & S Exploration Co., Inc. Durant 20-14 well, reached total depth of 12,460 feet. Logged and cored. Set 5½-inch production casing. Will complete the well as a major productive oil well. Repeat — major productive oil well.

The feeling for oilmen Elder and Shanks was like a World Series and Super Bowl victory. No crowd cheered at this isolated site in rural Alabama. Only tall pine trees surrounded this field, but the success was meaningful and sweet for the victors.

Three days later they began producing the well. It flowed five thousand barrels the first day and never slowed. The partners sold the first day's production for one hundred thousand dollars.

12

ZACK detected a pleasant excitement in the tone of his wife's voice. She tried never to interrupt his business day. "Zack, can you talk? There's an article in Sunday's *Times*. It's about the Durant family. And maybe Melvina Hawkins and the quadroons — the case you told me about."

"Talk."

"You remember the Cabildo down on Jackson Square in New Orleans?"

"Yeah. Well vaguely."

"It burned a few years ago. They've renovated it. Now they're reopening it. The *Times* story gives the details. And there's a special exhibit. Listen."

He enjoyed listening to Ann's reading aloud. The couple often read aloud to each other, but Ann particularly had the knack — clear enunciation with emphasis in the right places.

"Read the whole article."

NEW ORLEANS REOPENS CABILDO
The Cabildo, one of America's grand old buildings, restored to its former glory, reopened in New Orleans after the comple-

tion of years of renovations. A fire in 1988 gutted a major portion of the historic building. The Cabildo, a dramatic, mysterious building overlooking Jackson Square, is the most imposing structure built during Louisiana's days as a Spanish colony. Named for the city's government during Spanish rule, the Cabildo was the scene of ceremonies when Spain ceded Louisiana to France and when Napoleon ceded Louisiana to the United States in the Louisiana Purchase in 1803. Pierre Lafitte, brother of the pirate Jean Lafitte, was once jailed in the *Calaboose*, in the rear of the building.

The three-story building sits beside the Catholic Basilica St. Louis Cathedral and faces the Mississippi River. To visitors arriving in New Orleans by ship, the Cabildo and the other buildings along Jackson Square have offered a magnificent view.

Originally two stories when completed in 1799, an elegant third story composed of a mansard roof and dormers was added fifty years later. Splendid wrought iron gates and railings protect the entrance and windows.

To honor the restoration, the British government donated a historic document recently discovered in an abandoned bank vault in Bermuda. The document is an Indenture, a mortgage in current parlance. According to experts, the three-page handwritten document is a wonderful example of Victorian calligraphy.

The signatories to the document add to its interest and value: Raymond Durant, a Creole planter, who built a nineteenth-century financial empire; Thomas Moore, governor of Louisiana in 1860; and Benjamin Disraeli, president of the Bank of London and a later prime minister of Britain.

Of further interest is the strange story the Indenture tells of the relationship of Durant with a woman named Eugenie, his black concubine, who bore a son. Durant married a white woman, Michelle Bondurant, but based on the contents of the Indenture, the black concubine was the real mother of their son. The Indenture is displayed side-by-side with perhaps the Museum's most famous artifact, the death mask of Napoleon.

The French, Spanish, and British ambassadors to the U.S. and the governor of Bermuda will attend formal restoration ceremonies later this week.

"How about that!" He gasped, imitating an excited baseball announcer. "My God, my God. I gotta check this out. Let's go to New Orleans — tomorrow morning."

"Can't go. I'm hosting bridge club."

He wouldn't try to persuade her. Hosting the bridge club meant sixteen ladies as guests, four tables with lace table cloths, polished silver service, Wedgwood china, crystal, and the maid. He knew not to tamper with bridge club.

"But I'll make your reservations," she said. "A round-trip ticket on Amtrak. And a room at the Fairmont."

"Thanks. One more thing. Darling, you never cease to amaze me."

"Don't give me too much credit. It's in the *New York Times* for goodness sakes. Not exactly a momentous discovery."

"Momentous enough."

IAN LANGDALE and Lord Westcott stepped out of a limousine in front of the Monteleone Hotel in the French Quarter. The doorman held open glass doors at the hotel entrance. The men climbed the marble steps into the brightly lit lobby. A tall blond with a Scandinavian accent, the concierge, greeted them with a polite handshake and escorted the men to the front desk. Bellmen loaded their luggage on a dolly, except for a long metal tube that Langdale clutched.

Before they had finished registering for their rooms, the museum director appeared, escorted by an armed guard, to accept the tube with its contents from Langdale.

No city in the world celebrates more than New Orleans; no state celebrates more than Louisiana; and the reopening of

Louisiana's grandest museum was cause for celebration.

At eight o'clock, a white horse-drawn carriage driven by a soldier dressed in dazzling white with a three-cornered hat — a replica of a eighteenth-century French officer's uniform — arrived at the Monteleone to transport Langdale, the banker, and Westcott, the governor of Bermuda, through the French Quarter to the Cabildo. Wearing black ties and tuxes, the men drew curious looks from pedestrians on route to the museum.

Dignitaries arrived on the flagstone streets in front of the Cabildo in dozens of carriages. The eighteenth-century Spanish building was decorated to the hilt. Red, white, and blue bunting hung from all the windows. Six flags — the French fleur-de-lis, the French Tricolor, the eighteenth-century Spanish flag with two red lions and two white castles, the British Union Jack, the Confederate battle flag, and the Stars and Stripes — representing the nations which ruled Louisiana — floated from long poles jutting out over Jackson Square. A flotilla of decorated French, Spanish, and British frigates lay anchored in the Mississippi River opposite Jackson Square.

At the Cabildo entrance, the doorman accepted a card from Langdale's escort, then turned toward the growing crowd. He needed no microphone to amplify his strong voice, "Mr. Ian Langdale of Bermuda." Heads turned toward the Bermudian.

Langdale forced a slight smile onto his lips, and nodded politely.

He wished he were home. The past week had not been kind. Last Sunday, his fiancée telephoned from England to break their engagement. It wasn't unexpected. He met Sarah during Race Week — an annual sailboat race in Bermuda. They had corresponded, then traveled together — for two weeks through Kent, staying in B-and-B's in coastal towns from Rye to Dover. A few months later, they cruised the Baltic Sea, stopping at Scandinavian ports. They became engaged — at a cozy restaurant in Tivoli Gardens in Copenhagen. They shared so much, he thought. She was typically English in many respects — sophisticated with an attractively demure personality. She wore expensive but under-stated clothes. He loved the touch of her snow-white soft skin. Like him, she loved to travel.

But travel and shared wanderlust alone couldn't nourish the relationship. After the engagement, he took her to Bermuda — to the family house on Bostock Hill that overlooked Hamilton. The three weeks together in Bermuda hadn't gone badly, but they hadn't gone well. She seemed glad to leave. They talked by phone. He tried to save the engagement, but he hadn't been surprised to receive her Dear John call.

He wanted no part of the party he was entering. But he would play his role — represent the bank and Bermuda and, with as much dignity as he could muster, shake hands, engage in small talk, compliment the city fathers, deliver the speech written for him by the British foreign office, and then go home.

He had readily agreed to come to New Orleans at the request of and at the expense of the Bermuda tourist board and British foreign office. But that was before the breakup with his fiancée. This expenses-paid trip to New Orleans would have been wonder-ful with Sarah along. Without her, it was painfully lonely. He had an early flight tomorrow morning. He would excuse himself from the party after his speech, go to bed early, and be home tomorrow afternoon.

Curious how his gift was displayed, he asked the hostess to direct him to the Indenture display. They slipped through the elegantly dressed crowd up the two flights of stairs to a wooden display case in the center of the room. The Americans are like the British, he thought — queuing in a line in the civilized manner, rather than crowding and shoving like the French. The queue moved quickly, each person viewing the three pages for a few moments and reading the description printed above the display.

The Bermuda Indenture

This recently discovered document was donated to the State of Louisiana by the Waterloo Bank of Bermuda. The document is a Mortgage for a hundred thousand pounds. It is signed by Thomas Moore the Governor of Louisiana, Benjamin Disraeli, a future prime minister of Great Britain, and Herbert Durant, a prominent Creole planter in antebellum Louisiana. European banks financed development during the first century of America's history. Disraeli's signature on the final page of the Indenture is rare and distinctive.

The queue slowed. A tall silver-haired patrician gentleman peered down at the glass-encased document. He leaned over the display with his hands cupped against the sides of his face to reduce glare. For two, three, four minutes, his head moved from side to side while he studied the pages. Rather than a casual observer, he had the appearance of an expert scrutinizing each word. Several in the queue dropped away to sip champagne distributed by roving waiters or to sample seafood hors d'oeuvres. The gentleman viewing the exhibit finally stepped aside when a frustrated lady behind him forcefully tapped him on the shoulder, and broke his concentration.

Langdale accepted a glass of champagne from a waiter, and again followed his escort through the museum. The museum was washed with spectacular yellow light from hundreds of candles flickering from sconces, lanterns, and candelabra. The hall was fragrant with flowers and ladies' perfumes. Men in tuxes and women in evening gowns moved gracefully through the three floors. Like a whirlwind, his host escorted him from place to place introducing him to VIPs. Conversations were light and diplomatic. The crowd was loud, and the music lively. Empty spaces an hour before were now packed. Three bands — one for each floor — played Dixieland, jazz, and swing music. At 9:30 the music from the bands stopped. There was a ruffle of drums on Jackson Square, a blaring bugle, and the Marine band marched into the hall and burst into the "Halls of Montezuma."

When the martial music ended, the toasts and speeches began. Langdale delivered the brief words he had memorized, excused himself, and walked back to his hotel. A sparkling fireworks display had begun over the Mississippi in honor of the Cabildo's opening. He stopped at an all-night newsstand and bought the early edition of the Sunday *Times-Picayune*. His escort said the Cabildo celebration had made the front page and the social page.

Before turning in Langdale peered inside the hotel lounge. The lighting was dim, but he made out a lady playing a grand piano. A handful of people crowded around the piano in leather lounge chairs. His neck ached and his legs felt stiff from three hours of flight to Atlanta then New Orleans, and three more hours of shaking hands and making small talk. He wished he had been in the mood to enjoy it. The piano bar would be perfect for a quiet nightcap.

Langdale noticed two women — playful, animated, enjoying themselves — seated at the piano. One woman wore a wide-brimmed red hat with a black band pulled forward over her forehead. The other's sleek metallic silver dress sparkled. His fatigue waned.

An older couple sitting next to the women had almost finished their drinks. Langdale waited near the barroom entrance until the couple rose to leave. He tapped the empty seat at the piano next to the women.

"May I sit here, ladies?" He already knew the answer. The women nodded, and he relaxed in the soft leather chair snug next to the woman in silver.

"Does she take requests?" He pointed to the pianist.

The lady in silver heard him. "Yeah, her name's Janice, and she knows everything. She makes any song sound like she wrote it. Drop a few bills in the tip jar, and *voila.*"

"Where are you ladies from?"

She crossed her legs below the slit in the silver gown. "I'm in school working on an M.B.A. at Tulane. I'm a Yankee. My girlfriend's a Texan. But now we're both New Orleanians."

"How'd you end up in New Orleans?" He surprised himself with his aggressive question.

"Came South with my husband. Unfortunately — well maybe fortunately — we split up. I liked the city and stayed. Plus, Tulane's a fine school."

M.B.A. — that's American for Master's in Business. Close to her, with the light from the piano lamp shining on her face, Langdale studied her better. She was in her mid-thirties — a pretty woman. She had a high forehead but with smooth facial features. Her dark thick hair draped over her bare shoulders. Narrow straps held up the silver gown a couple of inches above her knee.

The music stopped for a moment. The woman turned and glanced at him. She nodded pleasantly, then resumed chatting with her girlfriend.

Langdale ordered a gin and tonic, took a pen from his pocket and jotted a request on a paper napkin, "New York, New York." He hoped the request didn't sound queer.

He handed the napkin to the lady in silver. "You mind passing this to the pianist?"

"No, neat song, too." She winked. "I'm from Long Island." She responded to his perplexed glance. "New York — Long Island, New York. So — what's your accent?" Her words slurred slightly from alcohol. "You must be from England."

"Actually I'm from Bermuda. We're British, but our accent's different from the English."

The lady cocked her head revealing long, dangling, silver earrings. "You musta been at the party at the Cabildo tonight. Good party. I saw the exhibit of that old document. I didn't read it, but it's all fascinating. We were there for the party. The history — not so much the history."

The dialog buoyed his confidence. "I'm the man who found it. The Governor of Bermuda and I flew here to donate the Indenture to the museum — to Louisiana."

Her charcoal eyes sparkled making her slightly freckled face seem exotic. "I saw you arrive in the carriage with the coachman. And being announced at the door with the Governor. That was you, wasn't it? I didn't notice in the light. Cool. I mean cool." She pronounced *cool* as though it were two syllables — so American.

The woman in silver turned to her companion and chatted a few moments. Langdale couldn't hear the conversation over the piano and other voices in the bar.

The two women simultaneously turned toward Langdale. "My name's Nancy," said the woman in silver, "and this is Maryanne Mitchell. We call her Mimi."

"My pleasure, ladies. I'm Ian Langdale."

Nancy turned toward the pianist, pulled a dollar bill from her purse, and dropped it in the tip jar. "What's a good British song? Our friend here's from Bermuda." The pianist began playing and sang, *Rule Britannia. Britannia Rules the Waves.* Langdale joined in the song, stood up, and gave a mock military salute. A few customers clapped when the song ended.

The pianist played British rock and roll, "Henry the Eighth" by the Hermits, and "Ferry Cross the Mersey" by Gerry and the Pacemakers. The bar crowd joined in.

Langdale overheard Mimi say, "Nancy, I gotta leave. If I order one more drink, I'll be trashed. Enjoyed the party. I'll call." Mimi pushed her chair back, smiled and waved a petite wave. Then she leaned over and murmured to Nancy, "Neat guy. Just go for it!"

Langdale heard the remark. He felt his face turning red. She would never notice in the dim light of the lounge. Mimi left.

Nancy leaned back in her chair away from the grand piano and turned toward Langdale. The slit of her dress slid farther up her thigh. She was wearing black leather sandals. Her fingernails and toenails were painted a light shade of red. "How 'bout a drink?"

she asked. "I'm buying. By the way, what's a Bermuda drink?"

"We're famous for rum and 'rum swizzles.' In Bermuda, we have a concoction called a 'Dark and Stormy.' I doubt they have it here, but it'll put you *'O-T-T.'*"

"What's *'O-T-T'*?"

"Over the top, of course. I'll ask if they make rum swizzles."

"I'll trust you. You catch the waitress, Ian. Guys are always better at catching a female waitress, especially a good-looking guy — like you."

Her comment excited him. He reached his hand under the piano and clutched her. She ran her fingers through his. His heartbeat danced.

"What's your favorite song, Nancy?"

"Love your accent, Ian." She squeezed his hand. "Maybe a Cole Porter song. Maybe 'I Get a Kick Out of You.' Cole Porter songs are wonderful, just wonderful, for the piano."

The waitress arrived and Langdale ordered the rum swizzles. "You ever met royalty? The Queen visits Bermuda, doesn't she?"

Ian wrote on a cocktail napkin and stuffed the napkin with a five-dollar bill in the fishbowl tip jar.

"Saw her on a *walkabout* once in Hamilton. That's where the royals stroll down the street meeting commoners."

He interrupted himself. His voice rose and his eyes blazed.

"Oh, of course I've met the Queen. Once in the U.K., I met her horseback riding. I was a boy visiting my grandfather, who lived in Eton, across the river from Windsor Castle. My grandfather and I were riding through the big park. We'd dismounted. The Queen and her party rode up. Grandfather kicked me on the bottom and told me to bow."

Ian laughed. "I made the best bow possible for an eight-year-old. Grandfather bowed and the Queen — Queen Elizabeth II, you know — stopped. She actually conversed with Grandfather for a minute or so. Charming lady. The Queen even complimented me on my manners. Funny thing, I hardly knew how to make a bow. When Grandfather kicked me, I just bent over." The story sounded awfully trite, but she laughed politely. Her laugh was soft and comfortable.

"God, I love that story, Ian." She talked at light speed. "You British are like Southerners with your manners. Yankees never like to admit the South is better — at anything. I am a Yankee, but Yankees could stand some Southern courtesy. It's civilized."

Nancy turned to the pianist, "Play 'That's What I Like about the South.'"

"You like it here?"

"Yeah, before we moved to Louisiana, I thought they were all mean — Southerners. Remember Neil Young? He cut the South down. Remember 'Southern Man'?"

Nancy sang the lyrics, "'Southern man, better keep your head. Don't forget what your Good Book said.' Neil Young, Huey Long, and George Wallace — that's what I knew about the South."

The waitress set two coasters and drinks on the piano bar. The couple sipped from the double old-fashion tumblers.

"I'm lost. Who's Neil Young?"

"Neil Young was a band member in Crosby, Stills, Nash, and Young. Come on, Ian. Get with it, man. That's American rock 'n roll."

He wondered at her energy.

"You ever heard of Lynyrd Skynyrd?"

"No."

"They had a song to answer Neil Young — 'Sweet Home Alabama.' Good song. A classic."

"Nancy, you're observant — this social commentary."

"South's an enigma, a riddle wrapped in a mystery inside an enigma."

Ian nodded. He enjoyed her knowledge. "You're bright. You must read a lot?"

"When I have time. The M.B.A. is demanding."

He placed his arm on the back of Nancy's chair, touching her bare shoulders and the silver lamé. She leaned toward him and he squeezed her.

"That means you have another degree."

"Yeah, BA in history from NYU. That's New York University, Mr. Ian Langdale." She said his name slowly and repeated. "Mr. Ian Langdale — from Bermuda. Tell me about the papers you donated. Gimme the details."

"It tells about a Louisiana family named Durant."

Nancy squeezed his hand to interrupt. "Durant. That's a big name — an influential family — in Louisiana. Mimi's had some dates with a guy named Durant — Peyton Durant. Mimi says Peyton's a direct descendant of a prominent, wealthy Frenchman named Herbert Durant. You pronounce it A-bear. Probably the same family."

"Tell me about him," said Langdale.

She continued. "He gets what he wants in this town. Big ego. Maybe he's entitled to a big ego. He's big into the cotton trading and international business. He's pleasant enough, but I never feel comfortable around him. It's like he never quite acknowledges your existence. When he talks to you, he seems to be looking over your shoulder to see if somebody more important is around."

She sipped her rum swizzle. "Brother, does he know how to entertain. And I mean lavish entertaining. Mimi and I were invited to a dinner that Peyton hosted at Commander's — that's Commander's Palace Restaurant in the Garden District. Before his clients arrived, Peyton pulled the head waiter aside, slipped him a hundred dollar bill, and told the waiter to keep the wine and drink glasses full. Drunkest crowd I ever saw. The whole night, there wasn't a glass less than half full. There were only twelve people at the table and they drank thirteen bottles of wine. But even when Peyton entertains, you just know he's doing it for some ulterior motive. You know the type."

"How old is Peyton Durant?"

"Forty or so. But he doesn't look it. He plays a lot of tennis."
She interrupted herself. "Do you play tennis?"

"Yeah, it's big in Bermuda. Very English. Bermuda had tennis
before the states."

"Peyton's like you — tall and athletic. He's a ranked player in
Louisiana. He hits an American twist serve with lots of spin. But
he's too competitive for me. He's notorious for cheating on line
calls. Mimi told me Peyton was playin' in the finals of a tournament out at the city park courts against the number one seed — a
real quick, fast player. The other guy was a cotton broker from
Mississippi. They were business competitors. Peyton wanted to
win so bad he went out to the courts — rubico courts — at
midnight and watered down the clay to slow down the surface."

She continued, "Strange thing happened tonight. Peyton's
lawyer, an older gentleman, was at the Cabildo tonight at the
party. After the dedication ceremony — by the way, you made a
nice speech, so gracious — guests were passing by the display of
your Indenture. Peyton's lawyer musta stood in front of the exhibit
five minutes. Seemed to be reading every word of the document.
He stared at the thing — his eyes fixed on the exhibit. Strange."

Nancy's eyes dazzled like diamonds.

"Is he tall with white hair?" he asked. "We musta been there at
the same place, at the same time."

Nancy didn't respond. She glanced down at his cummerbund
Her eyes dazzled like diamonds. Enamored with her eyes and the
slight scent of her perfume, he cared little about Durant or his
lawyer.

She changed the subject. "Mr. Langdale, I bet you wear Bermuda shorts."

"Every day. I wear 'em to work — with knee socks and a jacket
and tie."

"I always thought Bermuda shorts were tacky. But I bet you
look good in them."

His pulse jumped. American women, or at least this American, was so open, so brash, so sexy, so different from Sarah.

Nancy sipped the rum swizzle. The pianist's perky voice cut through the noise, "What y'all wanna hear?"

Ian didn't understand the pianist's accent — a combination of Deep South and New Orleanian. Nancy spoke up. "Play more Cole Porter, maybe some Buffett."

The lady at the piano bar launched into a medley that ended with 'Begin the Beguine.' Langdale dropped a ten in the jar, and the pianist asked for another request. "What's your most popular song?" She broke into "As Time Goes by." The crowd picked up in the lounge.

She played Buffett's version of "Stars Fell on Alabama," but the couple at the piano bar barely heard it.

"Ian, I don't know if it's the music or your accent. Sometimes I can't understand you."

He shrugged, "Two countries separated by a common language."

Nancy laughed. Her laugh was satisfying and sexy. She ran her fingers deep under the cuffs of his shirt.

He ignored his jet lag and weariness. "Why don't you show me the French Quarter?"

She smiled. "You got it. I've never been a tour guide."

She took his hand, stood up and playfully pulled him from his chair. The couple waved to the lady pianist and walked away, headed toward Bourbon Street — only a block away.

Most cities roll up the sidewalks at midnight. New Orleans starts rolling at midnight. New Orleans exudes a rhythm — music, lifestyle, architecture, cuisine.

Ian Langdale with his new acquaintance, the lady in silver lamé as his guide, willingly accepted the City's graces. Barricades had barred automobiles from Bourbon Street turning the street into a mass of partying pedestrians. Walking down the middle of the street, Langdale gently swung his right arm as Nancy clutched his left. He thought how long it was since he had felt so fit and strong.

He seemed to notice everything with fresh and alert senses — Nancy's perfume, her classy black sandals, the clinking of her silver earrings, and the enticing smile that never left her lips. He noticed everything at once on the street — music emanating from two bars on opposite sides of Bourbon Street, the smell of the Creole and Cajun food, the collage of potted plants and flowers lining wrought-iron balconies, the boozed crowd walking the pavement.

"Ian, you ever been married?" She interrupted herself. "You're not married, are you? I never saw a ring."

"No. Close one time. The lady dumped me."

"Seriously? You're a good-looking guy. Intelligent, fun. She must be a fool."

Langdale reached around her waist and squeezed her.

"Is Bourbon Street always so bizarre?"

"Every night."

"You have favorite places?"

"I like the jazz, myself. Bourbon Street's always changing. They say in the fifties jazz clubs were everywhere on the street. Then striptease acts took over. Now it's a mix of bars, restaurants, striptease joints, and all types of music — Cajun, rock, piano, and jazz. Myself, I like the jazz. And I hate those awful tee-shirt shops."

Ahead, a man in a black slick shirt and black trousers and a long ponytail stood in a doorway and hollered at the crowd to try his jazz club. Langdale stared.

"Those guys are the barkers. No microphones allowed on Bourbon, so the barkers cajole customers into the bars."

The barker noticed the couple watching him. He bawled in a deep, gravelly voice, "What y'all looking at? Buddy, get your ass and that good-looking chick in here. Best jazz in the damned universe." He made an easy catch and showed the couple to a front-row table.

The four-piece band, a piano, cornet, banjo, and clarinet, blared a couple of classics — "The Sheik of Araby" and "Basin

Street Blues." Nancy ordered two Dixies. Under the table, she massaged his forearm, hand, and fingers. Her touch was gentle, but it thrilled him throughout. A thin black man tried to sing the lyrics like Louis Armstrong: "You never know how nice it seems, Going down to the land of dreams, Going down to New Orleans."

The evening didn't end. The couple finished their beers, then strolled with the crowd down to St. Peter's Street for a set at Preservation Hall. At two o'clock, they sipped chicory coffee at the Café du Monde.

When the couple returned to the Monteleone, the lobby was empty except for a dozing clerk behind the desk. Langdale stammered for words to finish the evening. But he knew he wanted more of her. He acted as though their next date would merely be an extension of this evening. He slid his hand along her back and squeezed her bare arm. "When are your classes over?"

"Noon." She wrapped her arms around his waist.

"I'm scheduled to leave tomorrow. But I'm canceling the flight. You up for a liaison at lunch? I'll pick you up."

She smiled. "In what?" She clasped her hands behind his back.

"I'll rent a car — or take a taxi. I'll be there."

"You got a date, Ian Langdale. Call me."

With both hands, he pulled her body toward his and squeezed. He cocked his head and kissed her — hard. They embraced and drew it out — long.

She whispered, "A luncheon liaison. I like it."

"I want to ask you something," he said. "What are my chances of running into someone like you? You're the most interesting and beautiful girl I've ever met. You're articulate. You know music, history. You're well read."

She interrupted. "Hey, never say too much on the first date, Ian. Besides that could still be the rum swizzle talkin'."

She stuffed a piece of scrap paper with her name — Nancy Bolden — and phone number into his shirt pocket. "Romance is random, isn't it? Tomorrow. See you tomorrow."

13

THE ringing of the hotel telephone on the bedside table pierced Langdale's fog of sleep. Groggy from a restless sleep, he glanced at the digital clock on the bedside table — *8:17* in the morning — and struggled to grasp the receiver.

"Yes, hello."

The voice on the other end of the line carried a soft, gentle, deep Southern accent, "Sir, my name is Zack Whitcomb. Did I wake you up? The phone rang several times."

Langdale fibbed. "You caught me in the loo."

The voice in the telephone had a soothing quality. "Do you have a minute to talk?"

"Okay."

"I understand that you and your bank have donated an old Indenture to the Cabildo in New Orleans."

"Correct," Langdale answered curtly.

"I'm an Alabama lawyer — a 'barrister' or 'solicitor' you say in Britain. I've been studying the ownership of a large tract of land here. Yesterday, my wife happened to read a piece in the newspaper about your donating an Indenture."

The older man with the soft accent spoke clearly, "Mr. Langdale, the contents of the Indenture bear directly on the ownership of the tract of land I'm studying."

Now wide awake, Langdale interrupted, "How can a 150-year-old document possibly affect current ownership of property?"

The caller chose his words carefully. "Complicated question. Here's the simple answer. The contents of the Indenture support the claim of an elderly black woman that she is the heir to the mineral rights of the man who signed the Indenture — a man named Raymond Herbert Durant."

Before Langdale digested the answer and responded, the man's voice on the other end continued, "If convenient, I'd like to discuss this matter with you while you're visiting in the States. And, if possible, I'd like to see a copy of the Indenture. So you will be comfortable meeting me, I faxed my credentials to your hotel and to your bank in Bermuda." He hesitated again. "If convenient, I'd like to meet this evening."

Langdale fumbled for words. He didn't need the bother. "How'd you find me? How'd you know the hotel?"

"Called the Cabildo — the Museum. They told me you were staying at the Monteleone." Whitcomb's voice now conveyed an urgency. "Sir, this Indenture could be crucial to my client's case."

"Well, assuming your credentials are proper, I'll meet you — sometime. I'm not familiar with New Orleans." Langdale relented, "You sound sincere. All right. I'll have you a copy of the Indenture. Where?"

Whitcomb was quick. "How about Antoine's? It's within walking distance of your hotel in the French Quarter. You're my guest. Eight o'clock."

Langdale sounded reluctant. "Okay. Eight."

THE MAITRE D' at Antoine's escorted Langdale to a large dining room with polished brass, shining crystal chandeliers, bright tile floors full of customers, and busy waiters wearing tuxes. The older man, Whitcomb presumably, sat alone sipping a martini and reading the menu. His hat hung from a brass hat rack. The man held the *Times-Picayune* in his hands. He stood to greet his dinner guest. The pleasant expression on the man's face welcomed Langdale before a word was spoken. Until now Langdale wished he had declined the dinner invitation. Now he found himself glad to join the lawyer.

"Mr. Ian Langdale, I presume." Whitcomb offered his hand. "Pleasure to meet you."

"Call me *Ian*."

"Of course. Ian, I'm an Anglophile. I spent a lot of time in England during the War. I admired your people, especially Churchill. Nobody ever asked me, but when they choose the man of the century award, in 1999, it oughta go to Churchill."

"I've never been South before, but based on the women, whiskey and food last night at the museum, I'm coming back."

Whitcomb ordered Langdale a Scotch on the rocks and Oysters Rockefeller, an Antoine's invention. Two plates and a double old-fashioned glass appeared.

Langdale sipped from his glass. "Mr. Whitcomb, you're lucky I'm still in New Orleans. We planned to fly out this morning. I wouldn't have stayed if I hadn't met this woman last night at the hotel. We went to lunch today."

"Then give her my regards. And my client's. Call me Zack."

Langdale opened a file folder and handed Whitcomb several sheets of paper.

"Zack, this is a copy of the Indenture. Now, tell me about this Durant family, mineral rights, and the rest." Langdale sipped his drink. "I found the papers in the first place. I'm curious to learn what I've discovered."

Whitcomb spread the papers out on the table, then raised his glass. "What you have discovered is a piece of living history."

"How'd *you* become involved?"

"In my law practice, I'm hired to figure out ownership of mineral rights for oil companies." Whitcomb continued, explaining the case — describing Elder and Shanks, his search of the records, the dispute over ownership, and Hawkins's claim. "What brought this case to life is the oil find. Elder and Shanks hit a hell of a well in Choctaw County. The well's worth millions."

Whitcomb's voice rose. "Based on the recorded documentary evidence, a man named Durant from New Orleans is kin to the original owner of the land. He owns the mineral rights and the oil well. But Melvina Hawkins disputes Durant's ownership claim. She claims kinship to the original owner through family history and word-of-mouth. No record and no documentary evidence exists to support Melvina Hawkins's claim — until now. The Bermuda Indenture constitutes solid evidence that Mrs. Hawkins's story is true."

Langdale nodded his understanding. "Quite a story."

"Isn't it?" The lawyer formed a circle with his hands. "I'd like to ask you about the circumstances surrounding the document — the context."

"Context?" asked Langdale.

"Yeah. Context can mean everything when you're interpreting a document. Here's an example." Whitcomb eyes flashed in a manner indicating the example was more humorous than serious.

"I tried a divorce case a few years ago. The wife was on the stand. She said her husband used obscene language. The judge asked her, 'What did he say?' The lady replied, 'Nice people don't say such words.' The judge asked her to write it down. Cleaned up, the note read, 'I want to make love to you.' The active verb rhymes with *luck*. The judge passed the note to the foreman, who read it and passed it to the other jurors in the box. In the back row, there was a middle-aged woman sitting next to a man about the same age. The man had dozed off. The lady read the note, then tapped the man on the leg and passed him the note. The man immediately sat up straight and stuck the note in his pocket. The judge said, 'Sir, you need to hand that note to the bailiff.' The man said, 'Judge, this is a personal note between this nice lady and me.'"

Langdale broke into a laugh. "Context matters. I see your point."

Langdale explained how, when, and where he discovered the document.

Whitcomb ordered another martini. "I just appreciate your meeting with me and bringing the copy. I haven't actually read the contents. By the way, I'm sure the museum had experts examine the Indenture?"

Langdale shrugged. "No. Not really. Everything moved fast. They didn't see the original until yesterday."

Langdale motioned toward the copies on the tablecloth. "I had only sent copies to the museum. I brought the original with me."

Whitcomb ran his hands through his thin gray hair. His face showed concern. "God, I'll have to do some legal research to get the Indenture admitted into court."

Whitcomb scanned the pages for a full minute, then looked up. "Amazing, truly amazing. This old Indenture verifies Melvina's story. It even names her grandfather as Durant's son." Whitcomb leaned forward in his chair. His voice was serious. "If I gather information about the background and history of this document and prove it's authentic, then Mrs. Hawkins should own the mineral rights and the oil well."

Langdale's eyebrows raised. "Is your adversary a man called Peyton Durant?"

"Yeah." Whitcomb cocked his head wondering how the Bermudian knew.

"I hear he's a prominent man about town. Wealthy — with connections. You'd better have a solid case if you take him on."

Whitcomb gulped a drink of the gin and vermouth.

Langdale continued. "The woman I met last night — Nancy. She's an acquaintance of his. She said Durant's aggressive. He gets his way." Whitcomb's face reddened. "Zack, I didn't mean to unnerve you."

In a moment Whitcomb had regained his composure. "If the

case goes to trial, at least it'll be in Alabama."

Dinner arrived and the men helped themselves to flounder and Antoine's puffed potatoes. Enjoying each other's company, both men ate with deliberate slowness. The conversation drifted to other topics — food, sports and women.

Langdale told him more about Nancy and kiddingly asked for his advice. Whitcomb responded. "Men make a mistake when they try to be pals with a girl. If it's romance you're after, then act romantic. You call a girl and you ask her for a date. Be assertive. Plan an evening she'll enjoy. 'This is Ian Langdale. I'd like to invite you to lunch at Arnaud's — at noon.' Show up at a quarter 'til noon. Dress as well as you can. Use manners and don't apologize for it. Stand up whenever she stands up. You pay the whole bill. Being a buddy and a pal is worthless, if you want romance. These American men have let feminists change the rules. And kiss her, too. Women expect it. You're a likable fellow with good taste. You'll have it made."

Langdale didn't expect such a direct answer. "I need to make notes." Neither man hurried to finish his dinner.

14

BEFORE Zack left Butler, Melvina had asked him to call on her cousin in the Crescent City. Melvina had written her to expect Zack. Melvina said her cousin was the "storyman" of the family. She knew old family stories from way back, so everybody called her the "storyman."

Zack caught a cab the next day after he dined with Langdale. The taxi bumped along St. Charles Avenue past plantation homes and stately mansions of the Garden District, past Tulane and Audubon Park, then turned off St. Charles toward the river. The architecture changed to a mixture of raised cottages and two-story frame houses behind intricate cast-iron fences. Abruptly, the area changed again. A series of long, narrow shotgun cottages passed.

The taxi slowed. Whitcomb focused on the street numbers on the houses. "I'm looking for 216 Napoleon."

"Tips — Tipitina's, the music hall — is a block away. 216 Napoleon. You got it, man." The cabbie slowed and parked on the curb.

Doll's house sat on a block of identical houses. Each had a small porch with three columns holding up the roof. The narrow front allowed for only a door and one tall floor-to-ceiling window.

Doll's yard was barren except for a single wide-spreading oak tree with heavy limbs of twisted twigs towering above the roof. Smoke from the chimney rose in contorted forms above the gabled roof.

Before Whitcomb could knock, an elderly black woman opened the door. She wore a bright red dress, high heels, gold earrings, and a black beret over silver hair.

"Get in this house now, and get comfortable." Whitcomb stepped into the foyer. "You gotta be lawyer Whitcomb from Alabama. Melvina told me you were coming."

He nodded and tipped his hat. "Yes'm, you're right — exactly right." Whitcomb's eyes scanned the premises. Two ornate chairs faced the Victorian sofa. Heavy gold curtains covering the floor-to-ceiling windows blocked the sunlight. A huge wrought iron candelabrum with three burning candles sat on a chest in the corner. The candlelight was the only lighting in the room, and the leaping flames created dark corners and dancing shadows on the walls. The room smelled of fresh furniture polish.

"Everybody calls me 'Doll.'" Her eyes were dark, unearthly and glowing. They seemed to pierce his body as though she were looking right through him to another standing behind. Her eyes reminded him of a clairvoyant his family visited when he was a boy. After his mother lost her favorite cameo, they drove to Vinegar Bend in Washington County seeking the aid of a palmist. A wooden palm posted outside the house by the roadside advertised the palmist as "Madam Loo." His mother met the madam on the porch and explained the loss. His father handed her a five-dollar bill. Madam Loo's instructions were simple. "Look into my eyes and concentrate. Look into my eyes and concentrate on the cameo." Before you could say "Jack Robinson," she located the cameo. "Go home. Look inside — inside the sewing machine." Voila — the cameo was right there in a compartment in the sewing machine.

She poured Whitcomb and herself a glass of iced tea from a silver pitcher on the sideboard. He sat on the velvet sofa. She sat opposite him on a dark wooden chair with long carved arms. She handed him a teaspoon — long, sleek and polished to a bright luster with a "D" engraved on it. He inspected the spoon, but made no comment.

They engaged in small talk. Her warm personality contrasted with her cold, keen eyes. "Understand you wanna hear the story of Eugenie Durant and the *quadroon* balls."

"Yes'm, that's right. I represent Melvina. I'm trying to prove that Melvina is a descendant of Herbert Durant."

She interrupted. "I know all that."

"Okay. Melvina knew some vague stories, but she said you're the family historian — the storyman. She hopes — and I hope — you can enlighten me." Whitcomb pulled a pen and pad from his coat pocket.

"My pleasure," she said graciously.

The lady took her glass of tea, rose to her feet, paced the room, and began. "There was a time in New Orleans when colored girls — I mean women with light skin, born of a Negro mother and white father — would meet white men at wonderful balls. They called 'em the quadroon balls." Her accent was soft and sophisticated.

"The only people allowed at the balls were colored ladies and white men. The balls were held at the Orleans Ballroom in the Quarter — the *Salle d'Orleans* in French," she pronounced the words effortlessly. "They were brilliant parties with music and dancing. The colored girls dressed in gowns of the latest fashions and were chaperoned by their mothers. The balls were conducted with respectability and decorum. There was always romance in the air." She spoke and gestured like an actress reciting her lines.

"The balls were held two or three times a week, and they were so wonderful that no male visitor to New Orleans could afford to miss them." She threw her head back and waved her arms dramatically. "It was said that never in the world were women as beautiful as the quadroons of New Orleans."

Whitcomb already knew about the balls — from Ann. But he was enjoying her theatrical monologue.

She moved gracefully around the room, but her eyes remained fixed on him.

"The quadroon ladies lived in small houses like mine down on Rampart Street on the edge of the Quarter and were supported financially by their white gentlemen. The houses were neat and clean and the quadroon children were reared properly and educated. Some quadroons even owned slaves as cooks and maids. The quadroon ladies were known for good manners and behavior. They were beautiful to look at and captivating to everyone. Some practiced voodoo magic — maybe to capture lovers and keep them. Their white gentlemen would regularly visit the houses for tea and companionship. For the gentlemen, having a quadroon was a mark of social distinction, like possessions of fine horses and carriages."

The lady in the elegant red dress reached for her glass of iced tea from the sideboard. She paused for a sip, then continued her monologue.

"The quadroons were born and reared for love. They were said to be great lovers, taught the art of lovemaking by their mothers. The well-born white women were virtuous, but some white men wanted more. They found romance at the quadroon balls and the quarters on Rampart Street. They say young white men would drink champagne and absinthe and eat oysters to make better lovers."

She paused for effect. Her eyebrows rose. "New Orleans is a strange place, isn't it?"

He didn't answer her question. She waved a hand. The bright red paint on her long fingernails matched her dress.

"At the quadroon balls the young gentlemen, usually of French background, would meet and dance with the ladies. In diaries and journals, white men wrote of the fascination, the passion, and the temptation of the quadroon girls.

"If an acceptable young white man and a quadroon girl fell in love, the girl's mother would make sure he agreed to support her. Then the boy would buy her a house and set her up."

Doll stopped. "You looked startled."

Captivated by her delivery, Whitcomb shook his head. "You tell the story so beautifully. You remind me of a famous actress from Jasper — Tallulah Bankhead." Her eyebrows rose and she smiled in appreciation of the compliment. "Tell me, Doll — may I call you Doll? — why were the colored girls called quadroons?"

Now she sounded like a school teacher.

"When New Orleans was a French colony, the government registered people with black and white blood and gave a name to each. Quadroon meant one-fourth black and three-fourths white blood. In Louisiana, the term quadroon was used, in error I suppose, to cover all sorts of people with mixed blood."

"What were the years of the balls?" Whitcomb asked.

"Up to the time of the Civil War."

"Are there any well-known quadroon ladies?"

"Marie Laveau, the voodoo queen, is the most famous. They say she carried herself like royalty and cast a spell over everyone who met her. The whole city — black and white — was under her spell. Amazing woman."

"Did white ladies accept the situations?"

"No. White ladies deeply resented the quadroons and, I'm quite sure, denied their husbands participated."

"Doll, may I ask you something?"

She interrupted. Her eyes blazed. "You don't have to ask your question. I'm a descendant of a quadroon lady. When I was a little girl, I would hear the stories of the balls. It captivated me. When I was in school I used — still do — read everything about the quadroons. So, I'm part student but mostly storyteller."

"You read my mind."

"If you have questions, go ahead." She nestled into one of the chairs.

"Tell me, who held the balls?"

"Mothers of the girls. The mothers rented the Orleans Hall for their daughters' debut."

"Do you know when the balls were held?" he asked.

"During New Orleans' social season, from October to Ash Wednesday — the first day of Lent."

Her knowledge of details was impressive. She could make a good witness.

"Doll, you know why I'm here — to learn about Raymond Herbert Durant. Do you know anything about him — Raymond Herbert Durant?"

She corrected him. "It's pronounced Ra-mon A'bear in French. Yes, sir, I can tell the story. I've heard the story a hundred times." Her eyes sparkled with energy, and her voice sounded like a grandmother telling a fairy tale.

"Young Raymond Durant lived in a mansion on Esplanade, at the end in the French Quarter. House is still there. His family owned a plantation in the country, but they also had a fine, elegant house in the city. Like the other Creole boys, he longed to meet a beautiful quadroon rose. New Orleans' social season started in October. Raymond took a carriage through the narrow French Quarter streets. It was evening, and the night watchmen were lighting the street lamps. The carriage stopped outside the church-yard behind the St. Louis Cathedral. He and his best friend, Master Julien Poydras, walked up the stairs to the Salle d'Orleans. Admission was two dollars. They paid the slave boy with gold coins."

Doll's hands were lively, and silver bracelets on her wrists clinked with each movement. "The ballroom was large and beautifully decorated. Bright candelabra lighted the room. The chaperons sponsoring the ball were dressed in evening gowns seated on a *dais* covered with a thick crimson carpet. Above was a punka, a heavy fan, pulled back and forth by a slave boy to cool the ladies on the *dais*. The room was lavish and lively." Doll told the story like an eyewitness. His keen interest kindled her enthusiasm like pine on a fire.

"When the gentlemen entered the ballroom, they approached the *dais* and exchanged courtesies with the ladies. Raymond and Julien introduced themselves to ladies and gentlemen around the room."

"Raymond met Eugenie, a French name, pronounced 'you-genee.' They danced and drank champagne. Eugenie had dusty skin, like mine, and black eyes. She was dressed richly — that night she wore a long, flowing, mulberry-colored silk dress with kid gloves and slippers. Her hair was fixed with locks drawn gracefully back behind her neck. Eugenie was tall and lithe — a wonderful dancer. She and Raymond danced and danced all night. When they talked, her coquettish personality captured his heart. Eugenie and Raymond were in love from the beginning."

Doll paused for a sip of tea, but lost no enthusiasm.

"They followed the accepted code of behavior for courting. With approval of Eugenie's mother, Raymond entered into a financial arrangement. The Durant family was well-to-do. Raymond bought Eugenie a house on Rampart Street. The house is gone, but I remember it. Louis Armstrong Park covers that area now.

"Eugenie loved Raymond and they had a baby boy, Robert. Raymond later married a white lady, Michelle Bondurant. At first, Michelle resented Eugenie. But, eventually, Michelle accepted Eugenie and they even became fast friends. Michelle was kind to everyone. Michelle was barren, but she and Raymond treated Robert like their own son. With quadroon girls, it was rare that things worked out so well for everyone, but Raymond, Michelle, and Eugenie were extraordinary people."

Doll leaned back on her sofa signifying the end of the story.

"Well, Mr. Zack Whitcomb of Alabama, that's the story of the Durant family. Write your notes. I'll fix us a drink — something refreshing with a little bite."

Doll rose to walk to the kitchen. Whitcomb rose with her.

The lady's flowing dress grazed a small harp sitting on the floor, and the strings sounded a chord throughout the room. Whitcomb started to speak, then changed his mind.

She broke the silence. "Still a few real gentlemen left, I see."

They sipped the drinks from tall, ice-filled glasses and chatted. "The spoon — tell me about the silver spoon with the D."

Doll stopped at the kitchen door. "They say Michelle Durant ordered fifty silver spoons. She gave them away to all her relatives. Look on the back. 'W.H.' is the manufacturer — William Huntington, an Alabama silversmith, made those spoons out of melted-down coins after the Civil War."

He nodded, then took a deep breath. For a few moments, there was an uncomfortable silence in the room. Whitcomb's tone of voice became serious. "Doll, I feel like I can ask your advice. I've had two fears for many years. One's flying. The other is strange. There's a gravestone in Greensboro, an old town near Butler. The gravestone is in the shape of a harp, just like your little harp. The harp sits on the Coleman family plot. The family died out in the 1800s. Legend says that a passerby who hears the sounds of the harp playing is in grave danger or his loved ones are in danger. My wife swears she was walking through the cemetery years ago when she heard the strum of a harp. It was literally the day her brother died in battle. They got the telegram a week later."

Doll interrupted. "You didn't seem like a spiritual person." She motioned toward the harp. "The sounds of the harp bother you, don't they?"

He ran his hands across his face and through his hair. "I'm handling this case partly because of my friendship with Melvina's husband — " He stammered, then started the sentence over. "I'm handling this case." He stopped again. "Melvina says you're the seventh child of a seventh child. You see things, don't you? Can you tell me — is there danger in this case?"

A slight smile formed on her lips. She gently massaged the

sockets of her eyes with her index finger. "I see something. I see disaster on the Ides — the day of the full moon — the middle of the month — the Ides, perhaps, of October. Someone prominent in the case, has been struck by the bad fortune of the Ides."

He remembered studies of Roman history — the *Ides*, the fifteenth of the month, was considered an ominous, evil day.

She paused, then massaged her eyes again. "I do see danger. But I see glory, too. I detect self-doubt in you." She stood directly in front of him and placed her hand on his shoulder. "But you have no reason to doubt yourself. Why? Because you are a brighter man than the others." She dropped her hand and shrugged her shoulders. "That's what I see."

He finished the drink and rose to leave when a taxi arrived.

Whitcomb stepped out the front door onto the stoop, then turned around. "Doll, you amaze me with your knowledge," he stammered. "How can you know so much?"

"One of God's little gifts. I am a seventh of a seventh, you know."

"One more question, What's your name — your last name?"

"No one ever asks me." She turned and walked toward the house. "And I never say."

He walked to the car. He heard strains of fast-paced zydeco music coming in the distance from Tipitina's and smelled the aroma of boiling shrimp.

Whitcomb looked a last time at Doll's house. He could see the candlelight flickering against the curtains. *That's no little gift. And the damnedest story I ever heard. Her story's perfectly consistent with the Indenture. I believe every word, but, darn it — in the courtroom, you gotta have proof — hard cold facts. No judge admits legend into evidence.*

God, what have I gotten myself into? I could catch the morning train north, relax in the club car, fix a pitcher of martinis with friends, and forget it.

WHITCOMB WAS WAITING when the Tulane library opened

the next morning. A student directed him to the microfilm section.

For two hours, the lawyer scrolled through boxes of dark film of old New Orleans newspapers. He strained to focus on the screen. Copies of early eighteenth-century newspapers flashed history across the screen.

Doll said the quadroon balls were antebellum. Let's try May 1810; now 1820. Nothing. Try the social section. Nothing.

Try the classifieds. Nothing. Getting warm — here's an ad for an invitation to a ball at the Camp Street Theatre.

She said the balls were at the Orleans Ball Room on Orleans Street.

Check out the papers during the Mardi Gras season — from New Year's to Lent.

Here's Sunday, January 5, 1840. Perhaps the ball's advertised in the Sunday edition. Turn to Classified Ads.

His heart beat fast. He quickly scanned the three-inch advertisement in bold print from the *Picayune*.

Orleans Ball Room

**The public is respectfully informed that
Dress and Masquerade Balls
will take place every Monday, Wednesday, and
Saturday of each week until the Mardi Gras
Admittance — Two Dollars
Gentlemen only — to make the acquaintance
of quadroon ladies. Nothing shall be neglected to
maintain good order and decency, and to afford
guests the delights of a fashionable society of
ladies of color.**

Bingo! Now this is evidence. A piece of paper for a judge to hold in his hand and read. The ad supports Doll's story about the balls. That oil money belongs to Melvina. But can I prove it — with real evidence — admissible in court?

Whitcomb copied the page from the newspaper. As he looked at it once more to ensure it was legible, the adjoining column caught his attention. He closed his eyes hard. His stomach felt empty and he groaned. He forced himself to read the piece.

$50 Reward

Runaway. A negro named HARRY, about 23 years of age, 5 feet 7 inches; a round face, not perfectly black, but inclining to a dark copper color; small scar on his upper cheek. He is formerly the coachman of Mr. J. Dirger. He passes himself off as a free man, and has papers. He has been employed on board one of the steamboats in port and he was arrested on Tuesday, but made his escape. He has been seen within the last week about the steamboat landing. When last seen, he wore a light blue casinet jacket, pantaloons and a dark-colored jockey cap. He is a fellow of good appearance. Captains of steamboats are cautioned against employing him or carrying him away; no expense will be spared in prosecuting to the utmost extent of the law. The reward will be paid for said negro's apprehension and delivery to any jail. Apply at No. 84 Canal Street. Jan. 5, 1840

His mind focused on the content of the advertisement — reward for a runaway slave.

Isn't that grim reading? Slavery — cheap labor and greed. Burden — for blacks. And a burden of history for whites. Even grandfather and his forefathers owned slaves. For all their pioneering spirit; for creating a civilization from raw land with muscle, and sweat; for fighting to win independence and equality; why condone slavery?

Still, I can't change history. I can't right ancient wrongs. But, maybe, just maybe, I can right one wrong. Melvina Hawkins, I'm gonna win this case.

In disgust, he ripped the copy in half, crumpled the half about the runaway slave and tossed it in the garbage.

15

COMMODITIES traders recover quickly from the gloom of bad trading days. That's no surprise. They're optimistic by nature, otherwise they wouldn't choose such a risky profession.

After his debacle on the fifteenth of October, Peyton Durant paid off his debt, and, for the time being, quit trading. During his self-imposed sabbatical, he evaluated the market and his strategy. The cash price, known as the *spot price*, had closed at fifty-four cents on October 15. It fell to fifty-two by October 20.

Why had he been so wrong on October 15? He couldn't risk any more trading — even with access to Kruk's inside information — until he found out. Durant sought the answer from all sources — crop publications, raw data on supply and demand, his own charts he'd updated for years, phone conversations with farmers, brokers, textile mills, and retailers. Durant checked out the alleged rumor that moved the market.

Markets trade on rumors all the time. But to move the market, the rumor has got to make the rounds. This rumor — about a new artificial fiber — didn't make the rounds. It didn't make it past Canal Street. It was confined to the New Orleans Cotton Exchange Building — a small corner of the cotton business. Nobody in Chicago, New York, or London ever heard the rumor.

Still, the cotton market collapsed on October 15 — down to fifty-four cents — and hadn't recovered. Since October 15, the price hovered between fifty-two and fifty-four. Something caused the sell-off.

Durant discovered the cause of the collapse. The harvest in two principal cotton regions in the U.S., the Mississippi Delta and the San Joaquin Valley in California, had been strong — strong enough for American cotton production to hit a record high, and the news of the increased production had triggered the sell-off.

Durant bore his own blame. He was literally out to lunch, for two crucial hours on October 15, when the bearish harvest data appeared in trading offices driving the price down. Durant had sustained big losses on bad trading days but never experienced a day like October 15. To win in commodities, a trader must to do two things. One, maximize profits, two, minimize losses.

Durant had committed an error, a grievous self-destructive error in failing to minimize his loss. A simple trading technique — entering a *stop-loss* — designating a price to exit the market — would have limited the loss. More importantly, he abandoned the floor. Durant vowed that would never happen again.

DURANT AND HARVEY KRUK, the embassy attaché, talked by phone regularly — once a day at least. Durant believed the insider relationship with Kruk in Hong Kong would give him an edge, maybe the upper hand, even a whip hand of supremacy over competitors.

The Chinese crop figures prominently in international cotton markets. China produces on the average twenty million bales annually, which is over twenty-two percent of the total international crop. Traders crave accurate Chinese cotton data.

Kruk's insider Beijing connections would deliver to Durant a two-edged sword of an advantage. First, Kruk's disclosure to

Durant of accurate crop data prior to the release to the public would give Durant a slight advantage. Second, Kruk's disclosure through the embassy of inaccurate data for traders' consumption would give Durant a super advantage.

Everyday at noon Hong Kong time, one a.m. Central Time, Kruk called from a pay phone on Hennessey Street in Hong Kong to Durant's New Orleans' home. Kruk and Durant developed a comfortable relationship. Durant opened a bank account at Creditsuisse, a financial institution in Zurich. If their trading realized a profit, Kruk would receive ten percent of the profits — deposited in the Swiss account.

By mid-November, Kruk and Durant had perfected their plans. On November 14, the Chinese government was due to release reports of its actual fall cotton harvest. Through his Beijing connection, Kruk had acquired the results. The harvest had failed. Rainy weather had impaired the Chinese crop. The nation's harvest was seventeen million tons — a shortfall of three million tons below normal production. To make up the difference and maintain the operating capacity of its textile mills, the Beijing government would buy three million bales on the international markets. The release of this bullish report would immediately propel the cotton price upward.

On the 14th, the day before the release of the Chinese reports, Kruk would leak bogus data indicating a better-than-normal Chinese harvest. With luck, the bogus data would cause a sell-off, running the price down a few pennies. After the release of the bogus reports, Durant would buy the market with every dime he could garner. When the correct data emerged, the price would soar yielding Durant — and Kruk — a windfall profit.

AT SEVEN A.M. ON November 14 — a Monday — Durant already had the office up and running. He sat at his desk staring intensely at charts, graphs, and trading articles pinned on his office wall. His blue pin-striped suit jacket hung on the rack. His sleeves were rolled up past the elbow, and his hundred-dollar red silk tie was loosened at the collar. He was ready to trade.

Durant was in no mood for exchanging pleasantries when his secretary arrived at eight. "I'm lookin' for cotton articles."

He continually ran his hands through his hair — nervous energy. "Have the clerks scan this morning's papers — *Wall Street Journal*, *Financial Times*, the internet, everything we got. Tell them to tear out the cotton articles or copy 'em and bring 'em to me."

His secretary brewed coffee and delivered Durant's orders when the clerks — two college-aged men — entered. She set a steaming mug on Durant's desk. His cheeks were dark red like he had a fever.

"Hold all the calls. And nobody uses the fax. I don't want it occupied when Hong Kong faxes me."

In a few minutes, one of the clerks — wearing khakis, a black sport shirt buttoned to the collar, and polished penny loafers — hustled into Durant's office with a handful of newspaper pages and a print-out off the internet.

He sipped from a mug. "Pin those articles on the wall," Durant ordered.

Durant heard the fax machine beep. He hurried toward the sound. A sheet of thin fax paper advanced into the plastic tray.

At the top of the page was a representation of a flag. A large five-pointed star in the upper left-hand corner adjoined four smaller stars arranged in a semi-circle on a dark field. It was the flag of the People's Republic of China. Durant ripped the page from the tray.

FOR RELEASE TO THE PUBLIC

The Ministry of Agriculture of the People's Republic of China announces that the cotton crop for the 1994 growing season will approach 21 million bales. This production represents an increase of almost a million bales over the 1993 harvest.

Durant slipped his telephone headset over his ears and punched a button automatically dialing his floor broker. Stretching the cord taut, he walked toward the picture window overlooking the trading floor. He liked watching Hunter Morris, his broker, while they talked. "Hunter Morris here." Morris glanced up from the trading pit floor. Durant twisted the lever opening the blinds. "Hey Hunter. It looks quiet on the floor. I'm gonna shake things up. I'm trading big today, man."

Morris nodded. "Good news. It's been a little lonely down here without your business. Glad you raised the margin so quickly. Peyton, you just say the word, man. I'll make it happen."

"I'll call you in a bit. Be ready."

Durant pinned the fax on his wall. Then he sat at his desk and wrote with his Mont Blanc: "11-14-94. Buy 500 contracts. December delivery. At 55.50 or below. Target — 70.00. Potential Profit — 3.75 million."

He phoned the cotton pit again. "Hunter, here's my order. I wanna buy five hundred cotton contracts today."

Morris glanced at Durant with big eyes — surprised.

"Buy the market at fifty-five cents or below. For December delivery." Durant paused. "But keep it all low-key, Hunter. Buy in small lots. I don't want anybody to know that I'm trading big."

"Okay. You got it, Peyton. I'll confirm the order. During the trading day, I'll buy you five hundred cotton contracts for December delivery at fifty-five cents or below. You'll have five hundred Decs before the end of today's trading. Is that right?"

"Right, Hunter. Do it."

The trading bell rang at eight-thirty a.m. Morris started buying cotton in small lots — ten or twenty contracts on each trade. The price drifted lower, driven down by the bearish news of the bogus Chinese cotton data. Durant watched the fax and his computer screen. Any bullish news might offset the Chinese crop data.

Durant called trading offices around the country. The bogus Chinese cotton data made the rounds. The price drifted lower all day — *54.00, 54.50, 53.00, 52.50.* When the market closed at one-thirty, the cotton price had dropped to *52.00.*

At one thirty-five, Morris called Durant. "This is to confirm your trades for the day. You bought five hundred cotton contracts for December delivery. All the contracts are at prices below fifty-five cents." Morris nervously cleared his throat. "Peyton, I hope you know what you're doing. This is big league, man. You don't need a repeat of October 15."

Durant responded, "No problem. This deal is cooked. I can't lose."

NEXT DAY, at eight-thirty, Reuters broke the news:

> BEIJING — In a surprising development, the Chinese Ministry of Agriculture announced that the People's Republic of China has agreed to purchase three million bales of cotton for immediate delivery. Wang Li, Minister of Agriculture stated China's cotton harvest had failed because of an unexpectedly heavy rainfall during the autumn months. The shortfall in Chinese cotton production will be approximately 3 million bales.
>
> The minister announced, however, that China would continue full operation of its textile mills with the purchase and import of additional cotton supplies.
>
> Commodities experts share the opinion that the combination of these events will drive up the worldwide price when futures markets open.
>
> The announcement contradicts yesterday's announcement by the Chinese government of a favorable harvest.

Durant stopped reading. *Perfect.* He clapped his hands and clenched his fist in victory. *Kruk's pulled it off. Baby, I'm rockin' and rollin'. Big time. Cotton's a gold mine today.*

He printed the article off his computer and called his secretary. "I want you to get my directory. And fax this article to every broker in the book. E-mail it, too. Keep these machines hot. We're cooking."

Durant phoned Morris. "Hunter, I'm expecting a big rally." Durant's voice exuded enthusiasm. "I wanna take profits all day. Like yesterday, I want small lots. We're not trying to stun the market. Let's take nice little profits with nice little trading lots. I want you to wait 'til the market hits sixty-five. Then take me outta the market — a little at a time — until I'm out of all five hundred cotton contracts."

"Yes sir. I'll confirm. Sell five hundred cotton contracts December delivery at sixty-five or better." Morris wasn't convinced, "Peyton, what if the market goes against you? You gonna be around for instructions?"

"Man, it's gonna happen." Durant said flatly. "Just be ready to take the profits. Baby, the fix is in. The market's headed north."

The bell high above the floor sounded the opening. In the cotton pit at the New Orleans Commodities Exchange, and in cotton pits around the world, heavy buying propelled the market straight up. In the spot market, trading rules set no daily price limit.

Durant watched the pit and the electronic board above the floor — 55, 56, 57, 58. At ten a.m., the price stalled with market resistance at 58, but only for a half hour. The price moved again — 59, 60, 61, 62.

It stalled at sixty-two, then moved higher — 63, 64, 64.50, 65. When the price hit sixty-five cents Morris stepped into the middle of pit. He flashed hand signals, barked orders to traders encircled around him, and took profits — big profits — for Durant. The price surge seemed to lose its power. The price wavered — 66, 65, 66, 65.

Durant detected strong technical resistance at sixty-six. "Hogs get greedy," Durant remembered sage advice.

He called Morris. "Get me out. Now. I want out of every position."

Durant watched Morris in the center of the pit. In a minute, Morris walked away from the pit to his cubicle off the trading floor. He waved at Durant, gripped the phone and dialed.

Morris pumped out the words. "Peyton, you're back, I took you out at over sixty-five. You're back, man. Big time action. Big bucks. You're the man. You're running the show. Everybody's sayin' it. Durant's in control. I love it. Man, I'm proud to be your floor broker."

Durant didn't talk. He formed a pistol with his thumb and index finger of his right hand, whipped his hand forward like it came from a holster. He pantomimed six shots toward the floor and then raised the pistol to his mouth to blow the smoke away.

Morris nodded and grinned at Durant — high above the trading floor in his office box.

Durant had cleared a profit of $2.5 million. He wired Kruk his share into the account at Creditsuisse in Zurich.

16

DURANT celebrated his new success two weeks later — with a couple hundred friends. His house lies in New Orleans' Garden District. It's one of those magnificent three-story antebellum houses — the Greek Revival style with different sets of columns on each floor, detailed wooden brackets, cornices, arches, and cast-iron grillwork between columns on the porch and balcony. There's an intricate ironwork fence around the mansion and gardens. With the shutters painted black and the mansion painted a shiny bright white, the house looks like a huge wedding cake.

The living room and dining room are joined by French doors. Together the two rooms run down one entire side of the house. Durant had removed all the furniture, except for several sets of English dining chairs lining the wall, and converted the two rooms into a ballroom. The mansion bears the signs of nineteenth century and old-family opulence — eighteen-foot ceilings, crystal and silver doorknobs, wide cypress flooring, mahogany banisters, and marble mantels.

The house sits on Prytania, conveniently located just two blocks from Commander's Palace, which catered the party.

Cars were parked bumper to bumper for three blocks on all sides of the house. Couples dressed in formal evening clothes streamed up the front staircase, through the Ionic columns, and into the foyer. A dramatic entrance, the foyer has a marble floor with medieval tapestries hanging from the ceiling.

Durant sipped a vodka tonic in the foyer. This drink and a couple of earlier ones made his face glow. Two weeks of daily tennis had bleached his hair and bronzed his face. Durant played the perfect host. He wore a white dinner jacket, a starched white shirt, and a narrow black bow tie. He shook hands with every man and kissed every woman on the cheek. Mimi was there, too, at Durant's side. She greeted the partygoers in a flowing cream-colored gown and a strand of pearls from Hong Kong. Her high heels accentuated her trim and muscular legs.

The invitations said the party started at eight, and most of the guests arrived by 8:15. They knew to expect a good time at Durant's. The crowd — cotton brokers from New York, Chicago, and the Mississippi Delta, Durant's tennis buddies, Deke fraternity brothers, a handful of Saints players, the President of Tulane, the head football coach, his personal lawyers, stock brokers, and accountants, lots of politicos, and their ladies — covered the ballroom and overflowed into the garden.

There was plenty of food and drink. The caterers filled tables in every room with seafood — shrimp, oysters, crab, crayfish — like a Sunday brunch. Waiters in white jackets roamed the halls with silver trays of champagne and manned bars in every room and in the garden. Next to the garden bar, a man wearing heavy gloves and a Zephyrs baseball cap shucked oysters on the half shell. By eleven the party reached its zenith. In the ballroom, beneath bronze and crystal chandeliers, noisy chatter mingled with sounds from the jazz band. Durant, standing in the corner, holding Mimi around the waist, surveyed the jovial crowd with approving eyes.

There was dancing on the shiny wooden floor, men in tuxes leading ladies in gowns in jitterbugs, Cajun dances, Carolina shags, and fraternity sways. The party thundered with a jazz beat and the buzz of the throng.

A tall trim man with thinning silver hair — Louisiana's senior United States Senator — Roland Ratliff, approached Durant and motioned Durant to follow him into the study. The two men departed the ballroom, crossed the hallway and entered a large room with a walnut desk at one end. Durant shut the door behind them. The Senator leaned against a marble mantel above a fireplace. "Peyton, you got a good crowd and a good party."

Durant responded with small talk. "Glad you could make it. Nice of y'all to come. I wanted to thank you for moving along the sale of that radio station. I know you had to make a few calls. I was hurting for money."

The Senator nodded and strolled around the room. His face indicated he was having trouble forming the right sentence. The Senator spied a Degas original hanging on long wires from the molding. "Beautiful room you have here, Peyton." Durant noted the Senator's attention focused on the painting — the silky strokes of Degas's painting, "The Cotton Office, New Orleans."

"I give the New Orleans museum a few bucks, and they loan originals for the house. Beautiful art makes for an elegant party. That's a painting by the French artist Degas — when he lived in New Orleans. His brothers traded cotton. They're in the painting."

The Senator cut the small talk. "Peyton, I need a favor." The Senator chose his words carefully.

"My polls don't look good. I'm down ten points in the primary. And the campaign's broke. I mean busted. I can't buy any TV time. I need a boost." He looked in Durant's eyes. "We delivered the deal for your radio station. Can you pull up some cash for us?"

Durant ran his hand through his moussed blond hair. "I believe I've maxed out on my personal contributions, my brother and sister, too. We gave our thousand each."

The Senator responded. "I took care of the radio station deal.

We know commodities brokers can — shall we say — rearrange the books. Look what they pulled in Little Rock for the lady in Washington."

Durant nodded, "Lemme talk to my accountant." He turned on his heel and departed, "Stay here, Senator."

Durant found his accountant, Earl Blankenship, and his wife sitting in the corner of the ballroom. The older couple seemed to be the only guests not partying to the jazz. Durant sat next to Blankenship and the men talked for a minute. Then Durant rejoined the Senator in the study.

"Senator, my accountant tells me you have an account with us. I believe I can make things happen. Will 25K do the trick?" Senator Ratliff nodded in the affirmative and cracked a smile. "That's a damn good start."

"I'll see what I can do. Drawer trades. A few drawer trades and your account will look better." Durant grinned. "Check out the balance in your account tomorrow night after the trading day ends. You'll see a few more digits on your account balance."

They nodded. Durant opened the door. Sounds of the party filled the room. "Senator, thanks for coming. It's been an honor."

"Thanks, Peyton. Mimi's been a doll entertaining us."

The men shook hands.

A minute later, Peyton and Mimi were dancing in the crowd. Mimi, the former gymnast, moved with athletic grace. She wrapped her arms around Peyton's neck. He pulled her closer until he felt her body against his. He clasped his hands behind her waist, and the couple swayed in time to soft jazz.

She whispered in his ear. "I've been a good little girl, playin' hostess for you. When the party stops, I hope little Peyton can come out and play with me." He ran his hand along her back, then laid his hand underneath her collar on bare skin.

"You look good in your white dinner jacket, successful, tanned, gorgeous, so precious." She tugged at his cummerbund. "When you gonna take this off."

"Same time you take this off." He unzipped her dress a couple of inches.

"Peyton, your game's improving — every time we play. I like the racket you're using — that nice big oversized one." She giggled. The couple danced toward the center of the floor. "Next time we play, you wouldn't mind if I kissed that big, wide oversized head, now would you?"

He gently cupped his hand underneath her chin. "I don't play with an oversized head."

She rolled her tongue, wetting her lips. "I'm an expert on these things. And believe me, you're playing with an oversized head."

He grinned. "Somehow it's bigger when you and I play." She rolled her tongue again, then kissed him. "That firm rim, be-fore play. I'd love to hold it. It's the rim that's the hard part, isn't it?"

"It's steel. Can't be any harder."

"Honey, I believe I can make it harder. I'd like to try."

He squeezed her so close they could hardly breathe. "You're good for my game, Mimi."

"Next match, I play umpire. I keep the score and I hold the balls. Fifteen love. Thirty-love. Forty-five."

"Game." He gasped. "You're incredible."

They danced in silence until the song ended. She whispered. "You up for one piece of advice, Peyton?"

"What kind? Investment advice?"

She gently ruffled his blonde hair, then smoothed it back into place. "Keep things clean, Peyton. Please."

AT EIGHT O'CLOCK the next morning, Durant punched the phone button, automatically dialing his floor broker. From his office window, Durant watched Hunter Morris grab the telephone by the cotton pit after the first ring. "Hunter, you ready for a nice commission? I wanna enter a spread on the opening. Buy me twenty-five Decs. And sell twenty-five Mays at the market price."

"You got it, brother. Confirmation — buy twenty-five cotton

contracts at the market for December delivery. And sell twenty-five cotton contracts at the market for May delivery. That all?"

"There's more. Hold both trades. Let 'em slide for a couple of hours."

"You're talkin' about one of those first-lady spreads, aren't you? I can't pull that Arkansas crap, Peyton. You gotta put the trades in somebody's account. Floor rules say I gotta park the trades — somewhere."

"Come on, man. You brokers do it everyday. What's the big deal? I'll take the heat. Just let 'em slide for a couple of hours."

Morris didn't answer.

Durant broke the silence. "Grease these trades, Hunter. Tell 'em your clerk's busy. Or tell 'em your secretary screwed up. Just grease these trades for a couple of hours."

Morris was silent for a moment. "You got two hours. That's it. I'll blow this spread out in cyberspace 'til ten. Then we gotta park 'em in an account."

Morris dutifully entered the spread on the opening at eight a.m. He bought twenty-five December cotton contracts and sold twenty-five May cottons. By ten o'clock the price of both months had risen two cents.

Morris called Durant, "Peyton, you got a two-cent move on the spread. I gotta park these trades, man. And I mean now. I'm getting heat. Let's move."

"All right. Give me the loser. Put the winner in Ratliff's account. That's twenty-five thousand for the Senator in two hours. Not bad trading for a rank amateur."

"You're crazy, Peyton. Parkin' — just giving 25K to Ratliff. And you're taking a hit of twenty-five thousand."

"Just park the trades, Hunter."

"It's your money, man."

"One more thing, Hunter." Durant's voice became grim. "What's said between you and me stays between you and me. You got it?"

17

THE morning after he returned from New Orleans, Whitcomb secluded himself in his law library. The contents of the Bermuda Indenture confirmed Melvina's story. The difficulty in court would be getting the Indenture admitted into evidence. He shuffled through pages of Volume 32, Corpus Juris Secundum, The Law of Evidence, and then halted. The *rule of ancient documents* lay on the page before him.

> A document is admissible into evidence if (1) it bears a date before a period of thirty years prior to the time it is offered into evidence and (2) it is produced free from suspicious circumstances which indicate fraud or forgery.

The annotations below the black letter law referred to a Texas case. He read the holding. "An ancient document, meaning over thirty years, will be admitted to prove matters of heirship."

He underscored with his red pencil. *Good ruling.*

"Ancient documents are admissible for proof of the truth of facts recited therein."

Again he underscored in red. *Another good ruling.* He scanned the footnotes and circled an Alabama case. *What suspicious circumstances indicate fraud or forgery?* He turned the pages seeking the answer.

"It has been held that failure to record a document in the public records under probate recording statutes renders the document inadmissible without proof of the reasons for the failure to record."

Whitcomb grimaced. He re-read the statement of law. Then he scanned the cases below. Four cases, including one from Alabama, supported it. The rule of law stung. The Bermuda Indenture showed no marking that it had ever been recorded, and Whitcomb himself had checked the mortgage books from the probate office. No Indenture. Durant's lawyers would spot this rule of law whenever the case went to trial.

Maybe the Bermuda banker — Langdale — would testify to his discovery of the Indenture. It would be dramatic testimony. But finding evidence to prove the reasons why the Indenture was never recorded would be a formidable task. Digging up proof about a nineteenth-century document in Bermuda? A damned formidable task, for sure.

Whitcomb switched off the library light. He sat in darkness for a few minutes.

He pulled his suit jacket, overcoat, and hat from the rack and left his office through the back door. He hollered down the hall, "Going for a walk, Bea. I'm stymied."

The chilly November air swept the alley. *My ears always get cold first. Thanksgiving is this Thursday. And the boys will be home. It's Alabama-Auburn on Saturday.* He glanced at the bank's electronic billboard, "49 at 11:30." He tipped his hat to a lady passing by and shook hands with two black men outside P.P. Young's General Merchandise.

How'd I get involved in this mess? Taking on a New Orleans blue blood. Lord only knows the legal team he'll assemble. Wish I could call a couple of law profs. I'd call two — right now. Harrison and Farrah.

Leigh Harrison. He'd say, in his clearest distinguished voice, "Mr. Whitcomb, you must practice the art of preparation." The worst day of my life was in his class. "Mr. Whitcomb, state the reasoning for the Court's decision in Hochster versus de la Tour." I fumble for an answer. "In my opinion the Court was trying to broaden the law of contracts." Foolish answer. He knew I hadn't read the case. "Mr. Whitcomb, that answer is like the shifting sands of the desert. It has no meaning. And it has no place in a law school or in a courtroom. I expect you to be prepared next time." At least I knew to shut up. Believe me, Sir, I will practice the art of preparation.

Albert Farrah. They named the law school on University Avenue for him. Silver-haired, lecturing from behind the podium, wearing a dark three-piece suit with a gold pocket watch and the long-hanging chain, he seemed to be the voice of absolute reason. Lord, how he railed against Roosevelt's New Deal in constitutional law class. Seems archaic now. But the principles he taught are timeless. He spoke of justice for the common man. And he believed it. His charge at the beginning of school, delivered so clearly in a deep voice, was the same all three years. "Students, the law and justice afforded the Rockefellers, the Armours, and the Carnegies in the castles of wealth must be the same law and the same justice afforded to a poor man in the humble cottage. Equal, exact, and universal justice as contemplated by the founders — the apostles of democracy — rests with you, and you alone."

His heroes were progressives — William Jennings Bryan, Teddy Roosevelt, and Robert LaFollette. I'm getting old — nobody knows about Robert LaFollette anymore.

Farrah was proud of that law school. Why not? He raised the money to build it.

Alabama may not be Oxford or Cambridge. But I miss it. Gothic buildings around Woods quadrangle, Greek architecture around the main quadrangle, the chimes, the groves of trees, and flower gardens — everything arranged to create an atmosphere of introspection. Yeah, Alabama may not be Oxford or Cambridge, but it's as good as Yale. At least that's what Farrah believed.

That poor Yalie who transferred to 'Bama. Farrah calls him into his office. Everybody crowds around the door to the dean's office to see what happens. The guy from Yale comes out shaking his head. "Old man Farrah just reduced all my grades by one letter. I asked him, 'Why, for Christ's sake, are my grades being docked?'"

"Farrah says, 'Because Yale docked one of my student's grades by a letter when he transferred up there. And my law school is as good as anybody's.'"

He crossed the blacktop into the cemetery. Glowing gold leaves from the dogwoods bobbed in the breeze. Sidestepping stone markers, Whitcomb tramped across the freshly cut cemetery lawn. Anglo-Saxon, Scottish, Welsh, Scots-Irish names — Christopher, Lindsey, Sparrow, McPhearson — carved on weathered granite and marble covered the grassy ridge. He hiked down the hill toward the marshy area near the branch where slaves supposedly were buried without gravestones.

He exited the cemetery near the branch and stepped inside the pedestrian tunnel running under the street. He stopped halfway through the tunnel and shut his eyes.

That oil money belongs to Melvina Hawkins. There's no dispute about it. The Indenture confirms Melvina's story. Doll confirms Melvina's story. They're trying to beat her out of the property, out of the mineral rights, out of the oil well. And I may not be able to stop it. But Melvina owns the mineral rights — just as sure as oil's black. Doll's story is rank hearsay — never admissible in court. And, the Indenture's not admissible — unless I can prove why the document wasn't recorded. Lord, Lord.

Bermuda. A British colony in the Atlantic. We often sailed past her during the War. The merchant mariners on board feared her because of the coral reefs. The old Swedish captain called her the island of secrets. He wanted no part of her. Her secrets were deadly — unmarked and unmapped fragments of coral reefs that could gut a steel hull and sink a ship in minutes. He said three hundred shipwrecks lay sunk off Bermuda

— deadly evidence of the danger below the waves.

But Bermuda's where the answer lies. Way out yonder in the Atlantic. I'm too old for this. I used to prosecute criminals in three counties with a handful of lawmen and not a single investigator. Not now. No way. Doll detected my doubts. Maybe Melvina ought to hire a younger lawyer.

That's no good. I'm the only lawyer who understands what needs to be done. Bermuda. Maybe the banker — Langdale — knows something.

Bermuda. I need to go hunt up evidence out there. God, I hate to fly. Two hours over water. Scary. Ann could help. She loves airplanes, flying, and travel.

Farrah was right. The man in the cottage deserves the equal justice with the man in the castle. But I'm not Annie Sullivan, no miracle worker. The answer — it's not here in this town. It's not even in this country. Bermuda, the island of secrets. It's in Bermuda. My God, Bermuda. I gotta prepare this case. I gotta go. Maybe she'll yield one of her little secrets.

Whitcomb returned to the office. For a half hour, his fingers clattered on the keys of his ancient Royal typewriter. Bea faxed the letter to Bermuda.

December 2, 1994

Mr. Ian Langdale, President
Waterloo Bank of Bermuda, Ltd.
Front Street
Hamilton, Bermuda

Re: Interest of Melvina Hawkins

Dear Mr. Langdale:

I hope you returned safely to Bermuda. It was a pleasure to

meet with you. My client, Melvina Hawkins, and I genuinely appreciate your assistance in meeting me and in providing me a copy of the Indenture.

The discovery of the Indenture, to say the least, is providential for my client. As we discussed, language in the document confirms her claim to certain mineral rights. Since my return from New Orleans, I have researched the admissibility of the Indenture. Unfortunately, under the law, proving the authenticity of the document for purposes of admitting it to evidence will not be a simple task.

You may recall that the Indenture was never filed for record in the probate records in Choctaw County, Alabama. To admit the Indenture, I must present evidence explaining why it was not recorded. If I solve that mystery, then the mineral ownership is resolved. This requirement seems rather strict, but the courts have held that failure to record the Indenture places its authenticity in doubt because the document could be a fraud or a forgery.

Frankly, we need your help. I realize we are asking a lot of you, but I cannot possibly discover the necessary evidence without assistance. I am certain the Indenture is authentic and not a forgery, but I need to prove it.

Perhaps your bank's archives contain a promissory note or correspondence relating to the Indenture. Surely, there would have been correspondence for an Indenture securing such a large debt. Perhaps your bank records are stored in the state archives or in a library.

Flying is not my forté, but I am planning to travel to Bermuda as soon as possible. It's quite an expense, but if I can't admit the Indenture into evidence, my client's chances are nonexistent. If you can provide me a few leads, I will be grateful.

By the way, after reading the Indenture a number of times, I have noticed some interesting features: there is an unusual marking, a seal perhaps, in the right margin of the first page. Perhaps the marking has some meaning to you. The Indenture is executed in 1860, the year prior to the beginning of the Civil War. The date could be significant. Alabama joined the Confederacy in January 1861.

I appreciate your thoughts. I'll let you know my travel plans.

I often find historical background helpful. As a final request, could you direct me to a library or bookstore where I could read up on the history of Bermuda?

By the way, I'm glad you met an American girl while in New Orleans. More advice on dating Americans: wear Old Spice. It reminds girls of their daddies.

Sincerely,

Zack Whitcomb

18

WHEN Ian Langdale arrived at his bank office in Hamilton Whitcomb's fax lay on his desk. He read, then re-read it. He leaned far back in his dark leather, swivel chair, closed his eyes, cleared his mind and pondered. *Serious business. A big oil find in Alabama. Disputed ownership of mineral rights. Millions of dollars at stake. Now, the Alabama lawyer requests more, much more information about the document. It's all a bit overwhelming. Safest thing to do — simply not get involved. Stay out of this fight. I'm a banker for God's sakes, not some archivist or private detective.*

Yet the contents of the faxed letter indicated that Whitcomb had worked vigorously on this case — probably full time — since he returned to Alabama from New Orleans.

Ian reconsidered. *A nice bloke, Whitcomb. Soft-spoken. I like his warm Deep South accent. Pleasant personality. Honest. I can't feel his passion, but I respect him. He's the kind of man you want to please. The request is reasonable — even expected — from a thorough lawyer. I discovered the Indenture in the first place. Probably should carry the matter to a conclusion.*

Again, Ian picked up the fax and read it. He took a pencil from a desk drawer. For several minutes, he jotted notes on a yellow pad. Finally, he wrote on a separate page. "Get Zee's advice." At noon, Ian walked to the Par-la-ville Book Store — an old shipping warehouse near the water which the owner, Albert Zane, had transformed into an intimate book-browser's delight. Zane was in the back directing a customer through the nooks and crannies among the book cases. Ian browsed for a moment through the newspaper rack, bought the *Times of London*, then walked through the cozy maze of shelves toward the rear. The store smelled of yesterday's wine and cheese booksigning party. He found Zane standing on a wooden foot ladder pulling books off the top shelf. The elderly man's spectacles rested on his head, nearly hidden by his silver hair.

"I need information — that only you possess." Langdale stroked Zane's ego — Zane had taught history for twenty-five years. "I need a short course in Bermudian history. You're the master. Got a minute?"

"Always make time for my godson." Zane loosened his dark narrow tie and rolled up the sleeves of his white cotton shirt. He continued to pull books from the shelf and pack them in a cardboard box. Then he climbed down the ladder.

The two men walked through a forest of books to a makeshift kitchen in the storage room. With a wooden ladle, Zane dished out two steaming bowls of chowder, then led Langdale through a swinging screen door outside into the Par-la-ville Park. They sat on a bench under a colossal rubber tree, which shaded the St. Augustine lawn, green and thick, beneath palms, hibiscus, and bright blooming flower beds.

Ian pulled a folded fax from his pocket. "Zee, read this letter. It was faxed today from a lawyer in Alabama."

Zane placed his wire-rim reading glasses on the end of his nose. He concentrated on the letter. In a minute he folded the fax and handed it back to Ian. "Wonder why the mortgage never was recorded in the States? The lawyer says, solve that mystery and the mineral ownership is resolved as well."

"Zee, banks always record mortgages. In America, you record it in the county where the land lies. I can't imagine what happened. The lawyer wants me to find out. Frankly, I don't have a clue how to do so."

Langdale continued. "A mortgage securing a debt of a hundred thousand pounds sterling wouldn't have been overlooked. Whitcomb believes the execution of the document in 1860 and the outbreak of the American Civil War may be related."

Langdale took a few sips from the chowder and then looked up. "Eighteen sixty. Civil war. What's he got in mind? Tell me something about the history."

Zane tucked his tie inside his shirt to keep it out of the chowder. He sipped his chowder then talked. "The American Civil War was a brutal war. Casualties were shocking — hundreds of thousands. Lasted four years. The British government wanted to stop the war. Tried to get the two sides to negotiate a settlement. But settlement was impossible. Once that war started, it couldn't be stopped. It was a fight to the finish. The issues — abolition of slavery, right to secede — were too divisive. It was over an agrarian culture in the south versus an industrial culture in the north, and state sovereignty versus central power. The rebels would never submit to Union power. So the war couldn't end until the Union dropped dead from exhaustion or totally annihilated the South. Caused great bitterness for years."

He stopped. "But, you should know all of that."

"Yeah," said Langdale, " but what was Bermuda's involvement?"

Zane talked between sips. "That war was fought here, too. Bizarre goings-on. There was a physician here named Blackburn — a Southern sympathizer. The man got so bitter when the Confederacy started losing, he turned to a sort of germ warfare." He swirled his reading glasses. "A yellow fever epidemic had broken out in Bermuda and on ships in the Caribbean. Dr.

Blackburn practiced in St. George's and treated the patients without collecting for his services. People thought the good doctor was a savior. Actually, he was collecting clothes from the yellow fever patients. He hatched a plan to smuggle infected clothes through a Canadian contact into the U.S. Damned fool wanted to start a yellow fever epidemic. Rather heinous plot, wasn't it?"

"How do you know all this?" Ian asked. "Is it fact — or just legend?"

"Cold fact. The government here uncovered the plot and tried the conspirators in open court. Trial was in St. George's. So the evidence is a public record."

"You read it?" asked Langdale.

Zane nodded. "Yeah. Of course, the plot wouldn't have caused an epidemic. Mosquitoes infest humans with yellow fever — clothes of the patient don't."

Zane continued. "The Rebels must have been a very committed people. There's the story, a true story I presume, that the wife of a Confederate attaché here — a woman named Walker — was so committed to the South that when she bore a child here in Bermuda, she sprinkled dirt she'd brought with her onto the floor beneath the bed so she could say her son was born on Southern soil."

The ex-history professor's eyes sparkled with excitement. "Can you tell me, Ian, why does the lawyer think the Civil War is involved?"

"No idea. That's why I'm here to ask you."

"I thought you went to university to become an educated man." Zane sounded sarcastic. "You're too mercenary — all bank business and finances." He threw up his hands in mock frustration. "Visit the library. Look around my bookstore. Read something besides a banker's manual, son. You'd become a more interesting person. A learn-*ed* man."

"Spare me the sermon."

Langdale scanned his notes. "The mortgage has a faded seal on it. With a magnifying glass, you can barely make out a stamped number. It's five digits — two, three, three, six, three — that mean anything to you?"

Zane wrote the five digits on a note card. Then he scribbled slash marks between each of the digits — *23/3/63.*

"Yeah. it sure does."

He grinned.

"We've become so damned Americanized that we write dates like they do — day, month, year. The British way — the simplest way — is different. It's day, then month, then year. So twenty-three, three, sixty-three means the twenty third day of March, 1863." Zane looked at the fax again. "The Alabama lawyer could be right. The Civil War may be involved — somehow."

"Zee, you're smart."

"No, just old."

Langdale continued. "Also, there's a tiny marking in red ink — the letter 'B' with a circle around it on the face of the Indenture. That mean anything?"

Zane closed his eyes. "I know an old sea dog, a sailor, who lives on St. David's Island. Named Beauchamp. They say the Beauchamp family owned a successful shipping business in the nineteenth century. Their ships ran the blockade during the Civil War. They lost most of their business at the end of the war. The circle 'B' could be a shipping mark — a nineteenth-century shipping mark. Go talk to old man Beauchamp. Ask him about that marking."

Zane finished off the bowl of chowder then sat back in the cast-iron chair. "Ian, you're a clever fellow. Start with Beauchamp out on St. David's. Before you go, tell me — what happened between you and the lady you met in New Orleans."

Langdale ran his hand across his face, then spoke softly. "I haven't talked with her, Zee. Actually I'm a little embarrassed about it. I'm not sure what to do."

"Don't be too shy. When you first got back, you were excited about your trip. You told me all about her like it was first love."

"We're so different."

Zane rested his head on his hand as though he were reading Langdale's mind. "I'm no expert on women, but if you can accept the testimony of literature, then love can overcome the accidents of birth, class, time, or anything else."

"I didn't know you were so sentimental, Zee."

"You came to me for advice. I have two pieces of advice — Call on Beauchamp. See where that goes."

Langdale jotted Beauchamp's name on the back of a business card.

"And call New Orleans. See where that goes, too."

19

BERMUDA. It's a quiet, restful land where cars and motorcycles cruise at twenty-five miles per hour, max, on narrow roads bordered by limestone walls white as bleached linen. The atmosphere is pure. No industry means no soot, smog, or noise.

The Gulf Stream warms the islands, so even though they lie on the same latitude as Charleston, winters are not cold. Almost constant breezes limit the heat in summertime and the summer high never rises above 90 degrees.

Fog is rare and frost nonexistent.

Bermuda is prosperous, picturesque, and well-groomed with luxuriant gardens everywhere. No wonder tourists have loved the place for a hundred years.

There seems to be no poverty. Inhabited by hospitable people, Bermuda prospers with one of the world's highest standards of living.

A WEEK AFTER Zack Whitcomb wrote to banker Ian Langdale, Zack and Ann were flying to Bermuda. The traveler of the couple, Ann flew for TWA, Howard Hughes's airline, as a stewardess after

World War II. She planned trips well, and her husband left his business travel arrangements to her.

Ann actually visited Bermuda in the fall of 1945, just after V-J Day. She and her girlfriend, Sara McBride, had stayed a month.

As the plane climbed into the cool December air above the Atlanta airport, Ann told her husband details she could remember from the trip.

"Back then Bermuda barred automobiles. You rode in horse-drawn carriages, or on a bike. And they had a train that ran all the way from one end of the island at Somerset to the other end." Ann remembered Bermuda well enough to draw by hand a map for her husband on the back of a paper napkin. She marked sites on the napkin-map — Hamilton, St. George's, Gibb's Hill Lighthouse and the Dockyard. When the Bermuda stories faltered she occupied him with a quiz game.

"What's Woody Herman's band called?" she asked.

He clutched the arm rests so tightly that the veins in his hands bulged out. "Got it — the *Thundering Herd.*"

"Name a big band song about Birmingham."

Whitcomb ground his teeth and the muscles in his face drew taut. He forced an answer. "Tuxedo Junction."

"Who was Eddie Fisher's first wife?"

His hands were almost white from squeezing the armrests. "Don't know. Elizabeth Taylor?"

"Nope," Ann said. "It's Debbie Reynolds. Liz was his second."

The couple enjoyed trivia games. A few years before, on a tour of New England, they answered the final question of a quiz game: "Who was the second man on the moon?" and won the quiz game all the passengers played during the tour. The Whitcombs won a free weekend in New York City as a reward for their knowledge. But they never collected the prize. Zack wouldn't fly. Still, Ann kept the gift certificate for the two nights safely tucked away in her jewelry box — just in case.

Ann read aloud from the first page of a paperback tourist guide:

"Bermuda was discovered in 1503 by a Spanish explorer, Juan Bermudez. Early navigators called Bermuda *the Isles of Devils* — "

He interrupted. "What does it say about the *Triangle?*"

"What triangle?" She shook her head. "I'm not gonna talk about it. It's a myth. Nobody ever got lost in the Triangle. Whole thing is probably 'cause so many ships collided with the reefs around Bermuda. A simple explanation."

Exasperated, she slammed the book. "You're normally so logical. But this phobia about planes and about flying — "

"Ann, it's not the *flying*. It's the *crashing*. I've seen enough of the North Atlantic for six lifetimes. And on ships, at least you could get out and swim if they went down."

She rolled her eyes. "Ye Gods, I'm tired of quiz games. You win. I'm taking a boat next time."

He unbuckled his seat belt, tightened the strap and rebuckled the belt. He covered his face with both hands. Ann felt his anxiety, his acrophobia. She massaged his neck. "Relax. You talk for a while." She drew out her words in a soothing tone of voice. "Why don't you explain the case to me again."

He breathed several deep breaths, then wiped his face with a handkerchief, and for thirty minutes expounded on the intricacies of the case.

Bermuda lies six hundred miles due east of the Carolina coast. The flight from Atlanta — or from anywhere for that matter — is over a long stretch of water. For a man who perceives water to be concealing danger and an airplane to be a flying machine a single malfunction away from death, two hours of flight time over the Atlantic is interminable — painfully interminable. When the Delta 767 passed the Georgia coastline, heading east, Zack pulled the plastic shade down over the window so he couldn't see the expanse of water passing underneath.

TWO HOURS AFTER the plane left Atlanta Whitcomb felt relief. The long narrow island dotted with colorful houses and white roofs loomed out the airplane window.

The Delta jet touched the runway. Whitcomb peered out the plane's porthole. He saw tranquil aquamarine waters. It was Castle Harbor, with breathtaking rocky coral shores rising along the coastline.

The Civil Air Terminal, a pleasant, two-story stone building, lies on St. David's, the easternmost island of a chain of broken islands, divided by tiny inlets. The Whitcombs descended the plane onto the airport tarmac and passed through customs beneath a portrait of the Queen. They collected their luggage and hailed a cab. The black driver politely stowed their bags. The cab sped away from the airport at the speed limit — twenty-five miles per hour.

Zack leaned forward in the back seat. "Never laid my eyes on a more beautiful place, Ann." The clean and neat compact taxi crossed a narrow causeway, built of graying limestone blocks generations ago. Lavender waves lapped the shore. The ruins of ancient fortifications loomed high on Castle Island in the distance. He and Ann lowered the taxi's rear windows. A gentle breeze rolled in. The taxi crossed the causeway over the water and ascended a steep hill. The countryside was reminiscent of his war-days in Britain — groomed lawns, small gardens, cottages at the end of long lanes, so ordered, so English.

Hedges of rose-colored oleander, hibiscus, and purple bougainvillea bordered the narrow, winding road. The vanilla fragrance of the tropical plants, the cascade of flowering colors growing above stone walls along the road, the immaculate white roofs of the cottages along the road, the driver's calm Bermudian accent, and the light winds flowing through a grove of banana trees relaxed Whitcomb. His hands — white hot with tension on the plane — regained their color. "Why didn't you tell me about this place, Ann? I think we just landed in paradise. The houses, the walls, the yards, the trees — everything's beautiful. Even the bumps in the road feel good."

She rolled her eyes. "You're just glad to be on land. I've been telling you about Bermuda for years. And London. And Paris. I gave up talking you into serious traveling. It's not easy to go trans-world on the rails."

The Whitcombs joined Ian for dinner that evening at his residence in Paget, a few miles from Hamilton. The two-story residence, built in the eighteenth century, sat beside a narrow, lonesome lane at the crest of Bostock Hill. The stucco house, nestled between huge oak trees and surrounded by ten-foot olean-der hedges along a stone block wall, overlooked Hamilton Harbor on one side and the Atlantic on the other. After dinner — York-shire pudding — Ian called Zack and Ann to the study. He poured Zack and himself a glass of single malt Scotch and a crème de menthe for Ann.

He opened a leather briefcase and pulled out a handful of papers. "Read this, Zack, when you get a chance. I compiled information about the origin of the bank, the legal status of Bermuda, and of Bermuda's participation in your Civil War. Take the briefcase with you. Study the materials and drop by my office in the morning. I can have a notary public or a government official available to verify the documents."

He sipped the Scotch. "Unfortunately, I have nothing specific for you about the Bermuda Indenture. But, I have an appointment tomorrow for us to meet a retired sailor from St. David's. The man's name is Beauchamp. Maybe he can help."

The Whitcombs caught the last ferry back across the harbor to their hotel.

20

LANGDALE lay in bed, wide awake and restless. Whether the scotch whiskey he had shared with Whitcomb, the continuing saga of the Bermuda Indenture, or simply the horn from a distant ship kept him awake, he wasn't sure. He thought about New Orleans and Nancy.

Upon returning to Bermuda, Langdale tried to dismiss the brief romance with the American woman. But, he couldn't manage to forget her or New Orleans. Ten days after returning home he received a postcard from her. He never responded. His emotions were mixed. Nancy was fun-loving, witty, ambitious, bright and good-looking. But Nancy and he were different, and he knew it.

Langdale turned his head on his pillow to look at the bedside clock — 2 a.m.

His mind roamed and wandered to his week in New Orleans — the late night at the Monteleone Bar where he and Nancy had met, her sparkling silver dress, the dangling earrings, her quick wit. Then, strolling down crowded Bourbon Street at one in the morning. He had stayed in New Orleans for three days — because of her. It was two months ago, but the memories were fresh — clutching hands, leaning over the rail at the Fairgrounds Racetrack, hollering at the horses flying down the stretch. Sipping wine during the afternoon at a café patio on St. Charles Avenue. A midnight ride on the Victorian streetcars to the end-of-the-line on Carrollton. Partying with Nancy's buddies at a Sunday afternoon crawfish boil; dancing Cajun-style in the midst of the overflow crowd at the Maple Leaf Bar listening to Rockin' Dopsie, and the best part had been just chatting with her on subjects from the mundane to the serious. He doubted a long-distance relationship could ever develop between them. Their personalities clashed. He was British — reserved, formal, traditional. Nancy was an American, a Yank — bold, open, rebellious.

Tonight, Whitcomb had asked about her. A week ago, Zane had too.

"What the hell. Enough thinking. I'm acting."

He reached for the portable telephone by the bed.

"Nancy, wake you?"

"No, just lying down. It's midnight and I just hopped in bed." The sound of her voice rekindled his feelings for her.

"Got your postcard. Thanks."

"What time is it in Bermuda? You *are* in Bermuda?" she asked.

Langdale detected disappointment in her voice. "It's two in the morning. Nancy, I need to tell you something. I miss you dearly. I've made a mistake — not calling. I was scared after I got back home. I didn't tell everything. I told you that my fiancée broke our engagement. I didn't tell you that she had broken the engagement just a few weeks before I met you. It was mean for me not to call or write you. You are a fascinating woman. But I was scared to get too involved — so soon. I want you to know I'm sorry. And I want you to know I had a wonderful time with you in New Orleans. And I want to see you again soon."

Langdale couldn't believe his own words — he spoke so boldly. He hesitated, hoping for a positive response. He wasn't disappointed.

"That's a mouthful. I'm sorta shocked." She hesitated, then

collected her thoughts. "But I'm thrilled you called, Ian. I've had a horrible day. My corporate tax professor jumped all over me — for being late to class. I got a B-minus on a term paper in my finance class that I worked on day and night for two weeks. The worse news is that my summer internship in New York City fell through."

She hesitated again. "It's wonderful to hear a friendly voice, even at midnight."

"Nancy, may I ask you a question?"

"Shoot."

"What are you wearing? I mean right this second."

"Nothing but a Saints tee shirt."

"I like the 'nothing' part. Who are the Saints?"

"Get with the program, boy. American football — the New Orleans Saints. That's a pretty intimate question, Ian. What are you wearing?"

"A pair of white silk pajamas. The drawstring is untied. No, just kidding, Nancy. Actually I have on white sweatpants."

She laughed.

"Remember my lawyer friend from Alabama? The older gentleman. He is here in Bermuda working on that same case."

"About the Indenture?"

"Yeah. Zack asked about you."

"What did you tell him?"

"Said I would let him know later. So how are you, Nancy?"

"I just told you — bad and sleepy."

He fumbled with his words. "Tell me how — tell me about things. How's Mimi?"

"She's in Zurich with Peyton. He deals with a bank there, and he took Mimi along for the ride. Peyton's high living slowed for a while. Now he's rolling again — partying with the bigwigs. I'm among the hoi polloi — not big enough to be included. Mimi says he's not as much fun as he used to be. He's nervous and so impatient. They were playing mixed doubles last week. Mimi missed a few easy shots at the net, and Peyton went ballistic. He screamed at her and slammed a serve right past her head."

"Zack will be interested. What did Mimi do?"

"She takes it. She kept playing. But she's getting tired of Peyton's shenanigans. I tell her she oughta cool the relationship, but she's hung up on the guy."

"Are you good friends?"

"Good enough to know this — Peyton doesn't know how tough Mimi can be. She was dating a guy at Merrill Lynch last year. One night, she was having a party and he didn't show up. He just stood her up with no explanation. It embarrassed Mimi. Next thing — she started dating one of the guy's best clients and stole the client away."

Langdale searched for words, then he blurted out, "Nancy, you're coming to Bermuda for the summer."

"What? Sure. Right. And the moon's green cheese. Ian, at this moment, my checking account is in *single* digits. I'm talking eight dollars. With a little luck, my eight bucks will get me a Greyhound bus ticket to Whynot, Mississippi. So, Mr. Langdale, can you meet me in Whynot?"

Langdale laughed. He loved her sense of humor. "No, Nancy, here is my proposal. I'm buying you a round-trip ticket from New Orleans to Bermuda. There's a number of multinationals and big insurance companies out here. I know some people. Half the people in Tucker's Town own big businesses. Lots of 'em bank here. I'm finding you a summer job with a business here in Bermuda. You go to a fine school there at Tulane. We'll start on a work permit. Just get packed and you're off. I'll find you lodging." Langdale listened hoping for a positive response.

"Aren't you manna from heaven? Ian Langdale, you amaze me. We meet. Spend a glorious time together. You leave. The days pass. I don't hear a word. You call at midnight. You offer me a job, in Bermuda no less. You make my day, my week, my summer."

"Well, Nancy?"

"Get me that job and I'll row, man. I'll row a boat from Charleston."

"Excellent."

"By the way, Ian. Two things. Number one, do you mind faxing me tomorrow morning an answer to this question, 'How would economist John Maynard Keynes respond to Clinton's budget proposal?' Just kidding."

Ian laughed. "I'll try. What's your fax number?"

"Make it brief, but hard-hitting — if you know what I mean?"

"All right. What's number two?"

"I missed you, and I'm mad about you. And I'm so glad you called. Ian, I've got a confession to make. When we first met in the bar at the Monteleone, we both told each other about being in the line — the queue, you'd say — to see the old document. It seemed we were at the same place at the same time, purely by accident. Well, it wasn't an accident. When you arrived in that carriage, and they announced you at the door, I saw you in your tux. And I thought you were gorgeous. So I followed you and your escort up the stairs and got in line behind you."

"Why didn't you speak?"

"I chickened out. But then I asked the escort where you were stayin'. So Mimi and I went to the hotel kinda hoping to meet you. So, Ian, that means you're talking to a stalker. What do you think about that?"

"Flattered, actually. What man wouldn't be?"

"Ian, hold onto the phone a second."

He heard the phone hit the floor and the patter of feet.

"You left one of your Oxford-cloth shirts in the closet. Guess what? I'm wearing it! Goodnight, love."

21

LANGDALE drove his Peugeot past the American naval base — ceded by the British in 1940 during the days of Lend Lease. A high chainlink fence along the road separated the base from the rest of the island. The Peugeot picked up speed passing modest homes on the empty road.

Langdale slowed at an intersection. "I never come out here. May take a few minutes to find Beauchamp's place."

He turned off the main road and followed a curvy, narrow road bobbing and weaving through the landscape. The car climbed the hill past a field of Easter lilies and palmetto to the base of St. David's Lighthouse.

A simple white house with red trim sat beside the lighthouse. White sheets hanging from a clothes line waved in the breeze. Langdale stopped the car. He looked lost. "This is pretty isolated — for Bermuda. But we'll find it." He descended the lighthouse hill and turned onto the main road. A sign read Great Head Park.

Crumbling brick and mortar fortifications rose in the park forest. The road curved around an inlet of water called Great Bay. A half-sunken hull rotted in the water. A dinghy lay partly buried in sand on the beach.

"Let me warn you, Zack. People on St. David's can be rather cool — suspicious of visitors. The inhabitants out here keep to themselves. They don't have much contact with the rest of the islands. Beauchamp didn't say much when I phoned him. He sounded weak and rather aged."

"Why is this island different from the others?"

"For generations, St. David's was physically separated from the rest. There wasn't a bridge out here until the thirties. The people developed their own lifestyle. They had a strange mix out here — Portuguese farmers, Indian slaves from America, blacks, whalers. And probably a few pirates. Still, they're good, honest people. Damned good sailors. Just don't expect the warmest welcome."

Langdale parked in front of a two-story house in deteriorating condition. The windows were lifeless, like empty eyes, with no curtains or shutters. The smell of seaweed meant the ocean was just beyond a rocky hill behind the house. The sandy soil was barren of any lawn. Langdale opened the car door and two German Shepherds barked from the front porch, then keys jingled inside a two-key brass lock, and the heavy cedar door opened. A man, rusty-haired and tanned, wearing mud-spattered khaki trousers and a soiled white shirt with the top buttons missing, stood in the doorway. Bearded and hirsute, his tongue poking the side of his cheek, the blue-eyed man stared at the visitors.

He spoke after a long silence. "You Langdale?" The dogs barked at their master, expecting to be petted.

"Yes — yes, sir. I'm Langdale. I phoned."

"Come in. I'm Beauchamp, Tom Beauchamp." He shook hands with the visitors. They entered a large room, lit only by the sunshine beaming through the windows. Beauchamp petted his dogs and they trotted inside behind the visitors. He motioned for the men to sit on a wicker sofa with faded cloth cushions.

Langdale had it wrong, thought Whitcomb. Beauchamp moved athletically around the room, and with powerful, muscular arms, and he looked like he could still handle any job on a ship at sea. The room smelled of stale sweat. The underarms of Beauchamp's cotton shirt were stained with perspiration and the cotton shirt stuck to his skin revealing a muscular body.

"Mr. Beauchamp, you're in good health, I see. This is Zack Whitcomb from the States — state of Alabama." Langdale was nervous. He spoke quickly. "I explained the purpose of our visit on the telephone. Mr. Whitcomb is trying to learn the background of an 1860 bank document. Albert Zane, who's a good friend of mine, told me — "

Beauchamp interrupted. "I know Zane. I got his book."

Langdale continued. "Zane recognized a marking on the back of the document. He said it could be the ink stamp from the Beauchamp Company."

Beauchamp raised his eye brows. "You got the document. Let me see it."

"Don't have the original. Here's the copy," Ian placed the three pages side-by-side on top of a heavy wooden trunk.

Beauchamp didn't say a word. He walked across the room to an armoire, opened one of the massive doors and reached into a shelf full of bottles.

"Whiskey?"

"No, sir," said Langdale. "Never drink during the day." Langdale started to seat himself but drew a disapproving glance from Tom Beauchamp.

"You?" Beauchamp looked at Whitcomb.

"Why not? You got any bourbon — Kentucky or Tennessee bourbon? I'll take it with a little water."

Beauchamp looked surprised. "Good." He drew two glasses from the armoire, dirty, smudged, and of different sizes, and filled each glass halfway. Then he added water to each glass using a dipper to draw water from a wooden bucket. "I drink rainwater collected from the roof."

Ian winced.

"That's how granddaddy drank whiskey — lukewarm with a little water, 'cept he added some sugar," said Whitcomb.

Beauchamp handed Whitcomb a glass and lifted his own glass for a toast. While he thought of a toast, Beauchamp ran his fingers, crowned with long grimy fingernails, through his greasy hair.

"To American whiskey — the only good thing to come outta the place."

Whitcomb laughed and took a sip. "Mr. Beauchamp, you sure know your whiskey. Boy howdy, this is good stuff."

Beauchamp didn't smile. He spoke blandly. "Let's see this old paper."

Beauchamp retrieved a wide magnifying glass from the armoire. He knelt down on one knee and looked at a marking on the paper. Finally he scratched at his beard and stood up. His blue eyes grew large.

"I'll be damned. That marking is the seal of the Beauchamp Shipping Company Limited. Ain't no doubt about it." He looked at the lawyer. "What's your name — Zack?" He handed the magnifying glass to Whitcomb and pointed at the paper. "Zack, that's a *B* with a circle around it. You can barely make out the letter *B*. It was probably stamped on there with a wooden seal."

Whitcomb nodded. "Why do you reckon they stamped this particular document?"

Beauchamp drank from his glass. "They used to stamp on the seal just like they were posting a letter. That mark meant the Beauchamp Company was gonna deliver the paper. I ain't seen that marking in a long time. Interesting indeed."

Whitcomb sensed the Bermudian opening up. "Reckon you could tell me about the shipping company? Would there be any shipping records still around?"

Beauchamp freshened up his drink of whiskey with a splash of water from the bucket. "Where you from again?"

"Alabama."

"Alabama," Beauchamp cleared his throat. "That's where Joe Louis was from, wasn't he? The prizefighter. Alabama twister, that's what the English press called him." Beauchamp balled his hands into firsts, boxing-style, in front of his face. Whitcomb balled his fists too, his left in front of his nose, his right extended, as though he were preparing to defend himself. "LaFayette, Alabama," said Whitcomb, "That's where Louis was born."

The boxing talk aroused Beauchamp. He opened his eyes wide and threw a sharp jab into the air with his left. "I saw the Louis-Conn fight. During the war. I couldn't have been over sixteen. We were docked in New York, and I got shore leave. Conn — Billy Conn — the little Irishman, was a middleweight fighter. He beat Louis for twelve rounds. But Conn got overconfident. He tried to fight Louis straight up, and Louis knocked him out."

Whitcomb tilted his head as if he were evading a punch. "I saw the fight on the newsreels. Louis had terrific power. And perfect timing on defense. I saw him fight an exhibition in England during the war. You remember the rematch after the war? Louis KO'd Conn in the ninth."

"Alabama." The words rolled slowly out of Beauchamp's mouth. "The deep South."

"It's you damn Southerners who broke down the Beauchamp Company — during that Civil War you fought."

Whitcomb laughed aloud. He didn't want the conversation to get too serious. "Heck, the Civil War broke down Alabama, too — the whole state, the whole South."

The gruff Bermudian barely cracked a smile. "S'pose you're right. We all took a lickin'. You know something, I detest Americans. They're all so loud. And they think they know everything. Hell they tryin' to turn Bermuda into another damn state."

Whitcomb nodded. "Well, I got advice for Bermuda. Don't ever join the Union 'cause once you're in, you can't leave. That's one lesson of the Civil War. If you try to leave the Union, you're dead."

Langdale and Beauchamp laughed hard.

"You're a damned good fellow." Beauchamp sat down in a leather chair, and nodded for the visitors to be seated. "Let me tell you 'bout Bermuda and the Civil War. My family was the biggest company on the island running guns and supplies to the South. I know that era of history pretty well. I got boxes full of records out in the buttery tellin' all about it. Bet I've read every book ever printed about Bermuda and your Civil War. Like I said, that damned war pretty much broke the family business."

He finished his whiskey and continued. "In 1861, Bermuda became a blockade-running port for the Confederacy. Lincoln proclaimed a naval blockade of the South. The Federal navy had closed all Southern ports by the end of 1861. Being a colony of Great Britain, which was neutral, and located just six hundred miles off the coast, Bermuda was perfect for some gun-running."

Langdale looked bored with the narrative. But Whitcomb hung on every sentence. His drink forgotten, Whitcomb leaned forward.

"The Confederates shipped cotton to Bermuda to be exchanged for weapons. Raw cotton from the South was shipped to English textile mills. Gold and silver flowed like water in here. St. George's and Hamilton were sleepy little colonial outposts until the war broke out, but during 1861 they became centers of trade. The islands teemed with all sorts of men — sailors, traders, spies and ruffians looking for a quick farthing. They lived everywhere in the Islands — along wharves, in parklands, in public houses. Life quickened throughout Bermuda. The money pulled the tough adventurers, the speculators and especially sailors to Bermuda from over the world."

Whitcomb asked, "How did private sailors make such big money?"

"Hell, man. It was dangerous. And the Rebs had the gold. Just like the run to Murmansk during the War. You know 'bout that, don't you?"

"Yeah. Made for a rich merchant marine," answered Whitcomb.

"Same thing in the Civil War. For each run to the Confederacy, captains of blockade runners made five thousand dollars. Pilots made four thousand. Even sailors made three or four hundred. All fees were paid in gold and silver, not Confederate paper money, and half of the fee was a bounty, paid up front before the voyage began." He glanced at Langdale. "Banks flourished too — holding the wealth."

"St. George's was the primary harbor for the run to the Southern states. It's close to the open sea and it had a deep harbor. And blockade runners could commence their run past U.S. naval ships awaiting them in neutral waters. The Confederacy opened a trading office in the St. George's town square. I've got manifests. Almost two thousand ships, an average of over a ship a day, entered and departed Bermuda between 1861 and 1865 during the block-ade-running trade."

Whitcomb interrupted. "So Bermuda was allied with the South?"

"Not officially. Officially Britain was neutral. Queen Victoria wouldn't support slavery. Britain prohibited the slave trade years before. But the Bermudians supported the Confederacy. Not for principles. It was the money, the gold." Beauchamp raised his bushy eyebrows.

"And your family got involved?" Whitcomb asked.

"Up to their necks. Bermudians, like my family, bought their own fleet. From mother England. Liverpool mainly. And those Liverpudlians knew their craft. They built fast ships — beautiful ships with a low freeboard and draft for gun running. I've got drawings. The blockade runners had a humped back deck so they drew only ten feet of water. And they flew. They cruised at high speeds — fifteen knots, easily faster than the best ships in the U.S. navy. The ships were painted colors to make them invisible. At night, not a light was allowed, except for the helmsman. For quiet running, no animals, no cows and or chickens, were allowed on board. Builders were clever. The smokestack funnels could be lowered so the blockade runners would have little silhouette against the sky. Those four years were exciting, for certain. The Civil War brought riches to Bermuda — until the war ended. Unfortunately, my family was heavily — too heavily involved. My grandfather ran the company. The Beauchamps were always seafaring people. They made profits early, but kept investing. They invested big and lost big. Not too proud, myself, but there we are. You can't rewrite history. Can't rewrite facts."

The elderly man shook his head. "When the war ended, my family owed big debts. Never recovered. They had four ships in the fleet. And storehouses in St. George's. The banks sold off everything to pay debts. Out in the buttery I got journals, ships' logs, accounting records. I ain't got time to rummage in that mess, but I reckon you're welcome to 'em."

Without a word, Beauchamp opened a door, grabbed a dirty brown fishing cap with a long visor, and marched out the front door.

Langdale glanced at Whitcomb.

"Wonder where he's going?" asked Whitcomb.

"The rascal must have finished off all his whisky. And he's going for another bottle. Probably keeps his stash out in the buttery."

"The little square building?" asked Whitcomb.

"Yes, with the high, pointed roof. They used 'em to keep wine and things cool. Place is probably awful dirty, crawling with all kinds of vermin. Bet the old scamp hasn't cleaned it in decades." Langdale motioned outside. "Are you going to accept his offer — to examine Beauchamp's records?"

Whitcomb stood and walked across the room. He wiped dirt off a glass pane and peered out the window. It was the buttery — a one-room square building ten or twelve steps from the main house. Big chunks of limestone had peeled off. The roof sloped toward the crest above the center of the building.

"First thing, Ian, our Mr. Beauchamp is a lot smarter than he wants people to believe. He's like a lot of Southerners. He puts on a little act like he's a bumpkin. He's been around. He's got a nice vocabulary. And I could see into his bedroom when he opened the door — there was at least one bookcase, maybe more, full of books along the wall."

Whitcomb sounded reluctant. "Yeah, I gotta accept Beauchamp's offer. I gotta turn over every stone to try to solve the puzzle. The whole riddle may be solved right here, out in that room. The journals and logs are original papers, admissible in court. They're excellent proof in court. The Indenture itself, without more, won't win the case for Melvina. The authenticity of the Indenture needs to be proven by original documentary evidence like journal and log entries. So I gotta accept Mr. Beauchamp's offer to study the material."

He turned toward Langdale. "Does your bank store old records?"

"Yes, sir."

"Maybe your bank's archives will provide some clues on the authenticity of the Indenture. As I said in the letter I faxed to you, surely the bank attempted to record the Indenture in Alabama."

Langdale nodded in agreement. "Definitely. Without question, the bank would've recorded — or at least tried to record a mortgage securing a hundred thousand pound loan."

"We need bank records, if they exist, about the loan."

"I'll pull the records for you. But Lord knows, finding anything about the Indenture will be next to impossible."

"You ever heard the motto of the army engineers? 'The difficult we do immediately. The impossible takes a little longer.'"

Langdale laughed. "Have you always been so optimistic?"

"I like challenges."

"Good, because you certainly have one."

"I'll ask Ann for help. Ann's good at solving mysteries — at least murder mysteries."

"Zack, I appreciate your confidence. But for you to find any shred of paper explaining the old mortgage . . ." His voice trailed off. "Impossible."

"Can't be discouraged. I've made searches for years. Patience and careful, methodical work can pay off. One small clue leads to another. Your friend, Zane, referred us to Beauchamp. In turn, Beauchamp's knowledge of the blockade runners and his offer to allow us access to shipping records may yield clues. We'll see. At law, the truth is like a huge jigsaw puzzle. Every scrap of information is a piece of the puzzle. Diligence and patience will yield pieces. I can't be discouraged. Ann will help. She can find anything. Heck, she finds everything I lose. Who knows. If we're persistent, a clue will emerge."

He added, shrugging his shoulders, "I hope so anyway. By the way, I appreciate that information Nancy told you about Durant."

The door opened. Beauchamp entered ahead of the German Shepherds. He was holding an old whiskey crate.

"There're dozens of boxes like this one out yonder, all filled with old shipping records." He dropped it on the floor. "You might find something somewhere in the rubbish. That's the best I can do. I'll give you the key. You're on your own."

Beauchamp reached inside his pants and pulled out a gold pocket watch and chain. The crystal was cracked, but the watch was ticking. He gazed at the watch, signaling he was ready for his visitors to depart.

"Railroad watch?" asked Whitcomb.

"We say railway. I worked for 'em after the war. 'Til they shut down."

Whitcomb nodded. "I'll start tomorrow, if it's okay. Tell me something. Whatever happened to the Beauchamp Shipping Company? Why do you keep the records?"

"Hell, grandfather never quit sailing. Even when the business went broke, the Beauchamps kept sailing. All the family kept sailing. I've sailed every merchant ship in Bermuda. As far as I'm concerned, Beauchamp Shipping still exists. It's just taken us a little while to recover. Family's been here for a couple hundred years. Give it another hundred, we'll be sailing the main." He cracked a smile. "Don't know why all those records are still here. Reckon they were just waiting for some damn fool to come 'round."

22

THE next morning, the couple walked beside Hamilton Harbor along Front Street to Langdale's office. The weather was perfect, especially for early December — clear skies, slight breeze, seventy-five degrees. Small sailboats cruised Hamilton Harbor. Several freighters lay docked at the wharf. On the opposite side of the harbor, the hills gently rose from the water and houses with white roofs dotted the hills. Everywhere, vegetation was green and lush with blooming flowers and trees. Stone walls, built from quarries of the island's limestone rock, lined the street.

At intervals along the walls, stone gateways arched above the walls. These gateways — *moongates* to the Bermudians — were supposed to possess romantic qualities.

Ann reached and caught her husband's arm. "Tough working conditions. You expect me to actually work in this atmosphere?"

He didn't answer. Ann sensed her husband passing into a trance. After forty-one years of marriage, they understood each other's moods. Confronted with a serious problem, Zack often became single-minded, focusing on nothing but the problem before him. The outward signs were unmistakable — a fixed stare, curt responses, and distance between them. He considered focusing narrowly on a problem to be evidence of a disciplined mind. She considered it unhealthy for him to impose stress and anguish unnecessary to resolve a problem — particularly when he allowed everything else to go to pot. He would forget to pay the bills, skip meals and go without sleep. She used to think he was being selfish and inconsiderate. But they discussed their differences and he'd gotten better as he aged. He loved her and she knew it.

She kicked him behind the knee. Startled momentarily, he stopped abruptly. "Zack, relax. You're getting into a funk, a cloud. Look around. Smell the roses — well, oleander anyway. Enjoy. Remember what Luther says — don't take yourself too seriously. Okay?"

He held her hand. "I'm okay. Just a momentary lapse, babe." He kissed her.

"Question, Ann. Did Luther really say 'Don't take work too seriously?'"

"Not *Martin* Luther. I mean Luther at the Dixie station."

He smiled and rolled his eyes.

She returned the smile, took his hand, and squeezed it.

"So it's gonna be tough finding any records about this Indenture thing?" She made the sentence into a question.

"Yep. There's a mass of material to wade through."

They started walking again. Zack pointed to the bank building ahead — a modern five-story yellow and white edifice built beside a high sea wall. A Bermudian flag — red, with the British Union Jack in the upper corner — waved in the stiff breeze from a silver pole on top of the bank.

"Ann, I betcha there's a record in that bank tellin' what happened to the Indenture. We just gotta find it."

They walked for a moment.

"Zack, you're competitive. I'll make you a bet. We both make a wish. The first one to find a clue, gets the wish."

"Well, I never heard a bet called a *wish*. It's not a wish. But, fair enough. You get the bank records. I get Beauchamp's shipping records.

"What's your wish, Ann?"

"I don't come cheap. If I win, we spend two weeks in Europe — wherever I say."

He nodded.

"You got a wish?" she asked.

"We take a trip — by train — with a sleeper, the biggest sleeper they got — all the way from Meridian to Penn Station in Manhattan."

LANGDALE, DRESSED IN white Bermuda shorts, navy knee socks, a white shirt and club tie, unlocked the door. A conference table, laden with cardboard boxes, leather satchels, and bundles of papers of all sizes, sat before them.

"Any records or paper relating to the Indenture will be there — somewhere. It's all yours. Call if you have any questions." Langdale nodded, leaving the conference room to the lawyer and his wife.

The couple immediately started their research of the bank's records. They examined papers and organized the material until noon. Then Zack left the bank records to Ann and taxied to St. David's Island to work on the naval shipping records at Beauchamp's.

Meticulously, the couple combed the records. Each morning after breakfast they took the long walk along Hamilton Harbor from the hotel to the bank. Ann steadily pored through bank papers. Zack taxied to St. David's. After a week's work, the couple only had sore eyes for their labors. They took a respite from their research to enjoy the weekend — sunbathing on the pink sands at Horseshoe Bay, watching a soccer match in Somerset on the west end, and strolling the Royal Dockyards.

BERMUDA MUST HAVE more churches per capita than any country in the world. They're classic old churches with bell towers. It's comforting to a visitor. Churches convey a sense of morality.

There's an Anglican Church in every parish. African Methodist Episcopal, Church of Scotland, Roman Catholic, Seventh Day Adventists, the Salvation Army, churches of virtually all faiths, sit on every street corner in the capital and are scattered on roads throughout the country.

On Sunday the Whitcombs took in church services at the Hamilton cathedral. Ann held the church bulletin so both she and her husband could read it.

CATHEDRAL OF THE MOST HOLY TRINITY
16 DECEMBER 1994

The seat of the Anglican Church of Bermuda. The Cathedral was begun in 1884 to replace Trinity Church. The Gothic edifice dominates Hamilton . . .

The organist played the processional. Wearing scarlet robes, the choir marched from the rear of the church down the center aisle, followed by three clergymen. Brass and marble plaques commemorated heroes and churchmen. A row of tattered flags hung at the entrance to an adjoining chapel.

A storm blew up. It shook the palm trees outside the stained glass windows. The congregation was sparse. Whitcomb spotted a man in front of the church. The man's head was bowed — not in prayer, but in light sleep. His rusty hair was disheveled and his beard ungroomed. It was Beauchamp.

That old bird. Unpredictable. I ask him about the cathedral. He murmurs, 'the nearer to church, the farther from the Lord.' But there he sits, wearing the same old clothes. At least he washed 'em. Tough man. Survived five years in the Royal Navy during the war, with two ships shot out from under him I remember one, H.M.S. Prince of Wales. Jap airplanes shot it to pieces in the Pacific — near Singapore in '41.

Beauchamp doesn't care much for Langdale. No wonder. They live on the same island, but in different worlds. Langdale's world is modern — the island of tourism, international business, insurance firms, investment companies, British and American billionaires in Tucker's Town, the land with elegant shops on Front Street peddling English china, Irish crystal, and Scottish wool. Beauchamp's from a different world — an older, tougher Bermuda. A land of survivors. I see why they chose their motto: "Wherever the Fates lead us." I'll complete the sentence: "Wherever the Fates lead us, we will survive." They've done everything — farmed onions and lilies. They built these limestone houses that still survive. They built cedar ships and sailed the seas as traders, whalers, even privateers. Their fleet had two hundred ships — in 1820. They settled Turk's Island, way down near Hispanola, and for a century manufactured salt to sell, fighting off Frenchmen and Spaniards the whole time.

Beauchamp and his independent ilk are spiritual descendants of Englishmen who shipwrecked, created a parliament, rebelled against Cromwell and the Puritans, and survived.

I like Beauchamp's Bermuda. I just need his help.

The priest mounted the carved stone pulpit. He raised his voice over raindrops pelting the windows and read from Matthew. "You will know them by their fruits."

Whitcomb heard portions of the sermon. "Our appearance, our words, but especially our acts, are evidence to the world of what lies within us."

The wooden hood above the pulpit projected the priest's voice.

"Early Christians drew the sign of the fish in the dust and on walls. Their brothers knew the meaning — Jesus Christ, Son of God. Savior. Our forefathers identified themselves by their appearance — Scots with colorful tartans, English with their coat-of-arms worn over their armor, or woven in banners. Today some follow the tradition with buttons on our coats identifying a college or institution . . ."

Zack recalled the first day he saw Ann's brother Marley wearing his navy uniform. The brass buttons with the Naval Academy seal sparkled like stars against the dark blue coat. Zack ran his fingers across the niches and nooks on the brass buttons. They were as big as quarters and heavier — the carved eagle in the center — unconquerable. Ann had given Zack the buttons the year before. They lay in the top drawer of his chest. Maybe he'd have them sewn on a blazer.

The priest concluded the sermon: "And they will know by our love that we are Christians. Amen."

The lay reader read from prayer books. The congregation knelt on prayer cushions of intricate needlepoint. The priest prayed for Her Majesty the Queen and her subjects. Then Communion was over and the congregation strolled out of the cool stone building to ecclesiastical organ music. The church bells tolled midday. The storm had passed, leaving the streets wet and the air heavy. The clergy stood on the porch shaking hands with everyone.

The Whitcombs waited several minutes for Beauchamp to exit the church, but they never saw him. The couple strolled in silence down the hill toward the harbor waters at the foot of the street — Burnaby Street. The storm had churned the waters of Hamilton Harbor into whitecaps.

Ann closed her eyes and breathed a deep breath to savor the scents from the sea spray. She clutched Zack's hand.

"Too serious, Zack. You're getting too serious again."

"Yeah, maybe, but I wanna win this case." He kissed the back of her hand. "I'm dreading going back to Beauchamp's house. I'm sick of that buttery. It's the dirtiest room I've ever been in. It's dark, 'cept for two little windows. Filthy old crates with spider webs. And dust everywhere. You have to leave to get a decent breath of air." Whitcomb paused. "You learn a lot hanging around a man's house. Beauchamp has a big bag — a punching bag — hanging from the ceiling in the buttery. I've never seen him work out on the bag, but I know he does 'cause he leaves gloves out. And they're always warm and damp from his sweat. Imagine a sixty-nine year-old man boxing. That's what keeps him in shape. I kinda like Beauchamp. Just wish he'd clean up."

Ann wrapped her arm around his waist. "I didn't realize the records were in such bad conditions. Maybe we oughta give it up.

"I wanna do a good job. Durant's gonna hire the best in the business. If we're gonna win, I gotta have some more bullets to fire. We ain't gonna win in court with just the Indenture alone. I need some bullets. And we're running out of time and sources. Heck, we can't spend a fortune over here. And I'm sick of breathing dust."

They walked along the waterfront back toward their hotel. Zack shook his head. "We need a time limit. Let's hunt hard tomorrow. Then we'll decide whether to bail out."

ON MONDAY the first clue surfaced. Ann noticed from her work that nineteenth century bankers labeled a short piece of correspondence a *minute*. She learned to flip through the *minutes* — nineteenth century memoranda — quickly as she worked her way through the bank's records. Late Monday afternoon, Ann noticed a stack of unsealed envelopes bound and tied together in the back of a wooden wine box. The envelopes carried a London postmark over a stamp of Queen Victoria — the British monarch during most of the nineteenth century. A large circular seal of wax on each envelope was broken, but Ann could easily read the language on the seal when she pulled the top flap of the envelope down, matching the two halves of the waxed seal — *Bank of London*. She recognized the *Bank of London* to be one of the two banks loaning money to debtor Herbert Raymond Durant in the Indenture. She opened the first envelope in the package, pulled out a folded, tattered, dog-eared piece of paper and read the contents.

TO: J. Langdale, Pres. Waterloo Bank of Bermuda, Ltd.
              Hamilton, Ber.
FROM: W. Parson, Bank of London, London, Eng.
DATE: 1 Dec. 1859

An American, H.R. Durant from New Orleans, proposes through our agent in Louisiana to borrow 100,000 pounds. Mr. Durant's credit is excellent. He proposes to post as collateral for the debt his real estate holdings in Alabama, U.S. Our bank's board cannot accept such a large debt. The board has authorized me to offer your bank 1/2 of the loan, 50,000 pounds. We would appreciate a prompt reply.

Ann photocopied the minute and phoned her husband at Beauchamp's house in St. David's. "Good news, Zack. I believe I've found a clue — the first piece of the puzzle."

"Well done. What you got?"

She read it.

"You've done it, Ann. I always thought it curious that two separate banks made the loan. Simple explanation. The loan was too large for one bank. Copy the *minute*. Good work. I'll say it again — you never cease to amaze me. Stay with it. I'll read it tonight."

Ann feverishly rifled through the stack. Like the first envelope, most were sealed with wax and the deep, clear imprint *Bank of London*. They were postmarked *London* on a stamp of Queen Victoria, and addressed to *Waterloo Bank of Bermuda, Ltd., Hamilton, Bermuda*."

TO: J. Langdale, Pres. Waterloo Bank of Bermuda, Ltd.,
              Hamilton, Ber.
FROM: W. Parson, Bank of London, London, Eng.
DATE: 13 Jan. 1860

I am in receipt of your minute dated 17 Dec. 1859. Your bank having agreed to participate in the loan to H. R. Durant, we have posted a bank draft in the amount of $100,000 pounds to Mr. Durant, debtor, in New Orleans, La., U.S. Durant, et ux., will execute a promissory note secured by mortgage Indenture.

TO: J. Langdale, Pres. Waterloo Bank of Bermuda, Ltd.,
            Hamilton, Ber.
FROM: Bank of London, London, Eng.
DATE: 19 May 1861

I am attaching herewith a mortgage Indenture. The Indenture represents collateral security for loan of 100,000 pounds to H. R. Durant of New Orleans, La., U.S. Please post to U.S. for proper recordation.

TO: J. Langdale, Pres. Waterloo Bank of Bermuda, Ltd.,
            Hamilton, Ber.
FROM: B. Disraeli, Pres., Bank of London, London, Eng.
DATE: 31 July 1861

In response to yours of 30 June 1861, her Majesty's government advises that Alabama and other formerly states of the U.S. will accept foreign instruments with full faith and credit. Proceed with dispatch to post to Choctaw County, Ala. C.S.A. for recording. Failure to record the mortgage Indenture places the collateral at great risk.

TO: J. Langdale, Pres. Waterloo Bank of Bermuda, Ltd.,
            Hamilton, Ber.
FROM: B. Disraeli, Pres., Bank of London, London, Eng.
DATE: 11 Feb. 1863

I am in receipt of yours of 10 Jan. 1863. We agree with your attempt to post the mortgage Indenture through Wilmington. C.S.S. *Galveston* was built in Liverpool. She is reportedly among the fastest afloat with a fine crew (mostly British) and a fine captain. With good fortune, she will perhaps avoid U.S. blockade.

Ann photocopied all the *minutes*, dropped the copies in her briefcase, and gave the originals to Ian. He promptly placed them in the bank's vault.

She telephoned her husband again to share her find.

"Ann, you realize your discovery means you win a trip to — to wherever. Where we gonna go?" he asked.

"Somewhere in London. I wanna do two things — have high tea at the Savoy and tour Buckingham Palace."

"Fair enough, but you better work on lots of trivia questions."

"Why?"

"Cause, it's a six-hour flight across the Atlantic. I'll go insane."

"I got a tough one for you. Who betrayed John Dillinger?"

"Trick question — the lady in red."

BEAUCHAMP WAS SITTING alone at a table in the Hog Penny Pub. He stood to meet the couple. "Zack, this must be the sharp-eyed lady who found those bank minutes."

Ann looked quizzically at her husband. She hadn't expected Beauchamp to accept Zack's invitation to dinner and certainly hadn't expected the Bermudian sailor to be so polished and well-groomed. Beauchamp sat erect, his broad shoulders pushed against the back of the chair. With his gray hair combed, his beard neatly clipped, his charcoal tweed jacket pressed, and his shoes polished, Beauchamp looked quite handsome. She had expected a rough-looking, tough-talking, stubble-bearded man — not an Oxford don.

Zack wasn't surprised at Beauchamp's apparent transformation. At their first meeting Zack had recognized Beauchamp was more literate than he let on.

The Bermudian had opened up as the men became acquainted. They shared a great deal in common. Both spent much of World War II on the high seas of the Atlantic — Beauchamp as a sailor in the Royal Navy and Whitcomb as an Army officer on cargo ships. Zack had noticed Beauchamp's Royal Navy medal in a case in the buttery and inquired about it. Beauchamp served on the *HMS Prince of Wales* in 1940 during the four-day running battle between the British navy and the German battleship, *Bismarck*.

These men of the same generation shared war stories about shore liberty in European and northern African ports-of-call, Marseilles, Antwerp, Algiers, Casablanca, and Tripoli. They remembered a few of the same cafés and taverns and how customers would knock on the tavern door and wait for the owner to open the tiny wooden window to examine the customer before permitting entry. Neither man remembered the tavern keeper ever refusing. Maybe the Allied uniforms were the key.

Both men spent weeks at sea, running the gauntlet of the German U-boats — the sea wolves of the Atlantic. Powerful radios tuned to Axis Sally, the Nazi propagandist, presented the main entertainment for sailors on board the long gray convoy of Allied ships passing across the North Atlantic.

Zack saw signs that his host was well-read, well-traveled, and, at least years ago, well-mannered. After a couple of days, Beauchamp had felt comfortable with his guest and he gave Whitcomb the run of his house. The lawyer noticed Beauchamp's collection of books — worn from use — on a variety of subjects from history to literature. Scrapbooks of the sailor's schoolboy days, and old photographs portrayed Beauchamp as a younger, gentler man than he now presented himself.

The two men talked more as the week passed and became fond of each other. Beauchamp even showed Whitcomb the best food on the island — Dennis's Hideaway.

Years ago, Whitcomb's father had pulled him away from a fight with little Harvey Singer during a ball game in the pecan orchard behind the house. "In life, it's not how many runs you score. It's not how many dollars you make. What counts is how many friends you make."

Now Whitcomb slapped Beauchamp on the back, like an old friend.

"Ann's sharper than I am."

"I guarantee you she's sharper."

Whitcomb took a seat next to Beauchamp. "Before anybody else gets here and we get down to business, tell me, were you a boxer?"

"You saw the bag, didn't you? I boxed in the Royal Navy. It was a gentleman's sport then. It's a good work out. Keeps the blood flowing and your head clear. Preserves youth." Beauchamp turned toward Ann, "Pardon me, ma'am. And I'm ready if a smart arse kid thinks he's too big for his britches."

Langdale and Zane arrived together and joined the others for dinner at the Hog Penny — named for a local coin which honored the wild hogs populating the islands when the English first arrived. When everyone was seated, Whitcomb got down to business. He placed in the middle of the table copies of the minutes discovered in the bank's records.

"Ann has found this series of letters from the Bank of London to the Waterloo Bank of Bermuda. These *minutes* are admissible as evidence in court. I'll simply have Ian sign an affidavit testifying that these minutes are originals discovered in his bank's records."

"Is that the end of the case?" asked Langdale.

"No. I can't stop yet. The court will still want more. Those minutes tell the background of the Indenture. They're proof that the Indenture isn't some grand forgery. What we still need is proof — evidence showing why the Indenture wasn't recorded. That's what the judge will wanna know. Still gotta answer the question, why wasn't such a valuable mortgage ever recorded? I have Mr. Beauchamp's shipping records well organized. Think I'm on the verge of finding something."

Beauchamp rapped the table and spoke up. "Something's in those shipping records. I'm sure of it. I know it." Beauchamp's keen interest surprised everyone.

Beauchamp licked his thumb and began reading.

The waitress delivered five mugs of steaming tea to the table.

"Why are you so certain something's there?" asked Ann.

"It's the marking — the marking on the Indenture. The Beauchamp stamp on the Indenture meant the company was due to deliver the cargo. The Beauchamp Company stood behind that stamp. If granddaddy failed to deliver, there's an explanation." In silence, Beauchamp thumbed through the minutes. He read and re-read them.

He looked up. "Zack, how are the shipping records organized?"

Whitcomb explained his method. He began by gathering the records according to the vessels owned by Beauchamp Shipping Company, Limited. By the end of the first week, he had stacked all records in the buttery in four stacks — a stack for each of the four ships owned by the company. When Ann called today, he checked the records. No records existed for a ship called *Galveston*.

Beauchamp stopped reading. He took a pipe from his pocket and lit it. "Guarantee you something's in those shipping records about your mortgage Indenture. The marking of the Indenture was unmistakable. Granddaddy was thorough. Once he stamped cargo — crates, barrels, or even papers, he took custody. Treated his cargo like his own children. He meant to deliver it. Kept excellent records. Documented everything. That's why the buttery's so full of papers. Yes sir, there's some record, some journal entry, something in that buttery saying what happened. I guarantee it."

THE NEXT MORNING, at breakfast, the waiter delivered a note to the lawyer — "Meet at my house at one. J. Beauchamp."

Beauchamp stood in the doorway, waiting for the couple. "Come in this house." It was more like a command than an invitation. Beauchamp's cluttered antique furniture, the dark rooms, and the dusty floor didn't faze Zack anymore. He didn't bat an eye when Beauchamp drank rainwater with cupped hands from a wooden bucket. Ann sat next to Zack on a sturdy, intricately woven wicker sofa which obviously hadn't been painted in years. The clutter of antiques was straight out of a Dickens novel. *The Old Curiosity Shop* — right here on St. David's.

Beauchamp turned toward Ann when he detected her interest in his furnishings. Her roving sparkling eyes gave her away. "Look around, madam. Walk through the house. There ain't been a lady in *Laura Leigh* in five years at least."

"Thanks. Your place is perfectly fascinating." She stood to inspect the furniture. "Who's *Laura Leigh*?" she asked.

"That's the old girl's name — the name of the house and grounds. Named for the first ship purchased by the Beauchamp Shipping Company. In 1859."

Like a child in a toy shop, Ann moved among the clutter, running her hand along the Empire, Queen Anne, and Victorian pieces — two massive armoires, an elaborate roll-top desk, a cedar chest-of-drawers, wooden boxes of all sizes — as small as a candleholder and as large as a linen closet.

Whitcomb fidgeted on the sofa.

Beauchamp started talking again. "Zack, I used to read a lot."

"I know. I've seen your books."

Beauchamp reached into a cabinet underneath a dark Pemberton table and pulled out a pipe with a paper pouch of tobacco. He poked and twisted the long white pipe cleaner through the stem and then poured the tobacco into the bowl. The pipe smoker's ritual reminded Whitcomb of his father and Mr. Tollman Cammack from Mount Sterling smoking pipes and spinning tales about hunting.

"Zack, I been around you for a week. You're an interesting fellow. I wanna know what makes you tick?"

Whitcomb could barely believe the fellow before him — so open and gregarious — was the same dark and suspicious man who hardly let him inside a week ago.

The kettle on the pot-bellied stove whistled from the boiling water.

"Cup of tea?"

"Yes."

"Yes. Thank you."

"S'pose I'm like everybody else," Whitcomb said. "Money — the long green — is a good motivator."

Beauchamp snickered and shook his head. He poured the tea into three cups — all different sizes and patterns. "No. Don't believe it's money."

He puffed the pipe and smoke curled toward the ceiling. "Believe I'm a sharp observer of people. I like some people, but sometimes people bother me."

Beauchamp puffed hard and leaned back. "When young Langdale first asked me to meet with him and an American lawyer about looking at my shipping records — the papers out in the buttery — I said, 'You're crazy.' Only 'cause his bank loaned me money a couple of times that I let you come. Now, I'm glad I let you come. I think I got you figured out."

Ann interrupted. "What have you figured out? I'd like to know myself. I sure haven't figured him out and I've had forty-something years."

"Used to think Americans were the most money-hungry, greedy, tasteless, obnoxious people on earth. All Hollywood and Las Vegas glitz. People who'd do anything for money — sell their brother down the river to some tabloid newspaper, people who write and buy sensational, tell-all books. Hell, Donald Trump would fill up the Grand Canyon with concrete for a car park — if he could make money. You're different. Lee, your Confederate general — I like him. He took a bunch of cotton farmers, barefoot country boys, a few Mississippi riverboat gamblers and almost whipped the U.S. government. He was a good man. He wouldn't endorse an insurance company right after the Civil War ended, even though he and his family were totally penniless. Told the insurance company, 'My name's not for sale.' Now everybody's name's for sale. Just pay the price."

"Beauchamp, you know a lot of history. And you give me too

much credit. I'm no saint, believe you me."

Ann interrupted her husband, "Let him talk. Let him talk."

"Zack, this search for the records about the Indenture is not just business, not just a job. You're too intense, too enveloped in this. Never seen anybody concentrate like you. And for eight, nine hours straight. I appreciate hard work."

He puffed the pipe, relaxed in his chair and continued. "At first, I didn't care whether you found anything. You seemed to be a nice fellow, but it wasn't skin off my back. But your interest aroused my interest. I asked young Langdale to explain what this grand search was all about. He sent his correspondence to me. He told me about the oil well, the Indenture, the black woman, everything."

Ann sat on a wicker sofa and rested her chin on her hand to listen.

Beauchamp continued, "I usually don't say much. I listen a lot. And observe. And I've been listening. Maybe it's your military training — whatever it is, you do your duty."

Whitcomb noticed Ann silently mouth the word "duty" and then place her hands over her ears.

Beauchamp didn't notice. He reached down beside the chair. "I've been helping you out. I got something here for you."

He put down the pipe in the ashtray.

"You'd never have found this. It's a journal. Last night, at dinner, you showed those minutes to me. They said the Indenture was on the *Galveston* — the C.S.S. *Galveston*. I came back last night, lit myself a kerosene lantern, and went out to the buttery. You've done a fine job organizing everything, but it still took me 'til midnight. I found a manifest — a listing telling all the ships purchased by the Beauchamps — the Beauchamp Shipping Company. Five ships in all. They were built between 1855 and 1865. The C.S.S. *Galveston* wasn't included — under the name *Galveston*."

Beauchamp sipped his tea, then handed a worn, black leather-bound journal to Whitcomb.

"Open up the front cover."

Whitcomb slowly turned the cover with both hands to avoid ripping the bindings.

"About midnight, I noticed a notation — a notation that caused me ultimately to find this journal. The *Galveston* was the same ship as the S.S. *Deliverance*. Beauchamp Shipping Company bought the *Deliverance* in 1861, then sold her to the Confederates, who renamed her the C.S.S. *Galveston*. Granddaddy's records are under *Deliverance*. I told you my grandfather was incredibly thorough."

Zack opened the envelope just inside the cover.

"It's all there. Everything — a letter from a Confederate midshipman, Lieutenant Rivers Black, to my grandfather, telling about a package from Waterloo Bank of Bermuda for delivery to Wilmington, North Carolina. That's your Indenture that the midshipman refers to in the letter. Young Langdale told me that, under the Beauchamp marking — the letter B with the circle around it — was a barely legible date, 23 March 1863. That's the date grandfather gave the bank's package to Lieutenant Black.

"Read the journal. It's all about the *Galveston's* voyage to Wilmington, North Carolina — the closest Confederate port. The bank had it all worked out to deliver the Indenture for recording. The bank paid the Beauchamp Shipping Company to deliver the Indenture. Grandfather was a jack of all sailing trades. He was a carpenter, a chandler, a navigator, everything. He knew the *Deliverance* — now converted to the Confederate ship *Galveston* — was the strongest, fastest ship in St. George's Harbor to deliver the Indenture. Grandfather was well-acquainted with the Confederate agent here in Bermuda — a man named John T. Bourne of Rose Hill. Grandfather knew the Confederate Quartermaster agent — Major Norman Walker. He arranged for the Indenture to be shipped on the *Galveston*."

Beauchamp rose from his chair, walked across the room and pulled a leather-bound volume from the bookcase. "Here's a picture, a drawing actually, of the *Galveston* on the drawing board."

Beauchamp marked the page and handed the thick volume back

to the lawyer. "The *Galveston* departed St. George's Harbor on the morning of the 23rd of March, 1863. The lieutenant's journal tells what happened. The *Galveston* tried to run the blockade, but failed. Hell of a battle. The *Galveston* returned to Bermuda when she came under attack off the Carolina coast. The journal is detailed — and makes interesting reading. Even a bit philosophical. Read it, it's all there. Your proof. Everything."

"Amazing," said Whitcomb.

"I went to the library in town this morning. Did a little research. Turns out the Confederate — Bourne — kept good records. Kept money too. During the Civil War, his house was like a bank. Confederate gold and silver was piled a foot high on his dining table. Bourne's records are in the library. They have the original manifest of the *Galveston*. The Indenture is listed on the manifest. I copied it for you."

Manifest

C.S.S. Galveston

23 March 1863

32 cases of artillery harnesses	20 rifled cannon
4 tons steel bars	23 cwt. cartridges
45 tons of gunpowder	2640 ounces of quinine
265 pounds of chloroform	large quantities of boots
80 bales of woolen blankets	Confederate mail bag
1 sextant (in wooden box)	1 Indenture (in metal tube)

3 passengers

"Read the cover letter from Lieutenant Black and read the journal. It's all there," said Beauchamp.

1st day of May, 1863

James Beauchamp,
Proprietor Beauchamp Shipping Co., Ltd.
St. George's

Sir:

I attach herewith a journal of the attempt made by the C.S.S. *Galveston* to deliver to Wilmington, N.C., Confed. States of Amer., a certain bank Indenture. I regret to inform you that *Galveston* failed in her recent attempt to run U.S. naval blockade. C.S.S. *Galveston* was, therefore, unable to deliver Indenture to Wilmington. May I say, Sir, you sold my government a fine vessel. The *Galveston* is a marvelous ship, well built for speed and endurance. The *Galveston*, formerly The *Deliverance*, has been forged in the fiery furnace of battle. Again, Sir, I regret Confed. Navy was unable to deliver Indenture. As you are aware, I returned Indenture to you previously. Wishing you success,
I remain,
Your obedient servant

Rivers Black, Lieutenant
Confed. States Navy

Whitcomb offered his hand. "Beauchamp, you rascal, we've hit the motherlode. I'm grateful."
Whitcomb wrote Melvina that ownership of the mineral rights had been established — once and for all.
Four months ago, Whitcomb diagrammed the ownership of

1844	United States to Raymond Herbert Durant	Patent Deed from United States to Raymond Herbert Durant
1880	to	Raymond Herbert Durant reserves mineral rights to himself in 1880 deed.
1895	Robert Durant to	R.H. Durant dies without a will. Robert Durant, son of R.H. Durant, inherits.
1920	Calloway, Shields, and Ruth Durant to	Robert Durant dies without a will. His three children inherit.
1931	Calloway Durant to	Other two children deed the Durant Place to Calloway Durant.
1949	Melvina Durant Hawkins	Calloway Durant dies without a will. Daughter Melvina Durant Hawkins inherits.

Diagram written by Zack Whitcomb the night of December 18 — after his meeting with Tom Beauchamp.

the mineral rights. Now, he drew an updated diagram and circled the name of the rightful owner — *Melvina Durant Hawkins.*

THE NEXT DAY, a Delta jet ascended from the runway at the Bermuda Civil Air Terminal. Ann looked at her husband's hand — white knuckles gripped the armrest. She gently ran her fingers up his arm and along the back of his neck. His muscles felt like a rope pulled tight at both ends.

"Zack, I'm gonna find you a punching bag and boxing gloves. I could tell Mr. Beauchamp's workouts intrigued you. We'll hang the bag from the rafters in that smokehouse out back. I want you to stay robust — and virile."

He felt the erotic excitement of a man deeply in love. For a moment his phobia abated, and his arms relaxed. Then just as quickly, the phobia returned. When he clutched the armrest, Ann began peppering him with questions. "Whose band was called the *College of Musical Knowledge?*"

"I dunno. Give me a second. Okay. It's Kay Kyser. It's Kay Kyser and the College of Musical Knowledge."

23

RETURNING to Alabama, Whitcomb envisioned a simple trial. File a *Bill to Quiet Title* in Circuit Court. Arrange for the Bermuda Indenture to be delivered from the New Orleans Cabildo to the Butler courthouse. Prepare sworn affidavits for Langdale and Beauchamp to sign. Langdale's affidavit with the minutes from the Waterloo Bank, and especially Beauchamp's affidavit with the naval journal would authenticate the Bermuda Indenture. The testimony from the two Bermudians proved conclusively why the Indenture was never recorded. Introduce the Bermuda Indenture into evidence. Submit affidavits of Doll and Melvina. The trial would be over in minutes. A ruling in Melvina's favor was a lock.

A one-room log cabin sits in the edge of the woods fifty yards behind the Whitcomb's residence. The cabin's abandoned, but it was built to be a smokehouse for curing meats. For Christmas, Ann delivered on her gift of a punching bag, and arranged for it to be hung from the center roof beam in the smokehouse.

Zack didn't expect her to remember, much less find a bag — a *big bag* weighs sixty pounds and isn't for sale at McPhearson's Hardware.

After Christmas dinner, Ann laced up a pair of Everlast boxing gloves she'd given him, and he started punching. He moved around the bag tapping it lightly, then smashing a few blows. He danced around the bag raising dust on the dirt floor. He increased the pace, throwing steady punches. But after three minutes — one round of boxing — he hit a wall of fatigue. Sweat had formed on his forehead, and his arms hurt. Enough for a day.

The next day, he pounded the bag for three minutes again, then added a minute of jumping rope to the workout. The following day, he included a couple of minutes of shadow boxing. In a week, he had increased to a twenty-minute workout.

Ann added music. She brought a portable stereo — a *boom box* — to the sessions, like Mike Tyson or George Foreman training for a championship fight. But instead of James Brown and the Flames, Zack played Les Brown and the Band of Renown. Instead of Arrowsmith, Zack heard Kate Smith.

By the third week Whitcomb was thriving in the smokehouse, sweating through thirty minutes — tapping the dirt floor on the jump rope, parrying imaginary blows while shadow boxing, and smashing rhythmic blows into the big bag.

ZACK WHITCOMB's journey to Bermuda trip hadn't gone unnoticed. On the first business day of the new year, Tutt Sanford, Durant's lawyer, telephoned Durant's office at nine in the morning.

Durant's secretary spoke curtly. "Mr. Sanford, cotton's already open and Peyton doesn't take calls anymore when the market's open. Not unless it's life or death at stake. I'm sorry."

"Ma'am, just get Peyton on the phone," Sanford said. "Tell him there's a hell of a lot at stake. Tell him ownership of that Alabama oil well is at stake."

The line was quiet, then Peyton came on. "Tell me what you got, Tutt."

"Peyton, as you requested, one of the junior partners and I been studying title to your Alabama mineral rights." The lawyer chose his words with care. "There are recent developments that place your claim to title in serious jeopardy. A development has arisen," he hesitated. "It's bizarre. Bizarre."

"Several months ago a document was donated to the Cabildo — the Louisiana Museum."

Durant's voice urged Sanford to hurry. "Yeah, I know — I heard something about it."

"Turns out the document is about your family. Language in the document — it's called the Bermuda Indenture — disputes your heirship claim to the Alabama mineral rights."

Durant blurted, "That can't stand. I'm drawing twenty thousand a month in royalty checks from those oil wells."

Sanford continued, "I happened to see the document last fall when the Cabildo reopened. I never mentioned it. Sometimes you let sleepin' dogs lie. But we been poking around up in Choctaw County, Alabama. I'm afraid this lawyer up there has caught on. A sole practitioner named Whitcomb wrote the title opinion on the Durant place. We found out from the lawyer's secretary that he took a long business trip — to Bermuda, of all places — before Christmas."

Durant questioned, "Bermuda? So what?"

"That's where the Indenture originated," said Sanford. "If Whitcomb can prove facts about the origin of the Indenture, then we believe — I believe — you'll lose title to the oil well."

"Impossible. That's impossible."

"Peyton, I believe your title to the oil well in the Durant place is worthless with the discovery of that document, the Indenture."

"Who is this guy — Whitcomb?"

"He's a smalltown title lawyer in Butler — the county seat."

"Who's paying Whitcomb?"

"Whitcomb's checked the title for the oilmen — Elder and Shanks, who drilled the well. Now he represents a woman — a black woman named Hawkins."

"Write me a letter, Tutt. And give me the details. But I'm telling you — this won't stand."

A WEEK LATER, Durant sat alone in the back room at Casimento's, spooning from a bowl of dark, thick filé gumbo. Casimento's is the cleanest restaurant in New Orleans. It's a little uptown café on Magazine Street. The picture windows on the front and the tiled floor and walls bear the bright glow of a regular washing. Joe Casimento, the owner, lives upstairs and runs the place. The café lies a few blocks away from Peyton Durant's home in the Garden District. Durant regularly dropped by late in the afternoon after the close of the market.

The front door opened and a lean man wearing a threadbare short-sleeved tee shirt and a purple LSU baseball cap walked past the oyster bar toward Durant. A wide scar ran alongside his face. The man removed his cap and placed it on the table.

"I'm La Coste. I hear you wanna see me."

Durant sipped from the gumbo. He picked a piece of jagged crab from his mouth.

"You wanna eat, Mr. La Coste?"

"Just coffee."

Durant signaled the waitress — a tiny woman standing nearby — and a cup and saucer appeared.

The man in the tee shirt emptied three bags of sugar in his cup. "I hear you need a job done. What you need?"

Durant took a deep breath. "I got *two* jobs for you. One's complicated. Real complicated."

Durant left his spoon buried in the gumbo.

"I need to get a document out of a museum. There's a document on display at the Cabildo down on Jackson Square. It's sitting on the second floor in a glass case. I need it. The museum people have a label in front of it. They call it the Bermuda Indenture. Can you handle a job like that?"

The other man answered quickly. "If you got the money, I can get in there." He took a bottle of ketchup and played with it in his hands. "Cabildo. That's the place somebody burned up a few years ago."

Surprised, Durant glanced up. "I thought the fire was an accident."

"No way. Not in a fireproof building. Somebody wanted that fire. Believe me."

Durant nodded.

La Coste continued. "I've never done a job on a museum. And the Cabildo's a busy place down there in the Quarter. They probably got 'em a hot-shot security system. But I've never seen a security system I couldn't break. If I can get hold of the specs on the security system, I'll find a way. I got connections."

He tried to twist the top of the bottle. It didn't budge.

"Mr. Durant, you give me the money, and I'll get that document and whatever else you want outta that museum."

Durant coughed. "How do you get hold of the plans?"

"With enough cash, I'll get somebody — somebody who knows the system."

La Coste clutched the top of the ketchup bottle with an iron grip. He twisted hard and the top released.

"Mr. Durant, we'll get inside. And there won't be a trace. I guaran-damn-tee you. But it'll cost you. Just gimme a little time to work on this job."

Durant nodded. "Job two is a lot simpler. I wanna scare a couple of guys. I wanna scare 'em to death. But nobody gets hurt."

"Who's the bum?" asked La Coste.

Durant's eyebrows raised. He didn't understand.

"The bums. Who we after?"

Durant drained the bowl and drank half a glass of water.

"A lawyer. A hick, worn-out lawyer up in Alabama. Name's Whitcomb. Zack Whitcomb. And two Texas oilmen drilling up there — in Choctaw County. The details are in the envelope. Get 'em off my back."

"Okay, Mr. Durant. How's fifty thousand sound — $50K total for both jobs. That's my fee."

Durant nodded his acceptance of the offer. "Deal. But don't hurt anybody. Not yet."

Durant walked away leaving the envelope on the table.

SHANKS'S VOICE on the other end of the line sounded skittish.

"Zack, the motel clerk just gave me the message. What's the emergency?"

"There's been a burglary at the Cabildo in New Orleans. Guess what they stole — the Indenture." Whitcomb hesitated. "You, Jess and I need to talk. This is serious business."

"I'll be there in five minutes. Jess is flying into Meridian. I'm pickin' him up at the airport."

"Let's take my car." Said Whitcomb. "We'll talk on the road."

Whitcomb was waiting in his '55 Chevrolet when Shanks arrived. The oilman climbed into the front seat, and Whitcomb sped away.

"Read the article, Jim. Then I'll tell you what the NOPD says."

Shanks scanned the bottom half of the front page of *U.S.A. Today*.

THEFT AT CABILDO BAFFLES POLICE

The Cabildo, one of America's most historic buildings, was robbed Saturday night, as revelers played outside on Jackson Square.

According to a spokesman with the New Orleans Police Department the robbers stole several priceless items, including the death mask of Napoleon Bonaparte and the Louisiana Purchase treaty between the United States and France. The two items are considered to be worth millions of dollars.

Also stolen was a 19th century document, a mortgage involving a famous New Orleans family, recently donated to the museum by a bank in Bermuda.

A spokesman for the NOPD described the entry through the Cabildo's sophisticated security system as "bold and ingenious."

The trespasser scaled the St. Louis Cathedral and then shimmied on a rope over Pirate's Alley to the roof of the Cabildo. He dismantled a portion of the roof creating a small hole to gain entry.

The burglar apparently lowered a rope into museum space activating the motion detector alarm.

The alarm activated three times in one hour between eight and nine Saturday night. Museum security officials investigating the Cabildo discovered nothing suspicious. They thought the alarm system malfunctioned and deactivated the system. The burglar entered undetected Saturday night.

The police are investigating the possibility of an inside job.

Shanks stopped reading. "My God. My God. Knockin' over a museum. You think the robbery's connected with the ownership of the oil well?"

Whitcomb ran the Chevrolet through second and into third gear. "Probably. Ann saw the article in this morning's paper. I called the New Orleans police — first thing this morning. It was a strange conversation."

Whitcomb glanced at Shanks. "I got the distinct impression the cop was investigating me." He shut the vent window to block the wind noise. "I told him up front I might could help the investigation. Told him I used to be a circuit solicitor in Alabama and that I was involved in a civil case that could bear on the burglary. I told him about how the Indenture could resolve a dispute over ownership of an oil field.

"But the cop didn't care about my information. He wanted to know all about me, not about the burglary. When I asked for details, he basically told me to stay-the-hell outta the business of the NOPD."

Whitcomb and Shanks traveled in silence. They passed a sign

for a small community — Lisman. Whitcomb loosened his tie.

"All that time and work in Bermuda researching the Indenture. All wasted." Then he pounded his fist on the metal dashboard. "There's just so much money involved. And the Indenture is crucial. I been trying to keep things quiet. I didn't think anybody had made the connection between the Bermuda Indenture and the oil well. But, there were a couple of New Orleans lawyers in the courthouse a while back — checking title on the Durant property. Somebody mighta put two and two together. The cotton broker from New Orleans, Peyton Durant, could be behind it."

The Chevrolet passed another community sign — Pushmataha.

"Whoever committed the burglary must have figured it was too obvious to steal just the Indenture," said Whitcomb. "So they stole the treaty and the death mask."

"Jim, you and Jess need to be careful. A guy who would arrange this burglary would probably do something else." The lawyer sped along the empty road. "It's the same old story. When money gets involved, things can get ugly. And the bigger the money, the uglier it can get."

"Zack, what's the effect of the Indenture being stolen? Does Melvina Hawkins lose her claim?"

"I don't know. I gotta research that issue. It's doesn't look good. The Indenture was the linchpin of her case. Still, as a general proposition, the law doesn't allow a man to profit by his crime. Under some circumstances a copy might be admissible. But it'll be tough."

His voice became serious. "That's not my worry now. Jim, you guys need to be careful. A man who'll commit a burglary — y'all just need to be careful." Whitcomb turned to Shanks. "Can you handle a gun?"

Shanks breathed hard. "Yeah, maybe. I did ROTC at A&M, I did a tour in Vietnam — a long time ago."

"I'll get you a pistol."

The Chevrolet chugged westward toward the Mississippi line,

doing sixty. Several cars passed on straight stretches of highway.

Whitcomb glanced at the rearview mirror from time to time. Two cars followed on the narrow two-lane. The Chevrolet slowed to fifty, then forty-five. But neither of the cars moved to pass on the long straightaway.

The black Chevrolet followed by two sedans passed a small brick church set back from the road. Whitcomb waved the cars ahead, but they slowed with the Chevrolet.

"Jim, I may be imagining things, but I'd swear there are two cars following us."

Shanks looked behind. Two men rode in the front seat of a dirty gray Ford Taurus. Both men stared ahead, emotionless. The windshield was cracked. The other car behind was a solid black Camaro.

Whitcomb passed the Mississippi line. The road narrowed.

The gap closed between the Taurus and Whitcomb's car. The Taurus pulled to within fifteen feet, ten, then five feet.

"Zack, the fool's gonna ram us from behind."

Whitcomb's foot dug into the accelerator, and the Chevrolet leapt forward to fifty, then sixty miles per hour. Whitcomb pushed the engine revs up and up. The Taurus and Camaro fell behind. Whitcomb whipped the car faster — to sixty-five, then seventy.

At seventy-five, the steering wheel began to vibrate in Whitcomb's hands. The sound of the exhaust echoed through the car. Shanks yelled at Whitcomb over the high-pitch scream of the engine. "She won't take anymore. You can't hold the road at eighty in this thing."

Two hundred yards back, the black Camaro whipped into the left lane alongside the Taurus, and the two cars raced, side-by-side in pursuit of the Chevrolet.

Inside Whitcomb motioned with his head. "There's a gun in the glove compartment." Shanks opened and felt inside and took out a long-barreled World War II-vintage Colt pistol.

Behind them, the black Camaro raced ahead of the Taurus,

both cars gaining steadily on Whitcomb's Chevrolet.

Whitcomb floored the gas petal for maximum speed, and the engine's revolutions raised to a squeal. The speedometer hit ninety, but the black Camaro screamed toward the Chevrolet like a wildcat. The distance between the cars narrowed.

Suddenly, the engine of the black Camaro gunned. The Camaro shot into the left lane, and pulled parallel with Whitcomb's Chevrolet. The driver of the Camaro clenched his teeth as if he were preparing for a collision.

Shanks hollered, "He's gonna knock us off the road."

On an impulse, Whitcomb eased off the accelerator. "Hold on. I'm turning into that dirt road up yonder."

Whitcomb jammed the brake pedal. At a curve, he hurdled the Chevrolet off the highway onto a dirt road. Tall pine trees lined the one-lane road, their branches hanging over like long arms. Whitcomb was doing fifty as he approached a sharp bend. Riding the clutch, he coasted for a few seconds, then gave her more gas going into the bend. Ahead, the dirt road came to an abrupt dead end at an abandoned shack. Whitcomb jammed the brakes with all the strength in his leg, and the two men braced themselves for a crash. With brakes squealing and dust rising, the Chevrolet skidded to a stop on the dirt and gravel five steps from the shack.

Whitcomb and Shanks turned to look behind them. A moving cloud of dust was rising above the trees. In a moment, the black Camaro rounded the bend. The Camaro eased closer and closer and then tapped Whitcomb's bumper and stopped.

Whitcomb heard another car engine. The Taurus pulled behind the Camaro on the dirt road.

Whitcomb and Shanks were trapped.

"Jim, let's get out of here and see what's with these bastards."

Whitcomb and Shanks opened the car doors and stepped out on opposite sides of the Chevrolet, facing the Camaro from behind the open doors.

A tall man wearing a camouflaged army jacket and a purple

LSU baseball cap slowly emerged from the driver's side of the Camaro. His jet-black hair, long and thick under the cap, was slicked down. He right cheek bore a gruesome, discolored scar as long and as wide as a man's thumb, in the shape of a lightning bolt.

The man carried no gun, but the bulge in the jacket pocket looked ominous. A shotgun the length of a boy's baseball bat, with a pistol grip, lay on the dashboard in clear view through the lightly tinted windshield.

Whitcomb and Shanks stood behind the Chevrolet car doors and faced the man for a full minute. Whitcomb broke the silence. "Mister, if I were you, I'd back out of this road right now and move on."

The stranger spit on the ground. "Ol' Man, I don't think you're in a position to be tellin' me what I ought to be doin'." He spit again, then noticed Whitcomb's eyes focusing on the weapon lying on the dashboard. "Ol' Man, if you're smart, and I think you are, you and your buddy won't make any quick movements. That's a Mossberg 12-gauge riot gun. Holds seven big shells. I know. I just loaded it."

Shanks had lived in Lafayette, Louisiana, for three years and recognized the stranger's Cajun dialect.

"You're out of your territory aren't you? A *coonass* up here in south Alabama. A pretty haughty one, too."

The stranger cocked his head, spit out of the side of his mouth. He reached down and picked up a rock. He tossed the rock into the air and caught it several times. Then he straightened his cap and pointed his finger. "I'm gonna make this simple. I've got a job to do. We been hired by a man in New Orleans. You know him." The Cajun spoke slowly. "Stay out of his way. Leave things alone. Stay out of the man's way. Y'all understand? Lemme put it another way. If y'all don't understand. If y'all interfere, you'll wish you hadn't."

The Cajun patted the bulge in his coat pocket, stepped back into the Camaro and slammed the door.

The Camaro and the Taurus backed away, then turned around,

and sped away. Neither car carried license plates.

Without saying a word Whitcomb and Shanks resumed their trip to Meridian.

After a minute, Whitcomb spoke, "Jim, you realize that guy's a lackey for Durant in New Orleans? I'll give the guy credit for one thing. He was careful not to aim a gun at us. He showed the sawed-off shotgun on the dash and kept patting his coat pocket, but he never actually pointed a weapon at us. It's like a criminal lawyer advised him. Notice, he never mentioned Peyton Durant by name. Durant's just trying to scare us." Whitcomb spoke confidently.

"Yeah, Zack, damn right Durant's trying to scare us, and he's doing a good job of it. You said it right, when money gets involved, things get ugly."

Whitcomb laughed, then turned toward his passenger. Shanks opened the glove compartment and with a shaky hand laid the pistol inside. "You were smart not to try that," said Whitcomb. "His shotgun trumped that old thing."

Shanks's face was colorless. Above the collar of his work shirt, the pores on his face oozed a greasy sweat. Perspiration had wet the underarms of his cotton shirt into a growing dark spot. "You okay, Jim? You look white as a sheet."

Shanks dropped his head and placed his hand over his mouth. "Pull over. Stop the car, Zack."

Whitcomb eased the Chevrolet into knee-deep weeds on the side of the road. Shanks quickly opened the car door, leaned out, and vomited. For a full minute, Shanks heaved, coughing a pea-green liquid on the grass.

Finally, Shanks threw back his head and breathed a deep breath. "I'm a sorry sight — twenty years younger than you and fallin' apart at the seams. I thought I was pretty tough, being a Viet Nam vet. I'm pukin' up my guts, and you're rock hard, no sweat."

Whitcomb pulled a white handkerchief from his back pocket and handed it to Shanks. "Know something? You *are* a sorry sight, Jim. Let's get the hell out of here 'fore the Cajun shows up again."

Whitcomb cranked the engine. The antique car plowed through the weeds back onto the highway. After less than a minute, the car slowed and drifted to the right onto the shoulder into the weeds again.

Whitcomb braked to a stop. Without uttering a word, he glanced at Shanks, rolled down the window, leaned his head out, and vomited.

THAT NIGHT after his wife turned out the bedside light, Whitcomb lay awake. He heard every sound of a small town night — noisy crickets, barking of his neighbor's hunting dogs, and revved motors of eighteen-wheeler trucks passing through town. He felt anxiety, then fear. Then the more he thought about the day's events, the more his emotions changed to anger. His mind pondered. Durant — the egomania, the condescension, the arrogance of a man who would threaten him and the oilmen.

Whitcomb lay awake most of the night. He recalled his father's advice on fist fights — "Hold your left in front of your face for protection and punch hard with your right. Whitcombs don't start fights, but we defend ourselves." And Whitcomb remembered his grandfather's stories about the Sims War:

In the 1880s, a self-proclaimed minister named Bob Sims and about a hundred of his kinfolk and disciples decreed themselves independent of all earthly laws. A Confederate veteran, Sims was a tall, thin, brooding man with a booming preacher's voice and a Lincolnesque charisma. His fervent followers shared religious conviction, God-like worship of Sims, and antipathy toward their more conventional neighbors.

For a decade, the sect lived at peace on a large tract in the south end of Choctaw County. But the clan began distilling whiskey, ignoring tax laws, intercepting travelers, and harassing neighbors. Nobody took action at first. In December 1891, Sims and his followers attacked the home of an antagonist, a Scotsman named John MacMillan, who had reported Sims's illegal activities to the law. The clan, proudly calling themselves the "Simsites," set fire to MacMillan's home and shot MacMillan and three members of his family in cold blood as they escaped the flaming house.

The Simsites had crossed the Rubicon. Like a volcanic eruption, the citizens acted to purge the county of the dark stain. They formed a "vigilance committee," a posse of two hundred armed horsemen — Whitcomb's grandfather included. The horsemen surrounded the Sims compound and demanded surrender. When Bob Sims refused, the two sides shot it out, pistols, rifles, and shotguns blazing. The fight became known in Alabama history books as the Sims War. The "war" lasted twenty-four hours until Bob Sims realized his plight. He surrendered on Christmas Day 1891.

For better or worse, the posse hanged Sims and three followers in deadly retribution for the four innocents they had gunned down two days earlier.

Durant suffers from the same disease that afflicted Sims — fever of self-importance, delusions of power, reduced ability to reason, loss of humanity. The Greeks called it hubris. It's often fatal.

THE NEXT MORNING, Zack Whitcomb dictated a letter to his secretary. "Bea, this letter is to Durant in New Orleans. I want you to spell his name P-a-y-t-o-n." She chuckled. Her boss sometimes annoyed his opponents with an intentional misspelling.

February 16, 1995

Mr. Payton Durant
New Orleans Cotton Exchange Building, Suite 200
Carondelet Street
New Orleans, LA 70001

Re: Durant 20-14 well
Bladon Springs, Alabama

Dear Mr. Durant:

This is to notify you that I represent Melvina Durant Hawkins. Mrs. Hawkins is the rightful owner of the Durant well and the entire Bladon Springs Oil Field.

I have researched the matter in depth. Simply stated, I have determined that any claim you have to the Durant well and the mineral rights to the Durant place is bogus and fraudulent. I have attached herewith sworn affidavits and an accurate chain of title to the property indicating the rightful owner to be my client, Melvina Durant Hawkins.

Mrs. Hawkins, over my objection, has in the interest of compromise requested that I meet with you (and your attorneys) to discuss settlement of this case. If you wish to meet with me, I will be pleased to show you the evidence and authorities proving my client's case.

Sincerely,

Zack Whitcomb

"Bea, send the letter express mail."
"Yes. Anything else, Zack?"
He drew a breath. "Look up a telephone number for me. I wanna call the director of the FBI. In Washington."

Startled, she stared hard at him. "You sure? The FBI? Should we — should you — be involved in all this?"

He spoke with reluctance. "Bea, that's where this case needs to be. It's time to call the FBI. I just hope they still got some tough G-men like Hoover used to have."

WHEN DURANT received Whitcomb's letter, he phoned his lawyer. A soft feminine voice responded. "Sir, I believe he's away from his desk."

Durant's voice rose. "How far is he from his desk? Tell him Peyton Durant's on the line. And I'm mad as hell."

Momentary silence. Then Sanford answered. "Hello, Peyton. What are you mad about?"

"Tutt, I got a letter from Whitcomb — that yahoo who claims to be a lawyer up in Alabama. He says he represents the Bladon Springs woman. The letter is galling arrogant. Brazen. Whatever you want to call it. And he misspells my name to boot."

"Peyton, you're living a charmed life." He sounded skeptical. "I read about the big theft at Cabildo. Somebody cleaned out the museum. And they stole that Indenture."

"That sure helps my case, doesn't it?"

"Yep," said Sanford. "Tell me what the lawyer wants."

"He wants to meet with me and my lawyers to discuss settlement, of all things. Ridiculous. He's got no case and he wants to discuss settlement. I'm not gonna meet with him. You handle it."

"Peyton, this could be good news for us. If we could flush out his evidence, we'd know the strength of his client's case."

"What case, Tutt? I thought you told me he had no case without the museum document — the Indenture."

"The Indenture is the crux of his case. But he might have other evidence. I'd like to hear what he's got. Fax me his letter. I'll set up the meeting. When can you meet?"

"I can't meet during the day, when the markets are open. How about on a Sunday night?"

"Let's do it a week from Sunday. It's quiet around here. Get everybody — lawyers, the accountant. We'll intimidate the hell outta this guy."

24

NOBODY looks suspicious at the Maple Leaf Bar. It draws an eclectic crowd — Tulane students, Cajuns, merchant marines from ships docked in port, locals stepping out for a Saturday night — all avoiding the crush of tourists in the Quarter. The band, usually zydeco or Cajun, plays from a platform at the end of a long narrow hall with a concrete floor. A picture window is all that separates the band from the street. And when the crowd fills the bar, late arrivals will dance on the sidewalk. The walls bounce the music around the room and you can hardly hear the person next to you. Durant figured Saturday night at the Maple Leaf to be a safe place for the rendezvous.

He and Mimi sat on bar stools sipping long-neck Dixie beers. A slim black man singing and stroking a washboard led the zydeco band.

Durant felt a tap on his shoulder and wheeled around. His eyes met a scar-faced man wearing a greasy purple LSU baseball cap. Durant cocked his head beckoning the other man to follow him. The man in the purple cap slid through the crowd toward the back of the hall.

Before Durant could dismount the bar stood, Mimi reached her arm across Durant's chest as if to block him. "I wish you wouldn't."

"Wouldn't what?"

She leaned toward him to be certain he heard her. "You need to stop meeting these guys — these shady characters you've been dealing with."

He turned his head away, but she continued. "You're smart as a whip, as gifted as anybody. Handsome. Have tons of friends. I've heard the messages on voice mail — with Hong Kong, Switzerland. I'm a stock broker. I'm not an idiot. I know why you had business in Switzerland. For God's sake, I know insider trading when I see it."

Durant turned on his stool to face Mimi and raised both hands in front of her face. "Dammit. Enough. That's enough outta you." His voice rose above the crowd noise. "I don't see you turning down any parties or trips to Europe. I didn't notice you declining any presents I give you. Looks like your whole outfit you're wearing tonight is a gift from Durant Incorporated — from the twenty-four carat gold earrings down to the Neiman Marcus leather boots."

She balled her fists, then flashed a cynical smile. "Nobody talks to me that way, and gets away with it. Not even you. Jerk. You're just an arrogant jerk. I'm gone." She spun around on the bar stool and marched toward the front door.

Durant ignored her. He grabbed his beer, then slipped through the noisy, crowded dance floor to a quiet patio outside the bar. Durant joined the Cajun seated at an iron table in the corner surrounded by tall bamboo cane spreading out from the patio wall.

Durant drew a folded envelope from this wallet. "You did the job on the Cabildo. There's another $50K — for you — in the envelope. Now, I need a shooter. I'm meeting that hick Alabama lawyer next Sunday night — a week from tomorrow — in my office. I want you to be on my office floor from six o'clock on."

Durant whipped a miniature cellular telephone from the inside pocket of his jacket. "If I call you on the cell phone," he hesitated, "pump the lawyer. I mean pump him full."

The Cajun opened the envelope. "Fifty grand will do the job. You say the word. I'll fill his ass with lead."

25

THE NEXT Monday, Whitcomb arrived at his office early. The interior was dark, except for a blinking red light on the answering machine next to the telephone on Bea's desk. "Zack, this is Ian Langdale. It's Sunday night, eight Atlantic time, six your time. Something interesting you might want to know. My friend Nancy just landed in Bermuda for a week between quarters at Tulane. To my big surprise, Peyton Durant's girlfriend, Mimi Mitchell, got off the plane with Nancy. She says she and Peyton have broken up. She's going to stay here in Bermuda for at least a fortnight. I thought you would like to know." Whitcomb erased the message and immediately dialed Bermuda on the rotary.

Langdale answered his direct line. "Ian, I got your message. That's interesting about Mimi Mitchell. I sure would like to talk with her. Do you think she and Durant will get back together?"

"She says they're finished — she and Durant are finished. But I doubt if she would talk. She wants to sunbathe and see the islands. She didn't tell a single soul she was coming. I don't know if I could ask — " Langdale's voice trailed away. "What would you want to know?

"I'm not even sure. But believe you me, anything would help. I know it may be an imposition on you and her, but would you ask if I could talk with her — for a few minutes?"

Langdale didn't respond. "Just think about it, Ian."

The light on Whitcomb's answering machine was blinking red again the next morning. "Zack, I have good news. Mimi says she'll talk with you. She'll give you twenty minutes. Call her right now. At the Princess. It's nine-thirty Bermuda time — seven-thirty your time. I wouldn't wait long. She might change her mind. Good luck." Whitcomb erased the message and dialed.

When Bea arrived in a few minutes, Whitcomb was sitting in her chair. "Bea, I have a challenge for you. I wanna find an old deed — a deed on parchment, a handwritten deed that is as identical as possible with the Bermuda Indenture. I need one with the words *This Indenture* in large letters at the beginning exactly like the Indenture. We have a copy of it. Let's try to match it. Call all the lawyers in town — Ezell, Evans, May, Lee McPhearson, Utsey, and Christopher, maybe Ed Turner in Chatom. We may have to draft it ourselves. Heck, call Oxford University or Cambridge, if you have to."

She started jotting notes on a pad. "When do we need it?"

"By Sunday. This Sunday is the day."

"I'll try."

THE NEXT SUNDAY — February 21 — the Whitcombs drove to the Presbyterian church.

The minister rose from his chair behind the redwood lectern, said a prayer, then began his sermon. "I believe that God intervenes from time to time in the affairs of man. As a result, human lives are changed — for good or for evil. The consequences may be momentous, affecting the lives of millions. In 312 A.D., the Roman Emperor Constantine saw a flaming cross in the sky the night before a great battle. He converted to Christianity, defeated his enemies, and ultimately spread Christianity over the Roman

World. In 1588 the invincible Spanish Armada appeared off the English coast, threatening to invade England. But a massive storm destroyed most of the fleet, and Francis Drake led the English to victory over the Spanish, allowing democracy and the English rule of law to spread over the world. I believe that was the hand of God. The consequences of intervention are not generally so monumental. Usually, few lives are affected."

If the Lord's going to intervene, Whitcomb thought, *this is the case. I hope He's on our side. He'd better be. Maybe this is all predestined. It may take God and me to whip Peyton Durant. The discovery of the Indenture was providential. Bea did her job — she located an exact replica of the Indenture in Mobile and sweet-talked that collector into sending it to us.*

Whitcomb's mind wandered. After church, he would drive to Meridian. Meet two FBI agents at the depot. Ride the train with the agents to New Orleans. Tonight at eight o'clock, he would meet Peyton Durant face-to-face.

Whitcomb took a Bible from the pew and thumbed through Psalms, then stopped in Proverbs. "The Godly are as bold as lions." He recited the passage in his mind. He read Biblical passages to himself — verses that conveyed strength. The Twenty-third Psalm. The Beatitudes.

He turned in the hymnal to Luther's anthem. "A mighty fortress is our God, a bulwark never failing, protecting us with staff and rod, and power all prevailing." *This stuff may not turn the tide. But it sure doesn't hurt. If it was good enough for Martin Luther, it's good enough for me.*

Whitcomb turned the Chevrolet onto the Meridian highway. He handed Ann, sitting in the passenger seat, a folded letter handwritten on his personal stationery.

"What's this?" she asked. Her eyes scanned the handwritten letter:

February 21, 1995

Dear Ann,

I wanted you to know that I didn't forget this day. It was fifty years ago, at noon, I believe, in 1945, that the *Saratoga* was hit and Marley was killed. From your comments, however subtle, the last few days, I know you remembered. I saw on the vanity the worn-out telegram your family received from the War Department. You've seemed so pensive. I realize how difficult it may be for you remembering this day, even after all the years. Sometimes thoughts are too deep even for tears.

Frankly, Ann, I wasn't sure whether to write you and mention this, but I want to tell you how I feel. Maybe I can comfort you.

I'm your husband, friend, confidant, lover, all the time, forever. When anything causes you pain, it causes me pain, too. I didn't love Marley like a brother, but he was my best friend, and I loved him, sure enough.

Marley was the greatest man I ever knew. He had courage and fortitude. We know the Naval Academy confronted him with obstacles, a smalltown boy from Alabama competing with the nation's best and brightest. Some say Marley didn't deserve the appointment. Remember how he used to come home, worried sick about his studies?

But Marley wouldn't be deterred. He faced down and overcame all obstacles at the Academy and ultimately prevailed. He gave me confidence and I admire Marley to this day above all men.

When Japan bombed Pearl Harbor, Marley was ready to serve. I know we both wished things had worked out differently, but under the circumstances of war, we both also know that Marley was in the middle of the fight — just where he wanted to be. I must have heard him say a dozen times: a short life in the saddle beats a long life by the fire. Obviously, the Navy recognized Marley's qualities. They graduated him early and assigned him dangerous duty.

Marley was a genuine hero. Even though he perished off Iwo Jima, you and I know that our courtship and marriage would have made him happy. I never told you, but your gift of the brass buttons off Marley's Academy coat moved me to tears.

Marley Ashe, all honor to his name.

I want you to know, too, that since Marley introduced us, I never loved anyone else.

Love,

Zack

In a minute she dropped the letter onto the floorboard and shook her head. "You're nice to remember this. And this is a nice letter."

She raised her voice. "But this letter scares me to death. I know you too well. This sounds like you're going off to war. I've never gotten a letter like this from you." She read the letter: "'husband, friend, confidant, lover, all the time, forever,' — a little maudlin, don't you think? And it's so final."

She read some more: "'Hero. Duty.' I hate hearing about duty. When the sailor in Bermuda started talking about duty, I wanted to throw up. Too much duty gets people killed."

"I'm sorry, I guess," Zack mumbled.

She couldn't restrain herself. She spoke quickly. "Zack, you drive me nuts when you don't talk to me. You're gonna do something dangerous, aren't you? I know it, sure as can be. I thought I'd keep to myself and hope you'd be okay, but I'm worried. And now, this letter. You gotta tell me what's going on."

Zack looked his sixty-nine years. After all the years together, they both knew when he confided in her, it relieved his tension. He turned his head away from the two-lane road and faced her.

"How'd you know? I tried to hide it." Then he answered his own question. "I know you saw the article about the Cabildo being robbed. And you could tell I've been preoccupied."

He hoped she hadn't heard of the interrupted journey between Butler and Meridian.

With her left hand, Ann massaged his neck. "Lots of signs. Bea told me the FBI agent met with you at the office — twice during the week. You've been having a drink every night this week. And those martini's — so dry. Pure gin. And today you're wearing a blazer with Marley's Naval Academy buttons. I knew that meant something. And I saw the newspaper article." She hesitated. "And you leaving work early to — to practice with the high school baseball team? What's going on?"

"I threw batting practice. And hit a few. I did a little coaching. I'm just stayin' in shape."

"Do they listen?"

"I taught 'em a couple of things, like turning the double play — the pivot man's gotta be waiting for the throw. And the delayed steal."

She didn't respond. For a minute he drove ahead, oblivious to her presence.

"You're so observant, Ann. I didn't want you worried. It was easier just saying this was a business trip. It is a business trip — serious business."

He breathed deeply and then blew out the air in a rush, relieved to tell her. Although his eyes were sunken above the jut of his cheekbones, indicative of the recent strain, they were roving and lustrous.

"It always makes me feel better to tell you about a case. I shoulda told you before. Here goes.

"I phoned the FBI a couple of weeks ago. They had the special agent in charge in Jackson contact me. The FBI has been investigating a cotton broker, Peyton Durant, for five months. You know of Durant. He's the man who claims the oil under Melvina Hawkins's land.

"Durant allegedly bribed a foreign service officer to get access to crop information. That's illegal. That's insider trading. The

FBI's been looking at some other illegalities — violations of laws on campaign contributions. Durant may have laundered a campaign contribution through a commodities account. You already know about the Indenture on display in New Orleans. It's stolen. And that's the key document that proves Melvina Hawkins's claim to be valid."

He shrugged. "There's no doubt in my mind who stole it — Peyton Durant. Cops got no real clues about the theft. And New Orleans cops don't care. Durant's in bed with 'em."

He turned toward his wife's subdued face. "I reported everything to the FBI."

He glanced at Ann. The content of his words had flushed the color from her face. "Ann, everything's under control, getting the FBI involved. When I explained the connection between the dispute over the oil wells and the disappearance of the Indenture from the Cabildo, the FBI got involved. And I'm glad of it. Everything's okay."

She tried to relax. "I don't know how to handle this. Earlier. We should've talked earlier. Your letter says 'confidant.' So start confiding. Tell me, how in the world does the FBI get involved in a simple theft?"

"Several reasons. The FBI was already investigating Durant for the federal crimes — insider trading, securities violations, all that stuff. And there's a presumption — a legal fiction — that a theft of property worth over five thousand dollars is an interstate crime. FBI's got jurisdiction over interstate crimes. The Indenture's appraised at a hundred thousand. So the feds have jurisdiction."

His tone changed. "I should have told you. I'm sorry."

Ann nodded and turned to her husband. She massaged his neck again. "Zack, the FBI would never have connected the theft at the Cabildo with Durant if you hadn't contacted them, would they?"

"No doubt about it. I'm glad the FBI's in the case. Durant's too big and has too much influence in New Orleans and in Louisiana for the local police to handle this case. Ann, there's a hell of a lot more to this case than the FBI catching some sorry commodities broker bribing a bureaucrat over inside information on cotton. I don't appreciate some hot shot trying to beat somebody outta their money. The man thinks he runs the world. I wanna see Durant get his comeuppance."

She interrupted. "Control. Don't get too caught up. Stay under control."

"You're right," he continued in a more relaxed tone. "There's a rule of evidence called the *best evidence rule*. It says that the original document is the best evidence of the contents of the document. But copies are allowed in many situations. But the cases hold that if a document is central to a case, like Melvina's, then there must be strict proof about the loss of the document."

Ann stopped him, "Get to the point. Cut the law school lecture."

"I found a case called *Russell v. Bush*. It says that proof of the theft of the document is clear evidence allowing a copy of the original to be admitted."

Whitcomb nervously straightened his tie. "I talked to three judges outside the circuit about this. They say there's no assurance the copy will be admitted without proof of the theft. It's frustrating. You can't get a ruling up front. I gotta try this."

Ann shook her head, "Sometimes the law is so hard."

He hesitated, then spoke with determination. "If I prove Durant stole the Indenture, then Melvina owns the whole reservoir. I need to do this. And I'm the only guy that can do it."

She threw up her hands. "Why have *you* gotta do it? And for twenty percent — what a bargain Melvina's getting."

He cut his eyes toward her, as if to say, "How could you know?"

She continued, "Bea. From Bea. Zack, sometimes your focus is too narrow." Her voice rose to a high pitch. "By all rights, she and her family should've hired you to handle Abe's death case. God, you did all Abe's legal work dirt cheap. They took advantage of you. And now she hires you to represent her because you're the best property lawyer around — for a pittance, twenty percent. Doesn't every lawyer get at least a third? Some get a half. For once, maybe, *our* family ought to come out ahead."

She was right, as usual. He was silent for the next minute waiting for her scolding to end. She ended the silence. Her voice was soft, lustful. "Those boxing workouts, now baseball. I love watching you pound the dummy, putting your body into it. Sliding, dancing around. You're too handsome to get hurt. Forget the money. Survive. That'll be good enough for me. Just survive."

Zack stopped the car at the depot building constructed years ago when Meridian was a railroad hub.

Ann leaned across the car seat and kissed him on the cheek.

He nodded. "Okay. I promise to survive."

Zack opened the car door to leave. Ann tapped him on the shoulder, and he turned. Her eyes glowed. "Hey, big boy, I got a question for you. What band did Doris Day sing with?"

He grasped his briefcase, then winked. "Harry James."

AMTRAK'S SOUTHERN CRESCENT slowed until it stopped at the passenger depot in Meridian. The engine pulled six cars — four coaches, a dining car, and a sleeper at the end. Whitcomb wore a hat as usual, a blue blazer with shiny brass buttons over a starched white shirt, a red silk tie with a tight knot, and gray trousers. Carrying a briefcase, he chatted with the conductor, a black man in his fifties, dressed in uniform and cap.

When a smart-looking young couple walked through the depot doors toward the train, the conductor escorted the lawyer from the train and introduced him to the couple. They stood by a rusty steel baggage cart and waited for the Meridian passengers to board.

Then the conductor led his guests across several sets of tracks and climbed the steps onto a sleek, silver railroad car. The conductor was brisk and business-like. He spoke to Whitcomb and the couple. "I got three tickets from Meridian to New Orleans." He motioned the threesome to follow him toward the dining car, the opposite direction from the other passengers boarding. He twisted the heavy metal handle and pulled hard, opening the door leading into the dining car — closed until dinnertime. Waiters in red and gray uniforms busing the tables glanced at the special passengers escorted by the conductor. Waiters stood aside on the narrow aisle running down the center of the car between table booths allowing the conductor and the threesome to pass.

The blast of heat from the galley caused the passengers to pause momentarily. The conductor led them out of the dining car, across the platform and through the next door. Another uniformed black man stood at attention, his hands behind him, at the entrance to the sleeper.

The conductor turned to the three passengers. "Mr. Whitcomb, agents, welcome aboard. It's 3:30, only twenty minutes late. Probably make up that time and arrive on schedule at 7:30."

He motioned down the narrow corridor. "This car has private compartments. It's the last car on the train. There's no access, except through the dining car. You're the only ones with a compartment between Meridian and New Orleans. So you got the whole car to yourselves. Should be safe."

The conductor pointed to the other man in uniform. "The steward is Horace Wynn."

Wynn nodded and tipped his Amtrak cap. "I'll be stationed on the platform at the front of this car. Conductor tells me y'all want privacy. You got it. Nobody comes in this car without your permission. Y'all need anything, let me know." The steward and the conductor walked onto the platform between cars. The heavy metal door slammed shut leaving the passengers alone.

The two agents looked like a middle American married couple. The man spoke softly. "Sir, I'm agent Frank Johnstone." The man was six feet, about forty, hair cut conservatively. He wore charcoal slacks and a tweed jacket with an open collar shirt.

Whitcomb barely heard his name. "I'm Zack Whitcomb. Pleasure to meet you."

"Mr. Whitcomb, I'm agent Barbara Melton." She spoke with a stronger voice.

A whistle blew. A male voice called "All aboard." The engine cried a long wail, and the train lurched forward, headed south.

"Y'all call me Zack. Why don't we relax — get comfortable?"

Whitcomb had suggested he and the agents travel Amtrak to New Orleans. The four-hour train ride would allow time to rehearse their plans. An old hand at passenger trains, Whitcomb showed the agents into one of the compartments. Johnstone and Melton eased comfortably into an upholstered two-man sofa. Whitcomb dropped into a chair opposite the agents.

Whitcomb wasn't expecting a woman agent — particularly such a good-looking woman. About forty, with a nice figure, agent Melton wore a long sleek blue-jean skirt with a slit up the middle that flattered her legs. Long fringe hung Western-style from the top of the short, shiny white blouse. Her tanned skin showed between the shirt and blouse. The woman's hair, shoulder length, hung in bangs down over her forehead, above her warm, greenish eyes.

Whitcomb couldn't resist flirting. "Agent Melton, would it be improper to say 'You're the best looking G-man I ever saw'?"

She laughed, "Yeah, it's improper, but thanks. I've been assigned to the South a few months — based in Jackson. You Southern men are too much with those accents and manners. Geez, you're a pack of Rhett Butlers." She spoke with a sharp, rapid accent.

"You like the South?" Whitcomb asked, hanging his hat on a metal hook.

"It's different, for sure. People are friendly down here, but it's like a foreign country. I grew up near San Francisco. In Sausalito. You Southerners need to rejoin the Union. You *did* lose the Civil War, last time I read the history books. Wish Southern men would drop the manners BS. You guys overdo it."

"Spunky woman," thought Whitcomb, "typical Yankee, but

has a personality. She's the kind of woman who can handle herself in any situation."

Whitcomb chided her lightly, "Miss Melton, you ought to appreciate good manners. Don't be so blasé."

"It's a cop's job to be blasé."

"Maybe it's my *job* to be a gentleman." The lawyer smiled broadly.

Disarmed, she laughed, "Maybe you're right."

She leaned forward. Her voice became serious. "Mr. Whitcomb, Agent Johnstone and I are here to implement this plan, this operation. We appreciate your being willing to participate. Not many private citizens become involved to this degree." She paused. "This operation's been discussed high in the FBI hierarchy. Lots of people in the FBI are aware of your assistance. They appreciate it, and asked me to tell you so."

"A man does his duty."

The outskirts of Meridian passed by through the picture window. The train picked up speed and began its swaying motion. "We've read the dossier on you. Impressive. You've certainly had your share of success. 'Letter athlete at Alabama, officer in World War II, law degree, district attorney.'"

"Agents, I'll be frank. I'm not worried about me. I'm worried about Durant."

Agent Melton placed a briefcase on a built-in table attached to the wall and snapped the locks opening the briefcase. "Here's Durant's dossier. We already faxed you the principal conclusions. You get a chance to read it?"

Whitcomb took the dossier. He looked up at her, surprised that she, the woman agent, and not Johnstone, conducted the meeting. He loosened, then tightened the knot on his tie. "Yeah, I read it — probably fifty times."

"Good, I think that's an accurate profile of Durant."

Whitcomb flipped through the dossier. "Quite a character, isn't he? Comes from big money. Big ego. Drives flashy cars. High roller in commodities. I noticed that the dossier says 'quick tem-per,' 'difficult to work for.' I know the type. Lots of successful people — especially businessmen in high pressure jobs — demand instant action from workers. Impatient. Guys like Durant say 'jump' and workers say 'How high?' Probably hates lawyers."

Melton laughed and nodded. "You got it, Zack. I've been observing Durant since November for his alleged insider trading. Durant's the proactive type, but he's also impatient and demand-ing. The personality profile may help in your conference with him."

"Yeah. Always helps to understand your adversary — his thought process."

"Are you nervous?" asked Melton. "You keep messing with your tie."

"Don't let that bother you. I *am* nervous. So what? Who wouldn't be?"

Agent Melton leaned back in the sofa. She flashed a broad smile. "I gotta tell you, Zack. I'm a feminist. I went to Cal-Berkeley. I've been reading your correspondence. Do you realize, you always use the masculine pronouns — 'he,' 'his,' 'him'? You realize that's not cool anymore." She sounded part-hippie, part-Valley girl. "This is the nineties, man. It's 'he' or '*she*.' You got it?" She laughed and smiled at Johnstone.

Johnstone rolled his eyes and shook his head. "Barbara's been beating on me with that feminism junk ever since I met her. Agent Melton, can't you stay off the man's back? He went to college when, what do you call it, the 'masculine pronoun' was okay. What is this anyway — grammar school?"

Whitcomb laughed. The banter relieved tension. "Agent Johnstone, I thought for a while that you were a robot — a prototype of an FBI agent, a mechanical G-man. That's the first thing you've said." Whitcomb stood and stretched his arms. "Agent Melton, you're a pretty bright girl. I respect what you're saying — political correctness and all. But you can probably tell, I don't roll with the fads. I've been using the same grammar book since college. Believe you me, I'm not changing until they publish a new edition that says 'Change.'"

"Amen." Johnstone saluted the lawyer.

"Better get back to business, but I'm not giving up. By the way, Zack, it's *woman*, not *girl*."

"Agent Melton, I bet you always get in the last word."

Whitcomb and the agents discussed their plan. Whitcomb had scheduled a meeting with Durant and his lawyers for eight p.m. in the Cotton Exchange Building. Ostensibly, they would discuss settlement of the ownership dispute between Melvina Hawkins and Durant. Whitcomb had already been wired with a microphone and transmitter, and Agents Melton and Johnstone would record the conversation from a van parked nearby. "The microphone is embedded in a button on my jacket," said Whitcomb. He touched the top button — a quarter-sized brass button with a carved eagle in the center.

"The transmitter is here inside my coat pocket." He opened the coat, pulled a billfold from the high, inside pocket, and thumped the transmitter with his finger. "The transmitter is sewn into the lining of the pocket."

"We'll test the equipment in a few minutes," Johnstone said. "The equipment's simple. It works every time. But I got one instruction for you, Zack. Keep your jacket on, or we're dead."

Whitcomb chuckled.

"Mental chess," Melton said. "It'll be a game of mental chess. Zack, you'll try to probe, cajole Durant into a clue leading to proof of an illegality. Maybe Durant will admit an illegality."

Johnstone spoke up, "Sounds like a tall order. How you gonna make Durant admit anything? He's as smooth as anybody I've dealt with."

Whitcomb's eyes widened. "I view this meeting like a cross-exam of a witness." He pointed at Agent Melton. "As you say, it's like mental chess — a word game. I've prosecuted lots of cases. I deal with words. That's an advantage."

He continued. "Forcing an admission is a goal during cross-examination. I'll poke around — fish for some answers. In front of a jury, you normally act polite." The lawyer's voice rose. "But there are times when you try to beat out the truth. You just stampede a witness into blurting out the truth in spite of himself. It happens. Sort of a corollary to a Latin saying — Those whom God wishes to destroy, he first makes mad."

Melton's green eyes glowed. "Durant does have an ego. And he's gonna underestimate you. He won't like a small-town lawyer taking what he considers his money. It's an ego thing."

Whitcomb nodded in agreement. "That's my *modus operandi*."

Melton spoke seriously, "You know what you're doing, but don't get too cute."

Whitcomb continued. "I just hope Durant doesn't cancel this meeting. He doesn't have much to gain by meeting me."

Melton spoke up. "I just hope Durant hasn't read your dossier. You're a pretty sharp cookie."

Johnstone wondered, "Why *did* Durant agree to the meeting?"

"Two reasons," said Whitcomb. "One, Durant's lawyers will want to evaluate my case — Melvina's case. Two, they probably want to evaluate what kind of lawyer they're dealing with." Whitcomb tapped the coat button containing the microphone. "Y'all record everything well. As the old hymn says, 'One little word can fell him.'"

Melton shook her head. "Here we go again," she said. "You Southerners and your religion. What hymn?"

"It's a line from a Martin Luther hymn, 'A Mighty Fortress Is Our God.'" Whitcomb kidded her. "Surely, even you California New Agers oughta know about Luther — the Reformer."

"I'm Catholic. We don't talk much about Martin Luther. He sure wasn't big in Catechism class." Agent Melton spoke seriously again. "Now, Zack, you have another agenda beyond our criminal investigation."

Whitcomb explained that Melvina Hawkins's ownership claim to the oil well was largely based on the missing Indenture, and that a copy would be admissible if it were shown that the original was stolen. "If I could prove Durant stole the original, then the copy would prove Melvina's case."

Agent Johnstone shook his head, "Long shot. Big long shot, getting Durant to admit that."

"I have an idea that Durant never destroyed the original."

"I can't imagine he wouldn't get rid of it." responded Johnstone.Agent Melton looked quizzically at Whitcomb.

Whitcomb voice became intense. "Durant is the kind of man who collects trophies of his conquests — everything from tennis to trading profits, even girlfriends."

"That's not in the dossier," said Melton.

"It's a good source," said Whitcomb.

"Care to reveal it?" she asked.

"I can't — not now." Whitcomb's response seemed to close the subject.

"Maybe we oughta get a subpoena," said Melton.

"I thought of that, but it probably won't work. Durant's got a team of lawyers and connections all over town. They'd stifle the subpoena until he had time to destroy the Indenture."

Melton's eyes flashed with interest. "You gonna work that angle at the meeting, aren't you?"

"I'm gonna try." Whitcomb paused. "Now tell me something — what does the FBI have on Durant?"

"Durant lost everything last year on a bad day when the cotton market went against him. That was on October 15th."

"Fifteenth?" asked Whitcomb. "October 15th?"

"Yeah," Melton answered. "Why?"

Whitcomb recalled his meeting with Doll months ago and her vision about a disaster on the Ides of October — the fifteenth. Her vision had been eerily accurate.

He remembered Doll's parting prophesy, her comforting words

— Glory in the end. You are brighter than the others.

"Agent Melton," said Whitcomb in a pleasant tone of voice. "October fifteenth is the Ides of October. Did you know that?"

"I don't have a clue what you're talking about." His suddenly happy countenance had brought a smile to her lips. "Worlds apart, aren't we? We're worlds apart."

"Keep talking," Whitcomb said. "We're doing okay."

She shrugged and continued. "Soon after October fifteen, some cotton brokers in the upper Mississippi Delta reported rumors of all sorts of illegal trading by Durant. An American embassy attaché in China allegedly released bogus Chinese cotton crop numbers from the embassy — and gave Durant the accurate numbers. China and America are the two biggest cotton-producing countries in the world — about 20 million bales each. And the cotton markets can jump when the Chinese crop data — and the supply-demand reports are made public. Rumor has it Durant's been making big profits off the inside information. The attaché has an account in Switzerland. We suspect the account is worth hundreds of thousands. Durant's probably been transferring money into the sham account as a payoff for the inside information."

She paused. "We know for sure that the attaché has been living like a king — a lifestyle way beyond his government income. Man's racked up gambling debts in six figures at casinos in Macao. Durant went too far when his lackeys started harassing competitors — other cotton traders."

Agent Melton chuckled, "Funny thing I learned about cotton traders. It's like a fraternity. They don't care if somebody is trading on inside information. Seems to be a 'gentleman's agreement' that all's fair in love, war and the futures market — *until* you personally attack another trader. Durant got in bed with some New Orleans tough guys. He sent a couple of lackeys up to Memphis and the Delta to strongarm some traders for favors. That's when he stepped over the line. We've started getting tips."

Agent Melton pointed at Whitcomb.

"Zack, your call was the best, the most influential. You had the guts to get involved."

"As I said, a person does his — or *her* duty," said Whitcomb.

She glanced at Johnstone and motioned toward Whitcomb. "I like him."

THE CRESCENT ROLLED through farmlands and pine forests of east Mississippi, stopping at Laurel and Hattiesburg before crossing the Mississippi-Louisiana boundary. While Whitcomb studied the Durant dossier, the two agents sat silently in their private compartment. The train slowed, pulling into Slidell.

Agent Melton broke the quiet. "I'm gonna take a walk through the train — to check for anything suspicious. This is the last stop before New Orleans." The agent unbuckled her leather purse, reached inside, and pulled out a shiny 38-Special pistol. She checked the cylinder and the barrel and dropped the gun back in the purse.

"You ever used that thing?" Whitcomb asked.

"Never fired at anything other than a practice target," Melton responded.

"You ever *heard* a shot fired in anger?" Whitcomb asked.

"What do you mean, 'fired in anger'?"

"I mean 'been shot at.'"

"I've never been in a fight. I've been assigned white collar crime. That bother you, Zack?"

He didn't answer.

"What about you, Agent Johnstone?"

"Nope, but I can shoot straight. So can Barbara. All agents can shoot. We've been trained."

Whitcomb rolled his eyes and shook his head.

The woman rose, opened the compartment door, and turned to face the lawyer. "Zack, if you get an admission out of Durant, I guarantee you, we'll be there," she reassured. "We'll be there when you need us. Agent Johnstone and I are meeting a New

Orleans agent at the train station. He'll have the recording van ready. We've already got a spot a half block away from the Cotton Exchange. Agent Johnstone is a genius with listening equipment. We'll record everything. The moment you think you're in danger — any danger — you get the heck out of the building. We'll be in the building fast. You know this, but I'll remind you. If we're lucky — we probably do need some luck — and Durant makes an admission, no matter how subtle, then immediately excuse yourself under some pretense — any pretense — and get out. We'll be there. You can count on us."

She shut the compartment door.

Johnstone unzipped his suitcase and took out a black leather holster and slipped it over his left shoulder. It hung about three inches below his armpit. Then he took a Smith and Wesson .40-caliber automatic pistol from the suitcase, removed the clip and slid the action several times, He pulled the trigger, then reloaded the pistol, put up the safety catch and dropped it into the pouch of the holster.

Whitcomb nodded, pleased with the agent's firearm. "Now we're talking."

Daytime turned to dusk. The train slowed when it approached Lake Pontchartrain. For twenty minutes, the Crescent clicked along the tracks a few feet above the lake's choppy waters. The sun disappeared and the city lights glowed above the horizon.

The train slowed even further as familiar sights — the lights along Canal Street, the Superdome — passed by the picture windows. The three passengers gathered their belongings and walked the narrow corridor toward the front of the car.

Before the train stopped, agent Melton caught Whitcomb's arm. She pulled him into an empty compartment. "Zack, before you leave, I wanna say something. I should have said this earlier. The director approved this operation reluctantly. Frankly, he doubted one small-town lawyer could handle a man like Durant, with his high-powered corporate lawyers. We want Durant. You want Durant. We talked the director into this."

Agent Melton's voice became emotional. "You can get hurt. I know you're a tough-minded man. I've seen your war record. But man, that's fifty years ago." He'd become accustomed to the California accent.

She took a deep breath. "I like the heck out of you, Zack. Why put your life on the line for a client? You're not paid to get yourself killed. Durant is smart and dangerous. I've gotten to know him. I think he'd order you killed to keep that oil money."

Agent Melton regained her composure. "If you back out, no one at the FBI will secondguess you. When you walk in that Cotton Exchange, it's gonna be you, and you alone, versus Durant and his crowd. It'll be very difficult. Man, I just don't know about this." Her voice trailed.

Her speech moved the lawyer. He placed his hand on her shoulder and spoke to her like father-to-daughter. "Agent Melton, I appreciate your concern. I mean it. But I'll take care of myself. Remember, it only takes one word — one little word will fell him." Whitcomb picked up his briefcase and spoke confidently.

"You say this will be so difficult. You ever heard the World War II motto of the army engineers? That's the right attitude."

"What is it?"

"'The difficult, we do immediately. The impossible takes a little longer.' Let's go." He dismounted the platform between cars, turned and looked over his shoulder. "You and Johnstone — just get it all down on tape."

26

WHITCOMB stepped down from the yellow cab onto the curb in the New Orleans central business district. Across the street, the words "New Orleans Cotton Exchange – 1930" were carved into the stone near the top of the building. He stood on the sidewalk in dusky light, oblivious to the crowd gathering to catch the streetcar. The cold, gray stone hovered over him like a giant.

His palms sweating, Whitcomb almost dropped his briefcase. He stood on the sidewalk staring for a moment at the building. His pulse beat fast. His arms felt heavy and his feet numb. The sensation reminded him of the icy fear he felt in Westminster Abbey years ago.

He hadn't admitted it to her, but Agent Melton's warning bothered him. Was his life on the line? The money from the Durant well was so big that things were getting ugly, maybe too ugly.

Whitcomb steeled his mind against anxiety. He raced positive images through his mind — Westminster Abbey, Farrah Hall, the Demopolis ballfield, and Doll's comforting words.

He fortified himself with Biblical verses: "The Godly are as bold as lions — Yea, though I walk through the valley of the shadow of death."

He recited from Luther's hymn: "A mighty fortress is our God."

Whitcomb ran his index finger over the buttons on his blazer. Marley had always quoted Admiral Halsey — "Hit early. Hit often. Hit hard."

He reached inside his coat pocket, turned on the transmitter and walked into an empty alleyway. "I hope y'all can hear me. Frankly, I'm feeling shaky." He breathed deeply to relax himself. "I'm gonna test you. *Forsan et haec olim meminisse iuvabit.* That's Latin. Virgil, I think. If one of y'all can interpret that phrase, I'll buy you supper." He chuckled. "Let's go."

Whitcomb gripped his briefcase and strode toward the Cotton Exchange Building. The revolving door was locked. A security guard sitting on a stool inside the building motioned the late visitor to enter the lobby through a side door. The guard unlocked the door and held it open.

"Mr. Whitcomb?"

"Yeah."

"Mr. Durant's office is on the second floor, room 201. He's waiting for you."

Whitcomb ascended the marble stairs into a long wood-paneled hallway on the second floor. Room 201. Somebody opened the door, and Whitcomb stepped inside. The grandeur of the office setting overwhelmed him. The office overlooked the floor of the New Orleans Cotton Exchange through a long floor-to-ceiling glass wall. There were five men seated around the room. Whitcomb felt the unwavering stare of all eyes in the room. Clearly the moment, this confrontation, held significance for all.

Whitcomb's eyes flashed around the room in search of Peyton Durant, whose face Whitcomb would recognize from the FBI dossier. He found Durant sitting at his desk at the far end of the room. Whitcomb's body quivered for a moment. He was prepared, ready for the confrontation. He would survive, he told himself, but more, he would enjoy the moment.

He quivered again — like someone pricked him over his whole body. He controlled himself and concentrated on Durant. In the dossier Durant's features were pleasant, but in person, his face appeared grotesque. Durant's nose seemed crooked and his face misproportioned to his body. For a brief moment, Whitcomb felt sympathic. The thought passed quickly. Somewhere along life's road, the man had strayed and now instead of using his intelligence and talents to make money fairly, he was beating people out of their money. This man had hired another to threaten him. This man was desperate all right — to make more money and to gain more power.

Everyone in the room wore business suits except Durant, who wore a starched shirt with the sleeves rolled up to his elbows and a red silk tie. Durant slightly lifted his hand and nodded in Whitcomb's direction. *Durant looks bored. Probably wouldn't be here if his lawyers hadn't insisted.*

Whitcomb saw wisdom in the FBI profile. *Durant's success, but also his weakness, may lie in his impatience. Brilliant financial mind. Gathers facts and makes decisions quickly.*

Whitcomb glanced up at the wall behind Durant. The framed diplomas confirmed the FBI dossier: Economics degree from Tulane, Masters in Business Administration from Harvard. But other framed papers caught Whitcomb's attention. At least a dozen business statements recording millions of dollars of profits had been enlarged and framed. "Trading trophies," thought Whitcomb. "These must be the 'trading trophies' described by Mimi Mitchell. Whatever her motive, during one brief long distance call phone, Mimi Mitchell had laid it out for Whitcomb. She had no idea whether her ex-boyfriend had stolen the Indenture. But she was certain that if he stole it, then he kept it. It was in Peyton's makeup. From the day they had met, he kept all her notes in his wallet; he kept every tennis trophy from junior high on; and he kept those "trading trophies." She didn't know exactly where the Indenture was, but it was safe and secure. "Bet on it," she said.

"I'm Zack Whitcomb," Durant's newest visitor nervously drawled, "from Choctaw County, Alabama." The door shut behind him. Whitcomb felt a sense of claustrophobic unease. His sole protection was his wits and the wire connection with the agents.

In the van parked a block away, agents Melton and Johnstone heard Whitcomb's voice. "It's clear as a bell." Johnstone said, listening through a pair of headphones.

Whitcomb shook hands with the group assembled.

"Jay Morgganti. I'm with the Sanford law firm."

"I'm Byrd — John Byrd. I'm an associate with the firm, too."

"Tutt Sanford. I practice here in New Orleans. My pleasure, Mr. Whitcomb."

Sanford worried Whitcomb most. Whitcomb had checked out his adversaries in the Martindale-Hubbell directory. Morgganti and Byrd were hot shots right out of law school, Ivy Leaguers. Sanford, on the other hand, was older and probably wiser. Experienced urban lawyers learn not to underestimate their small-town brethren.

Durant interrupted. "Let's cut the formalities and get down to business."

"Excuse me. But I don't believe I've met this other gentleman yet." Whitcomb approached a shy-looking man sitting in the corner. Whitcomb offered his hand. "Pleased to meet you, sir. Didn't catch your name."

Durant's lawyers glanced at each other. No one ignored Peyton Durant or showed impertinence.

"My name's Blankenship. Earl Blankenship."

"What's your occupation?"

The fiftyish, balding man mumbled the words. "C.P.A. — for Mr. Durant." He sheepishly glanced at Durant, hoping not to upset his boss.

"Met everybody Mr. Whitcomb? You ready to talk yet?" Durant loosened his tie impatiently.

"Except you, sir."

"By the way it's pronounced, Du-RANT, accent on the second syllable. Got it? Du-RANT."

Durant spoke cynically. "And my name is spelled P-e-y-t-o-n. You got it wrong in your letter. Well, Mr. Whitcomb, you seem to want to shake everybody's hand. When are we gonna get down to business?" Durant was agitated. "My time is money."

"What's the hurry? The lights are out on the exchange. They don't trade by candlelight, do they?" Durant appeared surprised by the answer. Whitcomb reached to shake Durant's hand. Durant offered a limp hand.

Tutt Sanford spoke up. "Gentlemen, let's talk business."

A long conference table ran perpendicular to Durant's desk, and Sanford motioned everyone to take seats. Whitcomb sat at the end of the conference table facing Durant, who was seated at his desk.

Sanford, seated closest to Durant, pulled a piece of paper from his suit pocket and spoke methodically. "We received your letter requesting a meeting with Peyton and we have your affidavits." Sanford dropped the letter and let it settle softly onto the conference table. "Frankly, we see absolutely no merit in your client's claim. What's her name — Melvina Hawkins? No court in the world will accept your legal theory that this Melvina Hawkins — the black woman — is heir to the Durant mineral rights. Mr. Whitcomb, you're a property lawyer. You researched the ownership. You're the very lawyer who concluded in your title opinion that Peyton Durant owns the mineral rights to the Durant Well, and to the oil reservoir discovered in Choctaw County. No court in America will accept this oral history, family legend stuff in these affidavits you sent us."

Durant stared at Whitcomb. "That's it, Alabama. You have no case." Whitcomb returned the stare. Whitcomb had expected impatience, not blatant discourtesy from Durant. Samford's speech was expected. When discussing settlement with opposing attorneys, the surface reason for this meeting, lawyers usually state their case in its best light.

Whitcomb emptied the contents of a file folder onto the table. "Over the last few months, I have compiled these documents supporting my client's case. This includes affidavits, memoranda, deeds, which taken together, will prove by a preponderance of the evidence that my client's position prevails. I'll file the lawsuit in Alabama. Frankly, we might be the beneficiary of a little local favoritism." Whitcomb flashed a smile, "A little home-cooking."

Durant cocked his head and pointed his finger. "Spare me. Please spare me the rhetoric, Alabama." He spoke sarcastically shaking his head. "Lawyers' braggadocio. God, I hate it."

Whitcomb ignored the comment, stood up, and walked toward his briefcase sitting by the door. The interlude gave him the opportunity to scan the room. He had detected a shadowy figure at the end of the hallway — probably the Cajun henchman who intercepted Shanks and him on the road to Meridian. But Whitcomb detected no sign of danger in Durant's office. No violence would be attempted in the presence of Durant's lawyers or the accountant. A lawyer and an accountant might represent a scoundrel, but they wouldn't risk their careers by participating in crime.

While Whitcomb took a large sealed manila envelope from the pocket of his briefcase, he glimpsed Durant's roaming eyes critiquing his clothes. Whitcomb heard Durant whisper, "Catch the pathetic old blazer."

Durant pushed his chair back from the table, "Let's get going, Pops. I got things to do. You going to overwhelm us with paper?"

"You and these high-powered corporate boys shouldn't take life so seriously. It's only money. Gimme a minute."

"While you get it together, I wanna ask you a question." Durant rolled a pencil between his fingers, then spoke with sarcasm again. "Tell me, are you a *real* lawyer?" Durant yawned.

He seemed to be entertaining his lawyers. "I never saw a lawyer like you. You're not organized. You can't spell. And your clothes — pitiful. Where'd you buy that hat? Looks like a cheap imitation of Eliott Ness. Here in the big city, people wear real clothes, man. Things are a little more chic than backwater Dixie."

Durant looked around at his associates. "Where'd he buy that coat? Off a skid row bum? Somebody tell him those beat-up buttons don't fit." The two young lawyers snickered.

Ignoring the comment, Whitcomb coldly approached the conference table with the manila envelope in his hands. He felt the rhythm of his heart pumping.

"Let's get down to business." Whitcomb paused, then stared directly at Durant. Whitcomb's voice, carefully neutral, gave no inkling of the importance of the words. "I understand you have — shall we say — a close relationship with one Maryanne Mitchell, also known as Mimi Mitchell." Durant slumped in his chair, obviously surprised. His eyes held a hint of frenzy. Durant's lawyers didn't notice their client's unease.

Whitcomb pressed the metal clips on the envelope. "You are aware that Miss Mitchell has been unavailable for the last week." Durant's eyes seemed to grow larger and his mouth seemed to open wider with each word. "Miss Mitchell has — shall we say — been of enormous assistance to my client's case." A wave of apprehension, almost panic swept over him. Durant mouthed the word *Mimi* in silence. Only Whitcomb noticed the desperation written on Durant's face.

Whitcomb reached into the envelope, and slid the contents out. Three parchment pages in handwriting appeared. The words *This Indenture* were written in bold ink at the top of the first page. "The Indenture, it seems, has been resurrected," announced Whitcomb.

Durant's face turned crimson, as though there were a tight noose around his neck. He dropped his head into his hands, then turned toward Sanford. Calmly and clearly he said, "Mimi sold me out. A scorned woman, I guess. I don't know how she did it. But she got that Indenture out of my house."

Sanford covered his mouth with his hand signaling his client to stop talking, but Durant did not. "Mimi stole it out of my house. I let her know too much."

Whitcomb pushed the parchment pages back into the envelope, then rose to his feet. For a moment he started to walk away, then he turned again and faced Durant. "Mr. Durant, gentlemen. I like to think of myself as a gentleman. Until this meeting I never really gauged what kind of man you were. I thought when we met that you would act like a gentleman. I've been disappointed. You deserve no respect." Whitcomb's voice rose. "I will take no more of your discourtesy, your meanness. You hide behind these men. You are condescending and arrogant. If you were any part a man, I would whip you like a rented mule — even at my age. I oughta take the oil money out of your hide."

In the van agent Melton's eyes got large as marbles. "Whitcomb's won the case. He needs to get out of there."

Durant's eyes showed the surprise of a man who had never been physically challenged. He hesitated for a moment, clearly reluctant to retreat from the challenge. Durant began to untie and remove his tie. He rolled up his sleeves and gritted his teeth. His eyes narrowed. The muscles in his forearms tightened.

Durant began to take off his tie. "Old man, if you're gonna get any oil money outta me, you *are* gonna have to take it outta my hide." Durant ripped his tie from his collar like he was stripping for a fight.

Whitcomb's soft voice returned. "This is pointless, gentlemen. We're wasting our time."

He headed for the door, grabbed the doorknob, and turned to face Sanford, still sitting next to Durant. "When your boy gets over his tantrum, we'll talk."

Durant hollered, "Whitcomb, you think you're the smartest man in the world, don't you?"

Sanford grabbed Durant around the shoulders. "Control it, man."

A slight smile broke onto Whitcomb's face. "No, I don't. But I'm damn sure the smartest man in this *room*." He pushed open the door and exited the room.

In the van, Agent Melton yelled, "Go man. Go!" She and Johnstone exchanged high fives, low fives and a hug. "He's done it. Let's pull him out. He's in danger when the lawyers tell Durant how he screwed up." The agents grabbed their blue windbreaker jackets with "F.B.I." printed in yellow letters on the back and climbed from the van.

In Durant's office there was bedlam — everybody talking at once. Sanford finally caught Durant's attention. "Damn, Peyton, you told him you stole the Indenture. If he recorded your statement, you're busted!" Durant closed his eyes and dropped his head in his cupped hands. He regained his composure.

"Okay, I want everybody out." Durant reached for the phone.

Whitcomb walked briskly down the second floor hall past the elevator toward the metal door below the "exit" sign, hoping to see the agents. He saw no one and sensed the presence of danger behind the doors in the hallway. He opened the exit door onto the marble steps leading down to the lobby.

Melton and Johnstone sprinted, jackets flying behind them, toward the Cotton Exchange Building. Johnstone arrived first at the entrance, pulled his .44 pistol on the security guard. "F.B.I. Open the door!" The guard pushed the bar handle, slightly opening the door. Johnstone grabbed the door, pulled it wide open in time for agent Melton to rush through the doorway.

The agents hustled toward the marble staircase, then bounded up the stairs. They reached the landing between floors just when Whitcomb pushed open the metal door above them leading to the staircase. Whitcomb spotted the agents crouching low with guns on ready on the landing of the stairwell ten steps below him. He started down the stairs, but before he descended to the agent's protection, the stairwell door opened behind him and the barrel of a sawed-off shotgun appeared.

"Down, Zack," yelled Melton. Whitcomb dove headfirst onto the marble landing — a moment ahead of the fiery double-barrel blast from the shotgun. The sudden explosion surprised Whitcomb. It blew a hole in the plaster wall, and the sound reverberated throughout the stairwell.

Just as suddenly, the air crackled with more gunfire. Melton and Johnstone squeezed off several shots, pelting the shoulder and arm of the shadowy triggerman above them in the doorway.

The sawed-off shotgun fell onto the concrete steps.

"F.B.I., you're under arrest!" the agents yelled almost simultaneously.

The triggerman, the Cajun, instinctively raised his hands, one arm bloody from the shots.

Johnstone pulled a radio from his jacket pocket and called an ambulance and the NOPD. The agents cuffed the Cajun henchman. Immediately, the building teemed with New Orleans' finest.

Johnstone and Melton helped Whitcomb down the stairs and onto a stool in the lobby. His hair askew, his face pale, his eyes unfocused, he looked like he had fought his last battle. "Zack, you're gonna be awfully sore from the dive onto the marble. The ambulance will be here in a minute. You bleeding? Got any broken bones?"

Whitcomb ignored the question, untied the half-windsor knot on his tie. For a few minutes he sipped water from a Dixie cup Johnstone handed him. The water revived his spirit. He drew a deep breath.

"Okay, let's have it, G-men."

He cut his eyes toward the agents. "Did you get it?"

Before they answered, he reworded the question.

"Did y'all record it?"

A smile grew on Melton's face. She laughed out loud without control.

"You've done it. You've done it. The recording — it's perfect, just perfect."

"Durant — admitted the theft. Checkmate."

There are moments, usually rare and brief, when life is stirred to a frenzy and ecstasy overflows. Such moments reward our labor and lighten our lives.

Despite the pain from his headlong dive onto the marble floor, Zack Whitcomb arose, smiling ear-to-ear like a boy who hit his first home run. His face glowed like a torch.

Agent Melton hugged the lawyer like a daughter hugging her father.

"I didn't think G-men got excited,"

She ignored him. "You are all man, Zack Whitcomb. And a credit to the male race." She grinned. "Hey, I got the translation of the Latin — 'Someday this will be but a pleasant memory.'" She whispered, "I got a little help from D.C.'"

27

THREE months later I heard the case — *Melvina Durant Hawkins v. Peyton W. Durant. Bill to Quiet Title*, Civil Action No. 95-23, Circuit Court of Choctaw County. I'd never seen the courtroom in Butler full. Nobody had sat in the balcony since segregation ended. *Forbes, The Wall Street Journal, The Times-Picayune, Atlanta Constitution*, and all the big city papers in Alabama covered the trial. It was the biggest legal event in the circuit — at least since Judge Lindsey granted Onassis — Jackie's husband — a divorce at Chatom or since Aaron Burr was arrested outside McIntosh.

Peyton Durant sat at the defense table in the custody of two federal marshals. He had pleaded guilty to a series of federal crimes — securities violations for illegal trading practices, penal racketeering, conspiracy. I granted a motion for Durant's New Orleans lawyer, Tutt Sanford, to represent Durant in an Alabama courtroom.

The rules of ethics prohibit a lawyer from representing a party when the lawyer is a witness. Because Zack Whitcomb was due to be a witness — a key witness, primarily to testify about Durant's admission that he stole and destroyed the Indenture — he could not represent Melvina Hawkins. So, for all his work and sacrifice, and even a little blood, Zack Whitcomb didn't have the satisfaction of meeting Durant and his high-powered legal team in court. Zack directed the trial preparation, however. On his recommendation, the McCorquodale firm out of Jackson handled the case for plaintiff Melvina Durant Hawkins.

The Bermuda banker, Ian Langdale, sat in the gallery pews with Nancy — his recent fiancée. Luther Hawkins escorted his grandmother, Melvina Durant Hawkins, richly dressed in a red suit she bought for the trial, to the plaintiff's table. Melvina's cousin Doll, from New Orleans, wore a white satin dress with hat and gloves.

In his opening statement, Melvina's lawyer presented a chart of the chain of title to the mineral rights from the United States in 1844 to Melvina Hawkins.

In the defendant's opening statement, Tutt Sanford contended that Melvina's case was based on family legend — hearsay — with no hard evidence. But Zack had done a professional job of organizing the case. And the evidence was overwhelming — particularly the 1860 Indenture signed by Herbert Durant.

Sanford fought like a wildcat to keep the copy of the Bermuda Indenture out of evidence but the foundation for the document made its admissibility incontrovertible.

The testimony of Langdale, the Bermudian banker; Albert Zane, the Oxford professor and bookstore owner; the *minutes* from the bank records; and finally, the contents of the naval journal supported the authenticity of the Bermuda Indenture.

McCorquodale introduced the naval journal through Tom Beauchamp. The old sailor sounded like a character out of *Moby Dick*. Beauchamp authenticated the journal, which in turn, supported the authenticity of the Indenture.

But the most dramatic evidence allowing the Indenture to be admissible was the FBI tape recording by agents Melton and Johnstone.

Durant's lawyers put on their case during the second day, but it was weak. Everybody knew it. Melvina Hawkins's lawyers didn't even bother to cross-examine or present a rebuttal case.

The oil men, Shanks and Elder, testified. They've drilled five wells on the Durant property. Fifteen more are planned for the entire reservoir. The return — fifty thousand dollars a day to Shanks and Elder. Over six thousand a day in escrow to be paid to the royalty owner — the prevailing party in the lawsuit.

At the close, I ruled from the bench — in favor of Melvina Hawkins. Shanks and Elder cut her a check for over a million. She stands to receive one hundred eighty thousand a month. That will make for a nice trip to the mailbox.

Durant didn't appeal my ruling.

I RAN INTO Zack last week. He was taking a stroll past the courthouse. He'd just gotten a haircut and was wearing a new Brooks Brothers suit and even a new hat. I told him he looked ten years younger, like a king. He said he ought to look like a king. Melvina Hawkins gave him a third of her interest in the whole Bladon Springs Oil Reservoir.

Zack and I took a long walk around town. Zack resolved my curiosities about the case. First, on why Durant didn't destroy the Indenture, Zack says Durant simply couldn't bring himself to. The Indenture was the most valuable trophy in his collection. He had paid handsomely to have it stolen — and stolen from the grand Cabildo Museum, no less. The Indenture represented Durant's supremacy over lesser rivals to win the oil rights. It was beautiful and valuable and he couldn't part with it. Second, on why Durant, a brilliant man, could be tricked into admitting the theft of the Indenture, Zack says one word — hubris. I may have to go look that up. One thing I do understand is this — Zack believes Melvina and he might have been the beneficiary of an instance of divine intervention. The Great Eternal Judge above decreed this case deserving of a nudge of assistance. Otherwise, Zack says, how can we explain the hurricane that revealed the principal evidence, the Bermuda Indenture, and a string of apparent coincidences thereafter. We resolved to ponder these and other matters of great import over a gin with a splash of vermouth at Weidmann's Restaurant later in the week.

By the way, Zack and Ann are gonna buy a beach house — on St. David's Island in Bermuda.

Zack said Melvina Hawkins asked him to draw up a trust. She wants to restore Bladon Springs and turn it into a botanical garden — a garden with "white blossoms in the spring and gold leaves in the fall."

ACKNOWLEDGMENTS

I gratefully acknowledge the resources and assistance received from the Amelia Gorgas Library at the University of Alabama.

A number of individuals assisted me in particular areas:

- Blockade Running: Dr. Robert Johnson, retired professor of naval history; Colin Benbow of the Bermuda Historical Society.

- Cotton Trading: Rogers Varner of Varner Brothers Trading Company of Cleveland, Mississippi.

- Bermuda: Stuart Thompson and Jean Hammant. Before his untimely death, Kevin Stevenson, a former editor of *The Bermudian*, read my manuscript early on and encouraged me to persevere.

- Editing: Mindy Wilson, Ann Gay, and Dr. Joe Hornsby.

- Maps and Illustrations: Gary Crawford and Kathy Myers.

I also acknowledge for their support and encouragement: Zack Rogers, III, Dr. Culpepper Clark, Bill Black, Rosalie P. Pribbenow, and the entire English Department at the University of Alabama.

Others whom I gratefully acknowledge: Messrs. Metcalfe, Dampier, Findlay, Owen, Mason, Purvis, Broadhead, Bealle, Oldshue, and Jones; Doctors Pancake and Keever; Mmes. Graham, Underhill, Phillips, Gilmore, Doggett, Jefcoat, Homan-Watters, Edgar, Jackson, Cleary, Heaton, Allen, Owen, Chappelle, Ryder; Misses Dorough, Cheney; and the University of Wyoming Writer's Workshop.